Kidnapp...

Camille banged on the door with her fists, yelling Rogan's name.

A key scraped in the door. When Rogan's solid figure appeared in the doorway, instinct took over. She launched herself at him. Her fists thudded into his chest, and he staggered. Then he had both her wrists, holding her away with infuriating ease.

"Settle down!" he said sharply.

"The hell I will!"

She wrenched her gaze up to his face, to the accusing eyes and jutting jaw. His mouth was uncompromising. She could scarcely believe that it had wooed hers last night with tenderness and passion. His chest was bare, and she had to block out the memory of what it had felt like under her hands, against her breasts.

"What the hell," she demanded, "do you think you're doing?"

"Saving you."

Dear Reader,

The year may be coming to a close, but the excitement never flags here at Silhouette Intimate Moments. We've got four—yes, four—fabulous miniseries for you this month, starting with Carla Cassidy's CHEROKEE CORNERS and *Trace Evidence,* featuring a hero who's a crime scene investigator and now has to investigate the secrets of his own heart. Kathleen Creighton continues STARRS OF THE WEST with *The Top Gun's Return.* Tristan Bauer had been declared dead, but now he was back—and very much alive, as he walked back into true love Jessie Bauer's life. Maggie Price begins LINE OF DUTY with *Sure Bet* and a sham marriage between two undercover officers that suddenly starts feeling extremely real. And don't miss *Nowhere To Hide,* the first in RaeAnne Thayne's trilogy THE SEARCHERS. An on-the-run single mom finds love with the FBI agent next door, but there are still secrets to uncover at book's end.

We've also got two terrific stand-alone titles, starting with Laurey Bright's *Dangerous Waters.* Treasure hunting and a shared legacy provide the catalyst for the attraction of two opposites in an irresistible South Pacific setting. Finally, Jill Limber reveals *Secrets of an Old Flame* in a sexy, suspenseful reunion romance.

Enjoy—and look for more excitement next year, right here in Silhouette Intimate Moments.

Yours.

Leslie J. Wainger
Executive Editor

Please address questions and book requests to:
Silhouette Reader Service
U.S.: 3010 Walden Ave., P.O. Box 1325, Buffalo, NY 14269
Canadian: P.O. Box 609, Fort Erie, Ont. L2A 5X3

Dangerous Waters

LAUREY BRIGHT

INTIMATE MOMENTS™

Published by Silhouette Books

America's Publisher of Contemporary Romance

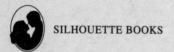 **SILHOUETTE BOOKS**

ISBN 0-373-27335-5

DANGEROUS WATERS

Copyright © 2003 by Daphne Clair de Jong

This edition published by arrangement with Harlequin Books S.A.

® and TM are trademarks of Harlequin Books S.A., used under license.
Trademarks indicated with ® are registered in the United States Patent
and Trademark Office, the Canadian Trade Marks Office and in other
countries.

Visit Silhouette at www.eHarlequin.com

Printed in U.S.A.

Books by Laurey Bright

Silhouette Intimate Moments

Summers Past #470
A Perfect Marriage #621
The Mother of His Child #918
Shadowing Shahna #1169
Dangerous Waters #1265

Silhouette Special Edition

Deep Waters #62
When Morning Comes #143
Fetters of the Past #213
A Sudden Sunlight #516
Games of Chance #564
A Guilty Passion #586
The Older Man #761
The Kindness of Strangers #820
An Interrupted Marriage #916

Silhouette Romance

Tears of Morning #107
Sweet Vengeance #125
Long Way from Home #356
The Rainbow Way #525
Jacinth #568
Marrying Marcus #1558
The Heiress Bride #1578
Life with Riley #1617
With His Kiss #1660

LAUREY BRIGHT

has held a number of different jobs, but has never wanted to be anything but a writer. She lives in New Zealand, where she creates the stories of contemporary people in love that have won her a following all over the world. Visit her at her Web site, http://www.laureybright.com.

Chapter 1

The woman knew he was watching her—Rogan Broderick was sure of it.

Rogan, perched on a stool with his forearm resting along the beer-stained counter, a whiskey glass in his hand, had seen her the moment she entered.

Dark-lashed ocean-green eyes clashed briefly with his as she looked about with the air of a cat entering a strange place and inspecting it for possibly hostile elements. Two plain gold clasps secured a sleek fall of shining brown hair, revealing a classically feminine face. An intriguing hint of strength about the jawline belied the tender, kissable curves of a luscious mouth.

Her shoulders were bare but for the narrow straps of a light, simple-seeming dress the same deep, mysterious green as her eyes. The thin fabric hung in symmetrically draped folds over nicely rounded breasts, skimmed her waist and hips, and moved tantalizingly about her thighs. A perfect beauty—and a city girl, he'd guess. She didn't seem to belong in the public bar of an old hotel on New Zealand's Northland coast.

A fish out of water. Or a mermaid.

No, not a mermaid. She had legs—the kind of legs other women would have killed for. Long, creamy and smooth, their fabulous shape emphasized by high-heeled sandals almost the exact color of the dress.

Giving her a friendly grin, he saw a slight widening of her eyes before the aloof green gaze roamed past him. She tucked her hand into her escort's arm as if for protection as they made for a corner table being abandoned by another couple.

He could hardly blame her, Rogan conceded, rubbing a knuckle over the three-day growth on his cheeks. Other men might look interesting and even glamorous unshaven, but he just looked unkempt and probably sinister. His thick, near-black hair was rust-colored on the haphazardly curling ends, overlong after weeks without seeing a barber, and the sea and sun of the Arabian Gulf had made it harsh and difficult to comb into submission.

He raised his glass to gulp a good shot of whiskey, not taking his eyes off the woman as her companion negotiated a passage through knots of tough, tanned fishermen, sunburned visiting yachties, and weathered locals in checked shirts and creased boots.

Sometimes holiday-makers from luxury yachts liked to hobnob with the regulars and soak up local color rather than patronize the classier lounge bar in the newer part of the building. These two didn't look like hobnobbers.

The man was slim, probably ten years older than Rogan's thirty-one, with neatly combed midbrown hair and smooth untanned cheeks. He wore precision-pressed sand-colored slacks, and a black blazer over a toothpaste-white, roll-collared shirt.

Rogan's T-shirt, long since faded from red to an uneven pink, was rumpled, and his jeans, softened with wear and washing, conformed comfortably to his body. When he'd heard about the old man he had packed his kit in a hurry and barely made the first available flight. Clothes had been the last thing on his mind.

After collecting a room key he'd deferred the long hot shower he planned, in favor of a bracing drink. One whiskey, he'd promised himself, then he'd go upstairs and make himself respectable. Or at least as respectable as he was ever likely to look.

Instead he found himself ordering another drink to give him an excuse to ogle a woman, his blood stirring when she leaned forward to speak over the noise of the bar to the man opposite her, revealing the upper slopes of her breasts, the velvet shadow between them. When a waiter approached the table she looked up and smiled. Rogan shifted on his bar stool. That smile would have brought a stone statue to life.

He made the second drink last until after she and her companion had been served with white wine. Her right hand closed around the stem of the glass while her left one rested on the table. Both were bare of rings.

Didn't mean a thing—she could be in a relationship. Rogan turned his attention to the man, who did sport a gleam of gold on the middle finger of a hand that obviously had scant acquaintance with manual labour. He looked like an accountant or a lawyer. Reminded of his brother and why he was here, Rogan tossed off the remains of his drink, not wanting to think about the reason he'd flown home. Easier to occupy his mind fantasizing about a pretty woman.

He placed the glass on the counter and the barman inquired, "Same again?"

"No. Thanks." His gaze returning to the woman, Rogan

got off the stool and hoisted the bulging pack at his feet up to his shoulder.

The movement must have caught her eye. She looked up and a faint rose color entered her cheeks. She blinked the deep-sea eyes and turned away to stare into her wine, a curve of burnished hair falling across her cheek. Her escort looked up too, his glance taking in Rogan's disreputable appearance before returning to his companion. He said something and the woman shook her head, then lifted the glass to her lips.

The man looked at Rogan again, warning him off with an ice-blue stare. Rogan slanted him a resigned grin and raised a hand in a half salute as he ambled to the door.

Granger was on time as always. Rogan, showered and shaved and in fresh jeans and a gray T-shirt, found him in the lobby, beside a large Christmas tree decorated with tinsel, colored gewgaws and, in defiance of the New Zealand summer, cotton-wool snowflakes.

The two men gripped hands and Rogan reached out to slap his brother's shoulder, noting signs of strain about eyes the same vivid aquamarine as his own. "You're looking pretty flash," he said, nodding at the suit and discreet silk tie.

Granger allowed himself a tight smile, his eyes glinting. "I don't suppose you even own a suit. I brought along a spare you can borrow. You'll be a pall-bearer, won't you?"

"Uh-huh." It was the least he could for the old man. "You haven't put *him* in a suit, have you?" At a guess, their father had never worn one in his life.

Granger shook his head. "He'd have died all over again."

Rogan's laughter cracked in the middle. He clamped his teeth shut and there was a small, awkward silence. Then he said, ''Let's eat.''

Camille Hartley saw two tall, dark-haired men, strikingly good-looking and bearing an unmistakable family resemblance, enter the dining room. It was a moment before she recognized the casually dressed one as the man who had stared at her earlier in the bar.

The piratical beard shadow was gone, revealing clear-cut bone structure and a stubborn jaw, and he'd ruthlessly combed back the unruly mane of his hair, its obstinate waves dampened and glossy under the artificial lights. She had a momentary picture of him standing in the shower, water sleeking his hair and cascading over his sun-browned body. A very good body—his clothes did little to hide the broad shoulders and chest, narrow hips, powerful legs. He looked superbly fit and strong—a man who did something physical for a living.

As if he'd felt her stare, his head turned. She saw an oddly bleak look in the blinding green-blue eyes, and then it vanished, replaced by a gleam of interest, a hint of bold inquiry.

She wrenched her gaze away, directing her attention to what James Drummond was saying. James, from their first meeting yesterday, had shown a rare respect for her mind, and a real though circumspect desire to get to know her more than superficially. Already they had established a tentative rapport. Yet still she was disconcertingly conscious of the other man, needing to breathe carefully, her heart beating faster and sending the blood to warm her cheeks.

Irritated, she inwardly shook herself. She wasn't in the habit of mentally undressing strange men, and had outgrown blushing years ago.

He was hardly the first male to stare at her, although few

were so frank about it. Aware that the gods had been generous to her, she had learned to be chary of men who were less interested in her personality than in flaunting her as some sort of trophy. She'd guess that the unsettling stranger, with his unabashed gaze and knowing grin, was the love-'em-and-leave-'em type, a genus she kept well clear of.

"Try concentrating," his brother advised as Rogan's eyes strayed again from the menu in his hands to the woman whose luminous gaze was now fixed on the man opposite her.

Granger half turned to see who he was looking at. "Not that I blame you," he admitted, "but I'm hungry and we've got things to talk about. I'm having the pepper steak." He closed his own menu.

"Wild pork," Rogan decided. "And a beer."

Granger ordered a bottle of red wine, and Rogan sipped his beer while they waited. "Thanks for booking me a room," he said. "I could have slept on board the *Sea-Rogue*."

"I thought you'd appreciate a real bed. Besides, I wasn't sure the boat would be available. I only collected the key from the police station just before I came here. Have you been down to the wharf?"

"I arrived less than half an hour ago," Rogan told him with a shake of his head. "Did you get all your business done?" Granger had said he had things to do but would be at the hotel in time for dinner.

"That's one of the things we should talk about," Granger said. "I checked out Dad's will."

Trust Granger to think of the legalities. Well, someone had to. "He made a will?" That didn't sound like Barney.

"Years ago. I persuaded him to get it fixed up with one

of my colleagues. The police needed to sight it before they would hand over the boat.'' Granger paused. ''You and I own half of the *Sea-Rogue* and everything in it.''

''Half each?''

''Half for us two together. He left the rest to Taff.''

''That's fair enough,'' Rogan conceded. Taff ''Taffrail'' McIndoe had been Barney's first mate and sailing partner for more than twenty years.

''But if Taff predeceased him,'' Granger continued, ''his share was to go to his legitimate descendants.''

''Taff isn't married, and anyway he hasn't prede-ceased—''

''He died two months ago. I only found out after the police called about Dad.''

Rogan's beer glass hit the table with a thud. ''*Taff* died?'' It was almost as big a shock as his father's sudden demise. ''How?''

''Liver disease. They were somewhere way out in the Pacific, and by the time Dad finally got him to a hospital at Rarotonga it was too late to do anything.''

While Rogan digested that, Granger added, ''You know how he used to put the booze away. It's a wonder either of them survived as long as they did.''

''Dad never drank at sea.''

''He made up for it on land. According to the pathologist there was enough alcohol in his body to sink a ship.''

''They cut him up?'' Rogan's voice went hoarse.

Granger eyed him levelly. ''They have to do an autopsy in a case of sudden death. Besides, he'd been in a fight.''

''You didn't tell me that!''

''You'd only have stewed about it all the way home. There could be manslaughter charges at least.''

Rogan's hand closed tightly about his beer. ''Against who?''

"Whom." Granger shrugged. "The police are investigating but they don't have any witnesses. He was found in an alleyway near here and he'd probably died in the early hours of Sunday. But the cause of death was a heart attack, not the beating he'd taken."

He'd taken a beating? "There must have been more than one of them." Barney Broderick had been a big man, toughened by a life at sea.

"Dad wasn't getting any younger," Granger reminded him, "and he'd have been reeling drunk."

"He never said anything about having a dicky heart…did he?"

"You know he wouldn't admit to being less than a hundred percent healthy." Barney had indiscriminately labeled all doctors quacks and used their services only in the direst need. "He might not even have known."

Rogan hoped that was so. And that Barney hadn't known he was dying when some thug—or thugs—left him alone and injured in a dark alley. His hand clenched harder on the beer glass. He'd like to beat the hell out of them in retaliation.

"It was probably pretty quick," Granger assured him. "The way he'd have liked to go. Without any fuss."

"Yeah." Rogan tossed off the remains of his drink, trying to drown an illogical remorse. It wasn't his fault, or Granger's, that the old man had lived and died far from his family. They didn't really owe him much at all, except the genes he'd bequeathed to them both, probably more or less by accident—of which Rogan seemed to have inherited the lion's share.

He signaled the waiter for another beer. "Does Taff have any descendants?" he asked.

"Possibly dozens—" Granger gave him a rare grin

"—scattered all around the Pacific, and none of them legitimate."

The waiter brought the beer and a fresh glass. Pouring the frothing stuff, Rogan looked up quizzically. "You don't think the old man fathered a few more children too?"

"I hope not. There's no mention in the will of any secret siblings."

Their food arrived and Rogan picked up his knife and fork. Real New Zealand wild pork and gravy with roasted vegetables. His mouth watered. He'd let his brother deal with the legal issues. Granger, after years specializing in corporate law with an international legal firm, had just launched his own practice in Auckland.

The thought of spending his days in an office, no matter how plush, made Rogan's blood run cold, but apparently Granger enjoyed it.

While Granger refilled his own glass Rogan stole another look at the woman he'd mentally nicknamed Ocean-eyes, and watched as she raised her fork to her mouth and opened perfect lips to slip the morsel in. The faintest ripple disturbed the smooth line of her throat, making him wonder how it would feel if he had his hand there, against the fine skin. Maybe with his thumb in the little groove at the base…

She reached for her wine and drank some, leaving a delicate sheen on her upper lip when she put down the glass and smiled at her companion.

Rogan had a dire urge to kiss the wine from her lips and taste it on the soft, warm mouth. A hot bolt of desire invaded his body, accompanied by a sharp envy of the man on the receiving end of that smile.

Too long without the company of women, he told himself, turning his attention to the pork and sawing at it with unwarranted vigor. The meat was tender and succulent, and he was determined to enjoy it to the exclusion of that other, inconvenient and less easily satisfied appetite.

He knew when Ocean-eyes left the dining room, but didn't look up. By that time Granger was talking about the funeral arrangements, and out of respect Rogan tried to blot everything else from his mind.

"He wanted his ashes scattered at sea," Granger said, "from the *Sea-Rogue*."

Rogan would have wondered at anything else. "What time is the service?"

"Eleven. Some of his old drinking mates have volunteered to help carry the coffin."

Rogan grinned. "Do you think they can stay sober until the wake? We are having a wake, aren't we?"

"It seems to be expected. The proprietor here's offered me a special rate for the private bar."

He probably wanted to shield his more refined clientele from a gathering of Barney Broderick's mates. Most of Barney's life had been spent on the ocean, but Mokohina was nominally his home port. From a sheltered deep-water cove and small shingly beach the old town straggled up the hills behind the bay. Formerly a mixture of settler cottages and modest villas, solid homes built by retired farmers, and a scattering of classic holiday "baches"—knocked-up boxes with few pretensions to architectural style—the port had been discovered in the last ten years by the owners of expensive oceangoing yachts, and land-based refugees from city life.

Semi-mansions had appeared on the higher slopes. New shops and food outlets aimed at the burgeoning tourist trade joined the modest stores that had served the district for decades. Two motels and a few bed-and-breakfasts catered to the summer influx, and trendy café bars had opened along the waterfront. But the permanent residents and reg-

ulars like Barney Broderick remained loyal to the old
Imperial, a two-story colonial relic, recently enlarged and
refurbished, boasting a creaking veranda on the top floor
and kauri wood paneling in the interior.

The new owners had wisely left virtually untouched the
well-used public bar. Its scarred, varnished timbers reeking
of generations of hard-drinking sailors and fishermen, it
was within staggering distance of the old wharves and the
Sea-Rogue's preferred berth when she was in port.

Granger picked up the wine bottle and offered it. Rogan
shook his head. After whiskey and beer he didn't fancy
adding wine to the mix. He watched his brother empty the
bottle into his glass, then quaff the lot. Granger seldom, if
ever, drank to excess, and the wine didn't seem to have
much effect, even when they left the restaurant.

In the lobby they paused by the elaborately carved, polished newel at the foot of the broad stairs. It was too early
to go to bed, and the air seemed thick and over-warm.

"Think I'll go for a walk," Rogan said.

"Good idea."

Outside, without discussion they strolled across the road
and turned along the curve of the waterfront. Rogan ducked
his head under a wide-spreading pohutukawa and skirted a
dinghy leaning bow-up against the tree.

The strip of sand gave way to a retaining wall where the
water slapped rhythmically at hard gray stones. Several
dozen boats lifted and dipped on the restless waves in the
bay. A high moon picked out the glimmer of metal here
and there, and cast white hulls and masts into relief, while
dark ones disappeared in the blackness.

Both men knew where they were headed.

The cheap cafés and fast-food bars, the shops selling
local handcrafts, gaudy sarongs and souvenir T-shirts, were
replaced by boating and fishing suppliers.

Rounding a curve, they reached a part of the shoreline where the streetlamps were fewer and the vessels tied at the weathered wharves were sturdy, battered working boats instead of glossy, greyhound pleasure craft. Past a warehouse, a marine engine repair shop and a malodorous fish-processing plant, they reached the mooring where the naked masts of the *Sea-Rogue* loomed against the stars.

Rogan scarcely hesitated before leaping lightly onto the deck below, followed by Granger. The ketch shifted against the wharf, the worn tires hanging from the boat's side to buffer the hull making soft bumping noises. Rogan went to the stern and ran his fingers along the old-style teak taffrail, paused as he found what he'd been searching for, and traced over the letters carved into the timber.

"Still there?" Granger came to stand beside him.

"Yep." Rogan had been eleven, Granger twelve, when they'd marked their initials with a pocketknife. They'd expected a blast from their father as soon as he discovered the defacement, but he'd just laughed and clapped them on the back with his big, rough hands.

A loose halyard flapped against the metal mizzen, and Rogan looked up, glancing at the furled sails. He remembered the thrill of the first time he'd been allowed to help hoist them, the wind cracking them free and blowing cool and strong on his face, while the ketch's bow forged blue-green water into a foamy V, throwing up a fine white spray that showered him with its salty blessing.

He'd fallen in love with the sea there and then. A love that had never left him. The only thing better than sailing was being underwater—a living, breathing part of the ocean itself. Between diving contracts he sometimes chartered a yacht with a buddy, exploring recreational dive sites. Or spent time on a tiny Pacific island where he and other professional divers supported a local dive school, giving financial and practical help.

"Want to go below?" Granger asked.

"Sure." Tomorrow they'd see their father's body in the funeral parlor before they carried his coffin to the seamen's chapel whose doors Barney Broderick had seldom darkened in life. But his beloved *Sea-Rogue* was where Barney's spirit lived. This was their real goodbye.

Granger dropped into the cockpit where the mizzen was stepped, a few feet forward of the wheel. He took a key ring from his pocket and opened up the deckhouse to descend the short, steep companionway to the dark interior.

Rogan followed him down. "Have you been aboard since the old man…?"

"No." Granger flicked a switch but nothing happened. Evidently Barney hadn't hooked the boat up to shore power. "Hang on a minute." He fumbled about the galley area behind the companionway.

A small flame flared, and within seconds he'd lit a kerosene lamp hanging from a gimbal. The light flickered, brightened, and steadied. Varnish gleamed on the mahogany interior; a slit-eyed mask from the Philippines leered from one of the few spaces on the bulkheads.

"Guess it hasn't changed much," Granger said.

The palm-leaf matting on the floor looked new, but otherwise was identical to what Rogan remembered from years back. So was everything else.

Seats that could serve as narrow berths formed an L at the table, their once-floral coverings faded and thin. A bank of instruments occupied the navigation desk near the companionway. Recessed shelves fitted with fiddle rails to safeguard the contents in rough weather held old volumes that Barney had treasured, along with some paperbacks, nautical knickknacks, and shells and carvings from islands around the Pacific.

In the galley a cutlery drawer sat half open, and a cupboard door hung ajar. Granger said, "The police searched the boat for ID and a contact address."

He unhooked the lamp and headed toward the stern, pausing at an open door to one side of the short passageway. Taff's cabin, with colorful pictures torn from *National Geographic* magazines pinned over the bunk, a battered peaked cap hanging on a hook, a rolled sleeping bag at the end of the mattress, looked as though he'd just stepped out on deck.

Granger moved on to what Barney had liked to call the master's stateroom in the stern, crammed with more books and a built-in desk. The attached wooden chair had a curved back, the varnish worn pale in the middle, its seat softened by a thin, indented cushion. Rogan had the absurd idea that if he put a hand on it he'd find it still warm.

A marine chart of the Pacific lay open on the desk, with a small pile of tide tables and almanacs. Items of clean clothing were heaped on the relatively roomy berth fitted at the stern, and books occupied the shelves above.

As Rogan followed him inside, Granger turned, lifting the lamp high. The framed picture of their mother still hung over the doorway, where Barney could see it every night before going to sleep.

Rogan swallowed, then blundered back to the saloon.

Granger said evenly, "I guess that's it." He rehung the lamp, and turned the flame down until it disappeared.

In the blackness Rogan groped for the companionway. Back on deck he breathed in the pungency of salt water and fish, and a whiff of diesel. "He didn't deserve to die like that," he said hoarsely. Like some bit of discarded flotsam, callously abandoned to the cold and dark.

"Nobody does," Granger agreed.

Rogan closed his fists, overwhelmed by a hot-eyed, skull-thumping rage. Whoever was responsible for causing his father's secretly damaged heart to finally stop beating—when he found them he'd bloody well tear them apart, limb from limb.

Chapter 2

Camille wasn't sure what to wear to the funeral of a man she'd never known.

The one dress she'd packed—lightweight, creaseless, and simple enough for any time of day—had been fine for dinner with James Drummond. But even with a beige silk cardigan to cover her shoulders it looked a bit frivolous for a somber church service.

Entering the historic seamen's chapel later, she was glad she'd settled for forest-green jean-style pants with a cream shirt and low-heeled braided-leather shoes.

Two men seated near the coffin wore impeccable dark suits, but other suits in evidence were of the ill-fitting, limp and unfashionable kind resurrected from some forgotten corner of a wardrobe, and the air was pervaded with a faint odor of naphthalene and mildew.

The service was simple and brief. When the minister paused, one of the men in the front pew went to the lectern, and only then Camille recognized her piratical stranger's dinner companion of the previous evening.

Shocked, she turned her gaze to the second man.

He'd had a haircut, but the broad shoulders straining at the jacket of the suit, and the confident tilt of his head, were already familiar. She half expected him to turn and grin at her with the same bold insouciance he'd shown last night.

But of course he wouldn't. This, she realized as his brother began to speak, was his father's funeral.

Camille hardly heard the eulogy, dimly registering words like "adventurous" and "indomitable" and "determined." She wondered if his sons had really known Barney Broderick. If they too had longed for a father who went to the office every day and came home for dinner every night and read the newspaper and watched TV before going off to bed. She swallowed, assailed by a familiar sensation—half sadness, half anger.

The man in the front pew dipped his head, momentarily out of her sight, but when he raised it again his big square shoulders were straighter than ever.

He didn't take up the minister's invitation for anyone to share their memories of the deceased, but a few gristly, weather-creased men spoke of a staunch friend, a fine sailor, a great bloke, and "one of nature's gentlemen." The last elderly raconteur told a couple of down-to-earth anecdotes about "old Barney" that had his cronies rocking with laughter and then wiping away tears.

His two sons as they helped lift and carry the coffin were tearless, seemingly emotionless. Outside, the coffin was slid into a hearse and the brothers stood shoulder to shoulder, fielding handshakes and condolences.

Camille waited for a gap and had almost decided to give up and return to the hotel when the pirate brother looked over the shoulder of a man who was shaking his hand, and she saw the quick flare of recognition in his eyes as they met hers.

He said something to the man and then he was pushing through the crowd, throwing a word here and there, moving inexorably toward Camille until he fetched up directly in front of her, so close she took a startled step backward.

Scowling down at her, he said, "Who *are* you?"

"Camille Hartley," she told him. "I'm sorry about your father, Mr. Broderick."

"Rogan," he said. "Or Rogue, if you like. Did you know him?"

"Not really. I was supposed to meet him here yesterday, but when I arrived I was told he'd…died. I'm sorry," she repeated.

"Why were you meeting him?"

"He asked me to. It concerned…my father."

"Your father?"

"Thomas McIndoe."

For a second he looked confused. Then he said, "Taff? Taff was your father?"

"Yes," she admitted stiffly.

"So old Taff does have descendants."

"One," she confirmed reluctantly.

There was a stir in the crowd behind him, and his brother came to his side. "Ready to go to the crematorium?" he quietly asked Rogan. The notice in the newspaper had said the cremation would be private. "I told everyone we'll see them later at the Imperial."

He nodded curtly to Camille and made to turn away and take his brother with him.

But Rogan stood his ground. "Granger," he said, "this is Taff's daughter."

Granger stared at his brother, then at Camille. He looked back at Rogan. "You're kidding."

"She's his daughter. So she says."

Slightly miffed at the addendum, Camille held out her hand to Granger. "Camille Hartley," she said. "I'm sorry about your father."

Granger took her hand and briefly clasped it in a firm, cool grip. "Hartley?" he queried. "You're married?"

Camille shook her head. "It's my mother's name."

The two brothers exchanged a fleeting glance that obscurely annoyed her with its hint of some secret joke.

Then Granger cast her a keen look. "You do know about Taff? I mean—"

"That he died, yes."

"Then may we return your condolences?"

"Thank you, but I scarcely remember him."

A woman touched Granger's arm. Middle-aged, with brass-colored curls and red-rimmed eyes. "Sorry to interrupt, love. I just want to say, your dad might have been a bit of a rough diamond, but he had a good heart. I won't go along to the pub, only I'd like to talk to you two boys sometime. You'll be in town for a while?"

Rogan said, "A couple more days anyway."

She moved off and Granger turned back to Camille. "Will we see you at the wake?"

"I wasn't intending to be there."

Rogan asked, "Are you staying at the Imperial?"

"Yes. But—"

"We have to talk to you," he said, "don't we, Granger?"

Granger said slowly, "I guess we do." He glanced back at the hearse, where the driver was showing signs of impatience.

"You're not leaving Mokohina yet, are you?" Rogan
pressed her.

After a small hesitation she conceded, "Not yet."

"Then we'll see you later."

Camille didn't answer, and as he moved away with his
brother he shot a glance over his shoulder as if willing her
to stay.

The wake was just the sort of send-off Barney would
have enjoyed. Drinks and stories flowed freely, and Rogan
lost count of the number of beer-breathing, teary-eyed old
salts who clapped him or his brother on the shoulder and
urged them to join in yet another toast to their father.

One white-bearded, purple-cheeked character whispered
hoarsely, "Did he tell you about his find then, boy?"

"What find?"

Rogan edged backward, but the beard only moved closer,
and the man squinted up at him through watery, bloodshot
eyes. "You don't know?"

"Know what?" The old guy was probably talking
through the bottom of his beer glass.

The man looked about them covertly and clutched at
Rogan's arm. "We gave Taff a send-off the night your dad
got his, y'know. In absentia, so to speak. Poor old Taff."
He shook his head in sorrow. "Barney was saying Taff had
missed out on a fortune."

Barney would say that. He'd always hoped someday to
uncover sunken treasure.

The beard leaned closer still. A whiff of tobacco breath
mingled with the beer. "I reckon," the man said porten-
tously, "him and Taff found something."

Rogan looked about for an escape route. "Then I guess
he died happy."

"And that's another thing." A broad, blunt finger poked

his chest. "Heart attack, they said, right? But what brought that on, eh? Someone jumped him, didden they? Barney didn't have an enemy in the world."

"It wasn't the first time he'd got in a…fight." Rogan avoided the words *drunken brawl.* Apparently Barney was already in line for the sainthood conferred by death, but he'd had minor brushes with the law in several Pacific ports after becoming involved in some pub scrap.

"Not for years," his friend averred. "He was getting a bit long in the tooth for that sort of caper, you know."

He was probably right, but Barney had been mourning his sailing companion, a man he'd spent way more time with over the years than he ever had with his wife or his sons. And he'd been drinking heavily. "Maybe he felt like getting in a fight that night."

The white-bearded chin protruded stubbornly. "Or maybe some bastard robbed him. Y'know, all night he kept feeling his breast pocket as if he had something in there he didn't want to lose."

"You think someone from Taff's wake beat up my father?"

The man looked shocked. Then he scowled. "Well, the pub was full and we were in the public bar. It wasn't a genteel private do like this." He looked about at the crowd splashing beer on the tables and the floor as they poured it from brimming jugs and brandished their glasses in raucous toasts. One man snored in a corner while his companions rocked in their chairs with laughter at another who stood on the table, declaiming a long and exceedingly ribald poem. In competition, a group being kept upright only by their affinity for the solid bar counter struggled through an off-key and heavily adapted version of "Shenandoah."

Rogan manfully kept a straight face. It was becoming obvious why the proprietor, after hosting Taff's send-off, had preferred to corral this particular group of patrons in a separate bar.

"Webby, you old piker!" Another enthusiastic mourner clapped the bearded man on the back. This one was taller and younger, with gingery whiskers peppering a long, creased face under a thistle-head of reddish hair. "Fill up, then!" He poured a stream of beer into Webby's glass, then waved the jug invitingly at Rogan. "What about yourself, Rogue?"

Rogan shook his head. Already he was feeling slightly unattached from his surroundings, the beer fumes and smoke and noisy revelry receding in an alcohol-induced haze.

Webby dug the newcomer in the ribs. "Hey, you remember old Barney at Taff's wake, don't you, Doll? Don't you reckon he was all fired up about something?"

Doll? Rogan blinked as the taller man pondered. "He was fired up about a lot of things—doctors, Taff dying on him, the government, customs regulations…"

Webby poked him again. "Wasn't he talking about getting rich at last?"

"Barney was always talking about getting rich."

"Yeah, but that night…"

Rogan edged away, leaving the two of them arguing. Granger, a slightly hunted look about him, caught his eye and came over. "Do you think anyone would notice if I left? This lot might keep going all day."

"And all night," Rogan speculated. "I've had enough, anyway. I don't suppose they'll miss us if we slip away."

Granger's look held veiled surprise. Then he grinned slightly. "Not much of a female presence here, is there?"

Rogan tried to look offended, suspecting he only looked sheepish. Sure, he liked female company when it was available. Came of being without it for so much of his working life. Even on shore, in some places where he'd worked just looking at a woman could get him thrown into jail or worse. Not to mention the even greater danger to any poor girl who might be tempted to return the compliment.

So in a free country where what a man and a woman did was a matter of mutual consent and no one else's business, he made the most of the sometimes brief periods he had to enjoy being with them.

He liked women. He liked their bodies, softly rounded or slender and supple, and their silky smooth skin, and their hair—how they kept it shiny and sweet-smelling, sometimes curled and plaited and decorated. He liked the way they moved, the subtle roll and sway of their hips and behinds as they walked. And how if they liked a man back, they touched their hair and tilted their heads and peeked at him with shy, flirty eyes. Or boldly looked at him and smiled, inviting him closer.

He specially liked their laughter, and their voices—light and pretty, or low and sexy. And how they listened, really listened when he talked. He liked the way they *cared,* about all sorts of things—children, the environment, their girl-friends' problems.

And he was awed by how capable they were. His mother had needed to be, but other women too seemed to just know things that men blundered through without a clue.

He liked being with them. For a while.

Sometimes a leisurely drink or two with a woman in a warm bar was as pleasurable in its own way as a wild romp in bed. Not that he wasn't open to offers…

He wondered if Ocean-eyes was around.

Camille, he remembered. Her name was Camille. Nice. Yeah, and it suited her. Although she didn't look consumptive like *The Lady of the Camellias.*

It wasn't easy escaping, and it was another hour before

the brothers slipped through a side door and Rogan gulped in a lungful of fresh air.

"Let's walk," Granger said.

Putting some distance between them and the revelry inside, they strolled randomly along the nearest street, then uphill, where for a while they silently observed the view, and finally by a roundabout route made their way back into the heart of the town.

Rogan told Granger about his conversation with Webby. "Do you think it's possible Dad had stumbled on something valuable?"

Granger snorted. "The old man chased after so many wild geese he could have started an egg farm."

That was certainly true. Except that he'd never actually caught one.

Granger's step faltered, then picked up, and Rogan said, "What?"

"Nothing." His brother looked grim. "That's the street where he…"

Died. Rogan stopped, looking back. The alley would be a shortcut from the hotel to the *Sea-Rogue,* a more direct diagonal route behind the buildings that meandered along the dog-leg line of the shore. "Show me."

Granger halted too. "There's nothing to see."

"Do you know exactly where?"

Granger studied the set of Rogan's jaw, and said tersely, "Come on, then."

It was a service alley between the unwindowed back walls of several business premises. Bags and boxes of rubbish sat against some, and a heavy smell of fish wafted from a rattling air-conditioner, mingling with the aroma of decaying fruit and vegetables spilling from an overfilled bin a little farther along where fat black flies droned lazily about.

"Here." Granger stopped at big double doors with peeling paint. On the wall, a faded sign above identified the premises as Tench and Whiteburn, Sailmakers Since 1899. A heap of sodden and stained canvas, rotted rope and collapsed cardboard boxes gave off a moldy fetor, and a couple of stubborn tufts of grass that had fought their way through uneven cracks in the tar-seal lent the only sign of life except for the flies.

"I told you," Granger said. "There's nothing to see."

A van roared into the alley, slowing as it lumbered by with barely enough room to pass them.

Rogan turned away, his throat tight. "Let's go," he said in an almost normal voice, leading the way and heading blindly toward the hotel. "I want to get out of this bloody suit." He stripped off the jacket that was stifling him and threw it over his shoulder, pulling irritably at the dark tie about his throat and stuffing it into a trouser pocket.

"It's my second-best suit," Granger told him. "And I'll thank you to treat it with respect."

Rogan snorted. "I don't know how you stand wearing them all the time."

"I guess your shoulders are wider than mine." Granger gripped one of them. "All that muscle-bound machismo stuff you do for a living," he mocked gruffly.

Rogan's reply was even less polite than before. Scowling, he shrugged off his brother's hand. He needed a stiff drink. Never mind that he'd already had more than enough beer. A whiskey was what he was after. Harsh, strong whiskey. Neat. Undiluted alcohol.

They reached the hotel, warily peering into the deserted lobby before entering.

Rogan headed for the doorway labeled Bottle Store, ignoring his brother's lifted eyebrow. "See you in fifteen minutes," he muttered.

He did too, feeling considerably better as he rapped on Granger's door exactly one minute early, having broached a bottle of Black Watch in his room.

"Here," he said, thrusting the borrowed clothes at his brother. "Thanks."

Granger took the suit and tie and motioned him in, going to the wardrobe.

"She's still here," Rogan said.

"Who? Oh—Whatsername McIndoe. You've seen her?"

"No, but I checked at the desk." He'd half expected her to have bolted. At the chapel she'd seemed uncertain, ambivalent. "Shouldn't we talk to her before we do anything else? And she's Camille Hartley, remember."

"Oh, yeah, Taff's illegitimate daughter."

"She can't help that."

"I wasn't being snide, Rogue." Granger finished hanging the suit and closed the wardrobe. "Facts are facts."

"Does that mean she doesn't inherit half the *Sea-Rogue?*"

"Extramarital children do have some rights. It's not my field, but she might have a case, if only morally. Did you get her room number?"

Rogan shook his head. "They wouldn't give it to me. Even wearing your suit."

"You weren't, any more," Granger pointed out, picking up the bedroom phone. "You'd already hauled half of it off." He'd taken off his own jacket but still wore shirt and tie.

He spoke into the receiver, asking to be put through to Miss Hartley's room.

After a brief conversation he reported, "She'll meet us down in the Garden Lounge in five minutes."

Somehow that made Rogan feel considerably lighter than he had all day.

* * *

The Garden Lounge looked seldom used. Its small, multipaned windows were curtained with loops of white lace, and when the men entered, Camille was in a cane armchair by a low table, watching them cross the carpet toward her. Her legs, neatly tucked to one side, were encased in dark green trousers. What a waste, Rogan thought regretfully, remembering those legs emerging from her dress last night.

Her gaze flicked across Granger and lit on Rogan. For some reason she looked apprehensive, and as the men drew closer her eyes grew larger, darker.

He was no Adonis, but surely he wasn't *that* intimidating? Suddenly he felt taller and bigger, as if he'd somehow expanded under her eyes, and he wondered if he should have put on something a bit more reputable than thin-kneed camouflage trousers and a khaki shirt with the sleeves ripped out.

Army surplus clothes were cheap and hard-wearing. And *comfortable,* for gosh sakes.

Heck, now he was even censoring his *thoughts.* As if she'd know what he was thinking.

He remembered her flushing last night as he watched her. She'd known what he was thinking then, all right. The gist of it anyhow.

Granger said, "Thank you for coming," and she actually smiled at him—not a wide smile, but a smile of sorts, and now she wasn't looking at Rogan at all.

The men sat down and a waiter brought coffee for three. Rogan would have liked a beer but his head was already floating inches above its normal position. And he figured, when Granger cast him a firm look before he ordered for them both, that as usual his big brother was right. He'd had enough to drink. At least for the next few hours.

"Why did you want to see me?" Camille asked.

She kept her attention on Granger while he explained the terms of Barney's will.

He reached the bit about Taff's descendants, and for a moment her delicious, tempting mouth fell softly open, making Rogan's blood stir as he wondered how it would feel to close it with his own.

"You may be able to make a claim," Granger was telling her, "if you have proof of your relationship."

She blinked at him.

"For instance, is his name on your birth certificate? Even though your parents weren't married—"

Her chin tilted. "My parents were married."

Rogan interjected. "*Taff* was *married?*"

She glanced at him with a hint of scorn. "He seems to have forgotten it, but he was once."

Granger said, "I'm sorry, I misunderstood." He fished in his pocket. "In that case you'd inherit half the boat and its contents—plus half of any profit still outstanding from voyages Taff made with our father. As executor I need your address and phone number." He handed her a card. "This is my office address. You'll need to produce your birth certificate to prove your right to your inheritance, and—"

"I don't want it." The rose-pink lips went tight.

"Why not?" Rogan demanded, making her look at him.

But not for long. Her gaze skittered away again to Granger. "Can't I just waive any rights I have?"

Granger looked at her curiously. "It would be simpler to let things take their course. Then you can dispose of your portion as you like. The boat might be worth quite a lot."

She opened her mouth again, then closed it, her eyes glazing in thought. "How much?"

"The market for classic wooden craft is apparently pretty lively. There are huge variations depending on a number of factors, but some fetch prices in six figures."

"Have you seen her?" Rogan asked Camille.

"I looked there for your father yesterday, but no one was on board. Someone from a fishing boat came over and told me what had happened."

Barney had been found by a delivery driver on Monday morning, and it was Tuesday before the police had identified him and tracked down Granger.

"Why did he want to see you?" Rogan asked.

Her face went stiff, expressionless. "He wanted to give me some things he thought I should have. I suppose he meant my father's…effects. He said he had to talk to me but he couldn't leave his boat for long. I was due for annual leave and it quite suited me to come north."

"Would you recognize your father's belongings?"

Camille shook her head. Dryly she said, "I'd have been hard put to recognize my father."

Granger asked, "Have the police talked to you?"

"No, why? I can't tell them anything."

"You should check in with them all the same. If you were supposed to be meeting Dad they'll want to see you." Granger pulled out a notebook. "Your contact details?"

She recited them stonily, and stood up. "Thank you for explaining the situation."

"We'll be in touch," Granger promised, rising too.

By the time Rogan had put down his coffee cup and started getting up she'd already left them. He sank back, watching her walk away, until he realized Granger was watching *him* with amused tolerance.

"Get your eyes back in your head, little bro'," Granger told him, "and your butt out of that chair, unless you plan to stay here." Eyeing him critically, he added, "Mind you, a second cup of coffee wouldn't do you any harm."

Rogan glared at him, hoisting himself from the chair. All the time they'd been talking Camille had scarcely glanced his way, her eyes pretty much fixed on his brother throughout. And Granger hadn't even seemed to notice. Did the man have ice water instead of good red Broderick blood in his veins?

Not fair, of course. Last night he'd shown a cursory appreciation, at least, of Camille's spectacular beauty. On the surface she was very similar to the women who occasionally, briefly, graced Granger's life—classy, polished, composed. Like him. Only better-looking.

Inexplicably, when he followed his brother into the lobby Rogan's heart settled somewhere near his midriff, as if he'd swallowed one of his lead diving weights.

His father had just died. It was natural to feel depressed. He *ought* to be feeling this way.

None of Granger's beloved laws said he had to like it.

Chapter 3

As Rogan and Granger crossed the lobby they were way-laid by a bunch of men erupting from the private bar. "Boys!" a solidly built man flushed with beer and bon-homie hailed them. He hooked an arm about Rogan's shoulder. "Bloody good do, this. Barney'd be proud."

The others milled around, one in an oversize suit asking peevishly where the effin' can was until his fellows shoved him in the right direction. Propelled back into the thick of the wake and obliged to drink yet another toast or three to Good Ol' Barney, it was some time before the brothers extricated themselves.

"What now?" Rogan asked.

"We could check over the *Sea-Rogue*," Granger suggested. "Pack up Dad's clothes, make sure there are no perishables on board. And decide how the boat's going to be looked after until we sort out the estate."

"Estate? He doesn't…didn't…own anything but the boat, did he?"

"It's a legal term," Granger said patiently. "You're probably right, but a standard clause in the will covers anything not specified, like bank accounts, bonds or other assets. He could owe money, or have some owed to him."

"Didn't he buy salvage rights to a wreck years ago?"

Granger laughed. "I don't suppose it's worth anything. The *Maiden's Prayer.* She disappeared in a storm in the 1850s with no survivors, carrying passengers returning from the Australian gold fields to America with the loot from their endeavors. There were chests full of gold on board—nuggets or bars—and several thousand dollars' worth of gold and silver coins. Not counting what passengers had in their luggage."

"A fortune," Rogan commented.

"If it were ever found," Granger said dryly. "The insurance company was happy to part with the salvage rights in return for a modest cut, particularly with the new laws about historic wrecks making recovery more difficult and expensive. Dad asked me to make sure his rights were solid and there'd be no counterclaims. The papers were with his will. But it'll take more than a maiden's prayer to pinpoint where she went down, with practically the whole of the Pacific to choose from."

Camille had returned to her room feeling rather dazed at the idea she'd inherited a share in a boat worth thousands of dollars. And through the generosity of a man she didn't remember even meeting.

Although he hadn't really left it to her, but to her father. She wondered if Barney had discussed the bequest with his mate. And if so, whose idea it had been to provide for Thomas McIndoe's family in the event of his death.

Staring out the window at the hill behind the hotel, she dredged up what she remembered about the seaport that had thrived in the days of sailing ships and sunk into obscurity with the advent of road and rail transport. One of the old houses crowding the slope featured a small tower with a railed enclosure around it. A widow's walk, similar to those in other historic ports around the world, from which women used to watch for their men coming home from the sea.

Like so many of those men, Camille's father had finally failed to return. But it was a long time since his wife had given up keeping vigil for him. Nobody had been waiting and hoping to welcome him home.

For a while she tried to work while the deep rumble of male voices penetrated the floor, and loud guffaws and occasional shouts or snatches of song floated clearly through the open window.

Distracted and restless, she left the room and ran down the stairs, her hand enjoying the smoothed curve of the baluster that ended at an ornate carved newel post, then hurried across the lobby into the dazzle of the sun.

Unthinkingly she directed her steps toward the seafront and then the old wharf, eventually finding the *Sea-Rogue* snugged against the massive wooden piles.

Camille didn't know much about boats, but this was a weatherworn veteran compared to the elegant yachts in front of the hotel. The deckhouse had a higher, squarer profile, with two steps leading from the wheel well to a narrow door, not a lift-up hatch cover. A waist-high timber rail instead of wire lines guarded the afterdeck, and a slender bowsprit like those on old sailing ships tapered forward from the bow.

After a brief hesitation she stepped across the small space to the rail almost level with her feet, and jumped onto the deck, pushing aside an uneasy feeling of trespass. After all, she'd been told she owned half of the craft.

The boards shifted under her feet. She touched a sun-warmed spar—or was it a boom? She was hazy about modern nautical terms.

A screeching gull drew her gaze upward. Two masts soared against the sky, and the sun glowing through a gauzy layer of cloud made her eyes water. The boat appeared bigger now she was on board. She stepped down onto one of the slatted seats in the wheel well to reach its floor.

Two farther steps led to the closed door. The wood around the brass lock had been splintered, fresh raw wounds showing through the varnish. As she reached out to investigate, a male voice from the dock said, "It's locked."

Camille jumped, flushing when she turned to confront the Broderick brothers, standing above her on the wharf. Rogan looked faintly amused, curious, and his brother noncommittal but a bit austere.

"Not anymore," she said. "It's been broken into."

"What?" Rogan jumped to the deck, followed by his brother.

Feeling she needed to apologize for her presence, she said, "I'm sorry, I just wondered…"

She didn't know what she'd wondered, what she'd been thinking. Only that her father had spent a good part of his life on this boat, sailing the Pacific with Barney Broderick.

They weren't listening to her anyway. Rogan let out one explosive word, Granger swung the door open and they plunged into the gloom inside.

After a moment's hesitation Camille entered the tiny compartment inside the door and descended a short, ladder-like companionway after the men, taking a few seconds to adjust from the light outside. Then she gasped in shock.

The foam squabs by the table were askew and the covers

ripped. Small carvings, shells and pieces of paper lay all over the place. Books had been wrenched from their shelves and some paperbacks torn in two, the matting on the floor shoved aside, and a conglomeration of sailing gear, food stores, ropes and objects that Camille couldn't begin to identify hauled from storage compartments that gaped open. The railed galley shelves were empty, cupboard doors hung wide and drawers had been upended, the contents of food scattered over everything.

Standing between the two men under the low ceiling, Camille could feel the anger emanating from them both, chill and focused from Granger, hot and fierce from Rogan.

"Who...?" Camille began, but it was probably an unanswerable question.

Rogan swore again before he said shortly, "No idea." He picked up a book, blowing a cloud of flour off its tooled leather cover, then rubbing his forearm over it. "Bastards."

His brother's expression was closed. "We probably shouldn't touch anything until the police get here."

The lone constable stationed in Mokohina surveyed the wreckage with Rogan and Granger before returning to the deck, where Camille waited to give him a brief statement.

"Probably teenagers," he told them, turning to the men. "Can you tell if anything's missing?"

Granger shook his head. "We were only here for a few minutes last night, and it was dark. Before that, as I told your detective yesterday, neither of us had been on board lately. But the police searched the boat on Tuesday."

The constable said he would contact the Criminal Investigation Branch in Whangarei. "They might want to take a look, since they're inquiring into your father's death." Suddenly thoughtful he added, "There's a rumor that he struck it lucky recently."

Granger gave a quiet, sardonic laugh. "My guess is his friends had some fanciful hindsight after he was…found."

Nodding as if his own suspicion was confirmed, the policeman closed his book. "Well, I'll secure the vessel and ask the wharf manager to keep an eye on it." He glanced at his watch. "If they need a scene examination it'll probably be tomorrow. We'll let you know when they've finished."

On the way back to the Imperial, flanked by the men, Camille didn't like to break the silence, grim on one side and seething on the other.

They were nearing the hotel when Rogan spoke over her head to his brother. "D'you reckon this has something to do with what happened to Dad?"

"I doubt it," Granger answered. "There are ghouls who study newspapers for death notices, and target homes when the families are at the funeral. This is probably the same sort of thing. Or maybe some young idiots heard the rumor and tried their luck, hoping to find a treasure chest on board." His scathing tone implied what he thought of them and their gullibility.

When they entered the lobby the noise from the private room had lessened considerably. Granger said, "Time to shoo the diehards into the public bar, I think."

The young Maori woman behind the desk called to Camille, "Miss Hartley…there's a package for you."

Camille excused herself from the men, and the receptionist handed her a small parcel and an envelope. "Have you decided how long you're staying?" the girl asked.

Having left her departure date open, Camille had become interested in the town and its little-known history, and on learning of Barney's death felt she should attend his funeral. Now things were complicated.

"We have a full house after the weekend," the receptionist explained. "It's the annual Mokohina big-game-fishing tournament. People come from all over for it."

"I'll remember that, thanks."

Opening the envelope, she bypassed the ancient, creaking elevator and started up the stairs. She drew out a single sheet of thick, elegant paper and unfolded a note written in a precise, almost copperplate hand.

This may interest you, it said. *Thank you for a very pleasant evening, which I hope to repeat before you leave.*

The signature was a flourishing, curlicued *James,* and he'd added his telephone number.

In the upper hallway she found Rogan lounging against the wall. Startled, she said, "I thought you were still downstairs."

He straightened. "Granger's taking care of things. I wondered what you're doing for dinner. We thought we'd try the Koffee 'n' Kai café along the road. Care to join us?"

It was extraordinary, the effect he had on her. Whenever they were within meters of each other she was totally aware of his presence. She could feel now the warm prickling on her skin, although he hadn't moved any closer.

He smiled at her and she reminded herself that Rogan Broderick wasn't her type, no matter how dazzling his male charisma. "Thank you," she said, "but I have other plans."

What plans? her mind scoffed. A lonely dinner in a discreet corner of the dining room or a snack in her own room, and a boring evening making research notes, talking to her tape recorder?

"Maybe some other time?" Rogan suggested.

"Maybe." She gave him a thin smile and went along the passageway to her room, telling herself not to hurry, and not to look back to check if her sense that he was watching her was right or wrong. But when she heard a door close as she unlocked hers she couldn't resist a covert glance.

The passage was empty.

"James," she said into the phone a few minutes later, "thank you so much! It's a gem." She placed the little volume on the night table, running her fingers over the gold-embossed pattern on the leather cover and the gilt title on the spine: *Journals and Letters of a Lady in New Zealand, 1835-7.* "I'll be sure to return it before I leave."

"No need," James Drummond's light, creamy voice assured her. "It's a gift. How was the funeral?"

"Oh, that's very generous. Um…" she said, "…crowded. Mr. Broderick had a lot of friends."

"And did any relatives turn up?"

Chatting over dinner, she'd told him she didn't know if Barney had relatives. "Two sons." *One who makes my hormones go crazy. And one who should but doesn't.* "They were in the dining room last night but I didn't know who they were."

"Those two big guys?" he asked curiously. "Have you spoken to them?"

"Yes, we had quite a talk."

"Really? What about?"

"Apparently I inherit part of the boat—the *Sea-Rogue*—through my father."

"How…interesting." He sounded genuinely intrigued. "Anything else?"

"Well, what's inside it, and possibly some outstanding payments from my father's last voyage."

"I'd love to hear all about it. Have dinner with me at my house?"

"Tonight?"

"Do you like fish? One thing about this town, you can

always get good fish. And my housekeeper is a very good cook. Or,'' he added teasingly, ''do you have a date with the brothers Broderick?''

She'd turned them down, but felt guilty about claiming other plans. Having dinner with James would validate that excuse. And he'd be an antidote to Rogan Broderick.

Cultured, intelligent, charming, with interests similar to hers and an obviously sympathetic nature, James was a total contrast to the bold-eyed pirate who was occupying far too much of her mind.

''No,'' she said, ''I don't have a date.''

''I'll pick you up at seven,'' he said, even though she told him she had her own car. ''No need to dress up for me.''

A quick sortie through her bag and she settled on light-blue cotton pants and a loose knitted top. James arrived on time, and whisked her away in a low-slung, polished white car that looked as though it had just driven off the advertising pages of a glossy magazine. It covered the winding uphill road to his house in barely five minutes.

Designed in colonial style but incorporating modern touches, the building soared three stories high, with broad verandas and big windows to take in the spectacular views.

Inside, real crystal chandeliers glowed on varnished timber walls and highlighted a breathtaking collection of antique furniture.

''Antiques are my business,'' James replied smilingly to Camille's admiring comment. ''Wholesale prices.''

''Your shop is very well stocked for such a small town.''

''Overseas visitors find prices here reasonable, and quite a few yachties get stuff shipped home. It's been worthwhile keeping the original store open for that reason, and for the retirees and newcomers who are building. But I have another store in Auckland, and a nice little apartment, so I divide my time between here and the city. Summers are pleasant in the north, and I do some entertaining here.''

Obviously the antique business was a lucrative one, or perhaps he'd inherited money as well.

She followed with a glass of wine in her hand while he showed her stunning examples of craftsmanship in furniture and fine porcelain, and equally impressive works of art, and a small collection of historic coins and thimbles in a glass-fronted cupboard. Surrounded by mementos of days past, she was enchanted.

Dinner was served by a gaunt middle-aged woman on a sheltered corner of the wide veranda, and when James brought up the subject, Camille felt sufficiently relaxed to talk about her unexpected inheritance.

His light eyes bright and interested, he said, ''I'd like to see your boat.''

''It's not mine. Well, only a part of it is. At the moment no one's allowed on board. It was burgled and police detectives from Whangarei may want to look at it.''

James looked surprised and concerned. ''Were there valuables on board that would have interested a burglar?''

''Rogan and Granger didn't seem to think so.''

He leaned over to pour her some more wine, and glanced up at her face. ''They should know. If so, they might be keeping it to themselves.'' He sat back and lifted his glass, regarding her steadily over it. ''You should keep an eye on your inheritance.''

''What do you mean?''

''Would you know if they'd removed anything?''

''I suppose not, but I don't think—''

James said, ''You'd be surprised what I see in my business. Families stripping furniture and valuables from a house before the body of their loved one is cold. How do the Brodericks feel about their father leaving a share to you?''

''They seem okay with it. One of them's a bit reserved, but I think that's just his nature.''

''Still, it pays not to be too trusting.'' He raised his glass again. ''Here's to your good fortune.''

James deposited her at the hotel well before midnight. If she'd given him the right signals he might have invited her to stay the night, but when she said she must leave he didn't demur beyond a polite expression of regret.

Although she had talked more than she'd meant to about the *Sea-Rogue* and the Brodericks, at least for part of the time she had managed to push Rogan Broderick and her astonishing reactions to him into the back of her mind.

When she went down for breakfast the following morning the brothers weren't about, and afterward she avoided the wharves, instead making a pilgrimage uphill to the tiny Settlers and Seafarers Museum run by a dedicated group of volunteers in an old missionary church. The elderly woman taking money from a desultory trickle of visitors was happy to impart her historical knowledge of the town and its environs, and Camille spent a couple of hours there.

After detouring to take a closer look at the widow's walk she'd seen from the hotel, and visit some obscure historic sites the museum volunteer had recommended, she returned to the hotel.

It was lunchtime. A bus occupied part of the hotel parking area, and the dining room was full of tourists chattering loudly in a dozen different languages.

Camille retreated, bought herself a sandwich and a paper cup of fresh orange juice, and found a park seat under a tree on the waterfront. She was on the second half of the sandwich when she became aware of someone standing before her, and looked up into Rogan's brilliant eyes.

"Hi," he said. "I saw you from my room. The cops have finished with the boat, and Granger and I are going to clean it up. We'll let you know if we find your father's stuff."

After a second's hesitation, she offered, "Can I help?" And then wondered guiltily if that had arisen from the faint suspicion James had planted last night rather than a genuine desire to be useful. Hadn't she decided to keep out of Rogan's way? But his brother's presence surely would dissipate the peculiar tension she felt around him.

Rogan's doubtful glance passed over her clothes, the same cotton pants and top she'd worn the previous night at James's house. "You don't need to—"

"I'll go and change," she said, "and be with you in about ten minutes." The sooner things were tidied up here and her father's belongings identified, the sooner she could get on with her life and remove herself from this man's disturbing orbit.

He gave her a slow smile, and oh Lord, it was devastating. "We'd appreciate that."

Rogan tapped on his brother's door. Granger opened it wearing a cream golf shirt and beige slacks that might have graced the pages of a fashion magazine. "What?" he asked as Rogan grinned.

"Nothing." Rogan himself wore his shabby khakis. Stuffing his tongue firmly in his cheek, he said, "You look very elegant."

"I wasn't expecting to be playing charladies."

"I could lend you something—" not that he had much in the way of clothes with him, his diving gear taking up most of the space ''—but you probably wouldn't be seen dead in—'' He came to an abrupt stop.

Granger said smoothly, scarcely missing a beat, ''Anything of yours, no.''

''You don't have to stay, you know. If you need to get back to work. Leave this to me.''

Granger shook his head. ''I'll shoot off tomorrow and be in the office on Monday. Shall we go?''

''Camille's coming too,'' Rogan told him.

Closing the door behind them, Granger lifted his brows.

''She volunteered,'' Rogan said. ''She'll meet us downstairs.''

They were waiting at the foot of the stairs when Camille came down, wearing sneakers and denim shorts with a pale yellow T-shirt. Watching her long legs descend toward them, Rogan swallowed hard, and noticed Granger too was staring with some interest, before he turned to Rogan to share a male moment.

On the boat the men surveyed the chaos with identical expressions of masculine cluelessness in the face of a mammoth housekeeping chore.

''Are there cleaning things on board?'' Camille asked. And when they turned to her, ''Brushes, cloths, detergents?''

Rogan said vaguely, ''There's a cupboard opposite the head.''

They worked for hours—stopping only briefly to have a drink, nibble on crackers that the vandals had surprisingly spared in the galley cupboards, or take short breathers on deck.

Rogan somehow managed to control his breathing and his blood pressure whenever he caught sight of Camille's curvy feminine behind stretching the fabric of her shorts as she bent to sift through the jumble on the floor, or when he couldn't help noticing how pretty and perky her breasts were as she reached to replace a book on a railed shelf.

When the daylight in the cabin began to dim, Rogan glanced at his watch. "Anyone hungry?" he asked.

Granger straightened from his task of mopping the galley floor. "Now you mention it…"

Rogan pulled off his sweat-dampened shirt and wiped his forehead with it, leaving a streak of something that might have been cocoa across the tanned skin. Camille dragged her gaze away as he lowered the shirt. "Shall we call it a day," he suggested, "and go back to the hotel?"

Camille said, "Couldn't we finish tonight?" The main cabin was no longer strewn with foodstuffs, and the men had dealt with the gear and miscellaneous sacks and boxes that had cluttered the hold in the bow. Although the two sleeping cabins tucked into the sides and the larger one at the stern had been vandalised, they weren't as bad.

"Sure," Rogan acquiesced, "but I need to eat."

Granger surveyed his brother, then himself, and finally Camille. The spilled condiments mixed with sauces, spreads and the water and detergent they'd used had left them all the worse for wear. "No decent establishment would have us," he deduced. "We'll have to buy hamburgers or something."

"You volunteering?" Rogan asked. "I'll have a double burger with egg and bacon, and plenty of fries. And a couple of doughnuts."

With good grace Granger accepted the request and turned to Camille, who asked for a cheeseburger. "You'd better start the generator," he advised Rogan, "so we can have some light." Then, throwing his brother a quizzical glance, he ascended to the deck.

* * *

Camille realized she and Rogan were alone. The cabin seemed small and increasingly dark, and he was gazing at her rather disconcertingly.

She put a hand to her hair, smoothing several strands that had escaped from their elastic band to fall stickily across her eyes. Pulling the hair tie off, she gathered up the ponytail again and secured it.

Rogan's eyes glazed. He cleared his throat and said, "I'll get that generator fired up."

He disappeared, and a few minutes later she heard and felt the throb of an engine. A light flickered on, and soon afterward Rogan came back.

Camille was carefully wiping down an old copy of Dumas's *Les Trois Mousquetaires,* handsomely bound in tooled leather. She glanced up. "Your father read *The Three Musketeers* in French?"

"He was fluent in French," Rogan said. "And a few other languages, including Pidgin." He nodded at the book in her hands. "I struggled through that when I was a kid."

"You did?"

"I'd already read it in English—but it was a challenge."

Camille could picture him welcoming physical challenges; it hadn't occurred to her he might enjoy intellectual ones.

She placed the book with others on a shelf. A lot of them seemed to be about disasters at sea. "You must have seen more of your father than I did of mine."

"He dropped by when he was in port—a couple of times a year—and took us sailing along the coast when we were old enough. My mother wouldn't let him go out of sight of the land when we were on board." Rogan laughed. "I stowed away once. I was fourteen, and when the old man found me he went ballistic. Turned right round and brought me back. He said if I ever did that to my mother again he'd flay the hide right off my backside.''

Camille looked at him curiously. ''Didn't she mind that he spent so much time away from her?''

''I guess she did. She went with him one time, before she had Granger and me, but she got so seasick they had to airlift her off before Dad could get her back to shore, because she was dangerously dehydrated. After that she couldn't face a boat again. But Dad lived for the sea. On land he was a fish out of water. I don't think she ever tried to change him.''

''Is she…?''

''She died,'' Rogan said abruptly. ''When I was nineteen.''

''I'm sorry.''

He looked down at the books still piled on the floor, waiting to be cleaned and replaced.

Camille picked up a copy of *Treasure Island*. ''I suppose you devoured this?''

''You bet. And this.'' He lifted another book and wiped the cover with his hand. ''*Coasts of Treachery* by Eugene Grayland. Great yarns, full of mayhem and murder.'' Meeting her level look, he added hastily, ''I mean, very well written. Educational,'' he told her. ''You should read it.''

''I have.'' She read every New Zealand history book she could get her hands on—those aimed at a general audience as well as weighty, heavily referenced tomes and professional journals. ''I'm a history lecturer.''

''Is that right? Where?''

His eyes were brilliant with interest and, Camille saw with satisfaction, respect. ''At Rusden.'' It was a small campus in the lower half of the North Island, a satellite of one of the larger universities.

She couldn't help noticing again what an unusual blue

his eyes were, like the inner curve of an incoming breaker at certain blue-water beaches. And his mouth was quite beautiful in a masculine way, the curves well-defined, his lips firm but not thin. Catching a glimpse of white, straight teeth, she felt her blood thicken. Her own mouth softened and parted infinitesimally.

Disturbed by a quick heat that made her legs weaken, Camille turned back to the task in hand. She thought Rogan moved closer, her skin signaling a simmering awareness.

To break the silence she said randomly, "All these books about shipwrecks...not exactly comfort reading for a sailor."

Rogan gave a quiet huffle of laughter. "Dad had a dream that he'd find a sunken treasure one day."

"I guess my father shared it."

They'd been cut from the same cloth. Both had neglected their families to drift about the Pacific, picking up cargoes and passengers, diving for pearls or *beche de mer* occasionally, working onshore only when necessary. And in between, hunting for an elusive, legendary prize.

Granger returned with their meal, and they went up to the cool air of the deck to eat. Rogan shrugged back into his shirt, to Camille's relief. She'd found his bare torso shamingly distracting.

"Camille teaches history," Rogan told his brother. "At Rusden."

"Really?" Granger looked at her thoughtfully.

"Mmm," she confirmed, swallowing a mouthful of cheeseburger.

Rogan asked curiously, "You enjoy it?"

"Very much." Teaching was a nice, steady occupation. If she needed excitement she could find it between the covers of a book about former times. And her salary was enough to keep her in reasonable comfort and help pay the mortgage on the house she shared with her mother. "What do you do?" she asked Granger.

"I'm a solicitor. And barrister, though I don't do a lot of court work."

"He likes playing with rorts and torts," Rogan said with a tolerant but puzzled air.

Granger slanted him a grin, and for a moment the likeness between them was extraordinary. "I bet you don't even know what they are," he said.

"Dead right!" Rogan agreed cheerfully, lifting one of the cans of beer that Granger had brought back from his foraging expedition. He drank thirstily, and Camille stared in fascination at the tilt of his chin, the tautness of his throat.

When she pulled her gaze away Granger was looking at her, his eyes assessing, attentive. "My little brother is a deep-sea diver," he said. "Fighting off sharks and giant squid for a living."

Rogan spluttered, and wiped his mouth with the back of his hand. "That's a load of sh…sugar," he said. "I've never had to fight off a squid, even a baby one. They're not aggressive anyway. You can stroke them."

Camille asked, "Does that mean you've fought sharks?" Her skin crawled.

"I've had some close encounters, but they're pretty harmless underwater as long as you don't do anything stupid."

Granger mocked, "And of course risking your life half a mile under the sea on a regular basis isn't stupid."

"No more stupid than sitting behind a desk all day," Rogan countered. "You're just as likely to die from an ulcer or heart attack there as I am putting in piles for a new oil rig or salvaging a wreck."

Sending a lazy grin in his brother's direction, Granger lifted his beer in acknowledgment. Camille deliberately watched him, waiting for a repeat of the small thrill, but it didn't come. They looked so much alike; in fact Granger was probably the better-looking one—less hard-edged, more sophisticated, well-groomed. And yet he aroused in her nothing more than mildly pleasant appreciation.

There was no doubt about Rogan's raw attraction. She was chagrined at being so susceptible to it.

To distract herself, she spoke to Granger about the first thing that came into her mind. "Do you think your father…and mine, might have discovered some kind of treasure?"

Granger looked amused. "Do you believe in fairy tales?"

Camille shook her head. She never had, even as a child. Her mother had taught her there was no such thing as Happy Ever After.

"To those two," Granger said, "finding sunken treasure was the gold at the end of the rainbow, the holy grail of the sea. And they had about as much chance of finding it."

When they returned to work Camille paused once to arch her stiffening back against her hands, and caught Rogan staring at the jut of her breasts. Quickly straightening, she turned away, hoping he hadn't noticed the peaks suddenly showing through her T-shirt, as if he'd physically touched her.

While she dealt with the rest of the books, Rogan and Granger cleaned up the two smaller cabins.

Then Granger emerged, saying, "Some things of your father's, Camille." He put a cardboard carton on the table as Rogan joined them. "There are clothes too. Do you want to—"

"No." She didn't want to look at them.

After a slight pause Granger said, "We could give them to the Salvation Army along with Dad's, if you like."

"Yes, thank you."

He gestured at the box. "You'd better have a look in here. It's all that was in his cabin."

Reluctantly she stepped closer, peering into the box. On top of a jumble of books, papers and miscellaneous items was a mounted photograph of a young woman smiling at the camera, holding a solemn-faced baby wearing a pink dress, with a matching bow in her short blond curls. Her mother and herself. Camille blinked and swallowed. Slowly she stretched out a hand and picked up the picture before placing it on the table.

Underneath it was another. She was older in this one, her fair hair in two pigtails, and she wore a party hat and clutched a balloon and a toy rabbit. Her sixth birthday party. The rabbit was the last gift she'd ever received from her father, and although she had thought it babyish at the time she'd cherished it for years. Until she realized he was never going to come home again.

"You were blond?" Rogan queried.

"It darkened as I got older."

Tucked to one side in the box were a number of envelopes, slit to reveal folded letters. She reached in and pulled out one. The address, care of a post office in Suva, was in her mother's writing—small, precise. Unexpectedly her eyes hazed with tears. She started to tremble.

"Hey!" Rogan's voice was in her ear, his arm about her waist. "Are you okay? Sit down."

He guided her to one of the seats by the table. "Can we get you something? Granger—?"

"It's all right." Camille blinked rapidly, only succeeding in forcing a tear to escape and run down her cheek. Furiously she rubbed at it with her fingers. "I'm fine," she reiterated loudly.

Granger said, "I didn't mean to upset you."

"I'm not upset! Just...surprised."

It was a weak excuse. She couldn't imagine why the sight of the meager keepsakes her father had hoarded should kindle a grief that was out of proportion. It wasn't as if he'd ever been a real father to her.

Maybe that was it. He never had, and now it was too late. "I'm sorry," she said. "I guess I'm tired."

Another pathetic excuse, but it galvanized the men into a flurry of apologies and self-blame. She'd worked too long and too hard, they should have realized, and Rogan would take her back to the hotel right now. Should they call a taxi?

"For a ten-minute walk?" She laughed shakily, embarrassed at their anxious outpouring. "Of course not. And I don't need an escort."

But soon she was walking along the seawall in darkness while Rogan kept a firm though careful hold on her arm, and Granger stayed behind to switch off the generator, secure the boat, and bring along the box of Taff's belongings.

As they reached the more populous area, where streetlamps glowed and were reflected in the water, Rogan said, "Granger shouldn't have sprung it on you like that."

"It wasn't his fault. I'm sorry I was such an idiot." She was mortified at her unexpected show of emotion.

"You weren't an idiot." He pushed a leafy twig aside as they walked under one of the pohutukawas, and in the shadow she stumbled on a root that had distorted the path.

Rogan's grip tightened. "You okay?"

His breath was warm on her temple. She caught a whiff of his male scent, the salty tang of fresh sweat and the less sharp aroma of musk, earthy but strangely not repellent. Was there nothing about this man that was unattractive?

"Yes," she said. "Thanks."

They walked on, but now she was tongue-tied, intensely conscious of the hand that still circled her arm, the masculine bulk of Rogan's body, the exact height of her head where it came to just above his shoulder.

She heard the intermittent slap of water on the seawall, its softer lapping about the anchored boats, the rhythmic splash and creak of someone rowing a dinghy back to their yacht. Music and the chatter of patrons at an outdoor café clearly carried on the night air. Nearby a bird chirruped sleepily, perhaps confused by the streetlights into thinking it was still day.

They reached the hotel and Rogan sighed, almost as if he were relieved. He released her arm and asked, "Would you like a drink? Brandy, maybe?"

Camille shook her head. "I need a shower." She looked down at her stained shirt and shorts. "And then I'll go to bed. I can get that box from your brother in the morning?"

"Sure. I'll see you to your room."

"You needn't, really."

But he steered her into the ancient elevator, and when it stopped he followed her out and padded down the corridor at her side, waiting while she unlocked the door.

"Thank you." She turned to him. "I don't know why he kept those things. They can't have meant much to him."

Rogan looked at her gravely. "They must have meant something."

Camille lifted her chin, her skin cold. Stupid sentimentalism would get her nowhere. She was grown up now, in no need of a father. Or any other man. "I'll go through them tomorrow," she said, "and see if there's anything that can't be burned."

Chapter 4

A line appeared between Rogan's dark brows. When Camille made to go into the room he caught her arm again, searching her face as she instinctively raised it in inquiry.

Then he bent toward her, and for a split second she knew she could refuse his kiss but didn't want to.

His mouth was gentle, questing but not demanding. He waited for her to reciprocate, and when her lips parted a fraction his arms slid about her, holding her close within them.

It was the nicest kiss Camille had ever had. But when he would have deepened it danger signals flared in her mind, and she made a little move of negation, pushing against his arms.

Reluctantly he let her go, and she looked up into a blaze of turquoise, returning his questioning, decidedly sexy smile with a small, shaky one of her own. "Good night, Rogan," she said, trying to sound firm and in control, but afraid she only sounded breathless.

As she opened the door wider he kissed her temple, barely touching her skin with his lips, and she had to hold the knob in a tight grip to prevent herself turning back into his arms. She hadn't been so affected by a man since…since she couldn't remember.

"Good night," he said, his gaze following her like a laser. He was still standing there with his hands thrust into the pockets of his stained and wrinkled khakis when she quietly closed the door.

Rogan had a quick shower, changed his clothes and, when Granger returned, pounced on his brother in the passageway.

"Does Camille want this tonight?" Granger asked, indicating the carton in his arms.

Rogan shook his head. "She said it'll keep until tomorrow." He followed as Granger entered his own room. "She also said she was going to burn most of it. At least, I think that's what she meant."

Granger shrugged. "Her prerogative."

"Yeah, but…" Standing by as Granger slid the box onto a small table, Rogan thrust his hands into his pockets, broodingly regarding the carton.

"What?" Granger queried.

"Suppose there is something in that story about Dad and Taff finding their treasure ship?"

"You don't really believe that, do you?" Granger scoffed.

"I guess not…" Rogan's gaze returned to the box on the table. "I wonder if Taff made a will."

"I doubt it," Granger answered. "Anyway, that's not our worry."

Camille woke early while the water in the harbor was sheened with cool silvery light, the shallow wavelets on the beach making scarcely a sound.

She went for a short walk before breakfast, turning away from the wharves and heading in the other direction until the path petered out at a small park and the beach ended in a tumble of craggy rocks under a headland. For a while she watched the waves foaming against the rocks, and when the sun began to climb and shimmer on the water she started back to the town.

The seamen's chapel was open and she went inside, finding it deserted. She sat in one of the pews, remembering Barney's funeral, and wondering what kind of service, if any, her own father had been accorded.

Barney would have told her, but he'd never had the chance. She should feel sad. Instead she felt empty. How could she mourn a father she scarcely remembered?

When she returned to the hotel the staff was serving breakfast in the dining room and the Broderick brothers were seated at a table, Granger consulting the menu while Rogan gave the teenage waitress the benefit of his stunning eyes and rogue's grin as he ordered bacon, sausages and eggs with hash browns.

As the waitress turned to his brother Rogan saw Camille in the doorway. Immediately he was on his feet and crossing the room. ''Join us,'' he said, reaching out a hand to take her arm. ''It's a bit better than hamburgers on the deck.''

He left her no choice unless she was to be unnecessarily rude. She took the chair he pulled out for her, and after saying good morning to Granger ordered orange juice, toast and marmalade.

Rogan said, ''That's not breakfast!''

''Maybe not for you. It's plenty for me,'' she retorted.

Granger said, ''How are you feeling this morning?''

Camille turned to him with relief. "There's nothing wrong with me."

He gave her one of his restrained smiles. "I'd concur with that."

Rogan shot him a look that was almost suspicious, and said rather loudly, "Granger's got that box of your father's things for you. When would you like to look through it?"

She glanced at him and then back at Granger. "Anytime it suits you."

"Before I check out I'll bring it along to your room—or send Rogan." His fleeting glance at his brother held a hint of amusement.

"You're leaving today?" Camille asked. Did that mean Rogan too?

"I've done all I can here, for now anyway." He looked at Rogan. "You'll take care of the ashes, then?"

Rogan nodded and Granger turned to Camille. "Can you get a copy of your birth certificate sent to my office? And of your parents' marriage certificate too?"

The waitress brought their breakfasts. By the time Camille finished, Rogan had nearly demolished his meal and Granger was well on the way to disposing of his bacon, eggs and tomatoes.

As Rogan cut his last sausage in pieces he said, "Granger reckons it could be weeks before you can claim your half of the *Sea-Rogue*. Meantime I hope you won't object if I sleep aboard."

"Of course not." She surely had no right to object.

"If you'd like one of the cabins," he said, "it's cheaper than a hotel."

"Thank you, but I don't think I'll be staying in Mokohina." She should have checked out, herself, but it was Sunday and the sky was blue now with a few insubstantial clouds drifting across it, the harbor a deep satiny green, and after yesterday's exertions she felt lazy. Maybe she could stay a day longer.

Rogan pushed away his plate as the waitress came with coffee and poured for all of them. Rogan took his black, Granger added a dash of cream.

Rogan asked Camille, "Aren't you on holiday?"

"A working one." She stirred cream and brown sugar crystals into her cup. "I'm preparing a presentation on the interaction of Maori and European women during the early settlement period."

When Barney had been so insistent that she come to Mokohina she'd decided to make the trip an opportunity for research. The Bay of Islands, first visited by Europeans in the late eighteenth century and with missionary settlement since 1814, was a good place to find obscure local material.

"So where are you off to next?" Rogan inquired.

"Maybe Kerikeri." The town was home to some of New Zealand's oldest buildings and had a charming river. But its views didn't compete with those of Mokohina. "My plans aren't fixed."

Granger warned, "The holiday season's starting. You could have trouble finding casual accommodation." He pushed back his chair and stood up, glancing at his watch. "I'll be off shortly," he said to Rogan, and nodded pleasantly to Camille. "Thanks for your help yesterday."

"No problem," she murmured, and began to move, herself.

Rogan stood too. "I'll bring along that box for you."

He left her at the reception desk, where she managed to extend her stay to the following day. Ten minutes later she opened her door to Rogan's knock.

"Where do you want it?" he asked, ignoring her attempt to take the box from his arms.

"On the table, I suppose." There was a round glass-topped table by the window, flanked by two cushioned wicker chairs that had been freshly painted white.

The telephone on the night table burred. Camille hurried to answer it as Rogan edged a vase of artificial flowers away from the center of the table to ease the box down.

Camille picked up the phone. "James here," his voice said quietly in her ear. "I wondered if you'd like to meet a retired headmaster who's made almost a lifetime study of the history of this area. He buys old books from me and has a collection of family papers and other original documents he's amassed over the years. But perhaps you're not interested in talking with amateurs."

She'd been intrigued on her visit to the tiny museum, her interest in localized history piqued. "I'd be very interested," she assured him, watching Rogan rescue the vase as it toppled, and look around for somewhere safe to put it.

James was saying, "He'll be at church this morning, but I could take you to his place this afternoon."

"I don't like to impose on you, James."

"It will be a pleasure. Please don't deprive me of it."

James sometimes seemed like a gentleman from another era. She laughed quietly. "If you put it like that…"

Rogan carefully placed the vase on the 1930s dressing table and sent her a piercing look.

"Good," James said. "Is one-thirty too early?"

"Not too early at all. I'll be ready."

"Ready for what?" Rogan shot at her as she replaced the receiver, and when she raised her brows in surprise he looked mulish for a moment before muttering, "Sorry, none of my business." He looked down at the box. "Well, there it is."

"Thank you."

Rogan still didn't move. "You won't...um...you won't throw out anything that might..."

"Might what?"

"There could be some clue here, if Dad and Taff really found treasure..."

Camille didn't believe for a minute that there was any treasure, much less that her father's pathetic belongings would hold the key to its whereabouts. "If you like," she said indifferently, "you can go through it with me."

She wasn't sure why she made the offer, but perhaps it was because somehow she was dreading tackling this task, and company—any company—might ease it.

Later she would have to phone her mother and ask her to find the certificates Granger had asked for—and explain why. At least Rogan's presence was a good excuse to stave that off for a while. Although she was wary of the potent sexuality he exuded, the undeniably pleasurable if unsettling sensations she experienced whenever he was around were an antidote to the depressive mood that threatened her.

She sat staring at the box for a second or two, then lifted out the pictures she'd already seen, removed the bundle of letters beneath, and after glancing through the envelopes laid them aside.

"You're not going to read them?" Rogan asked.

Camille shook her head. "They're from my mother." The postmarks showed they had been sent more than twenty years ago. "I'll ask her what she wants done with them." But she could guess anyway. *Burn them,* Mona would say with a brittle laugh. *Throw away everything.* The way Thomas McIndoe had thrown away their marriage, their daughter's love.

Camille wished she had the courage to do it without looking any further, but a small, niggling, useless curiosity made her keep digging into the box.

She withdrew a battered peaked cap that gave off a faint whiff of salt water and tobacco and another elusive odor, bringing an instant memory of a big laughing man lifting her off her feet when she must have been only a tot, giving her a bear hug and planting a smacking kiss on her cheek, his skin like rough sandpaper. And a voice, with that same rasping quality, "How's my little girl?"

The picture was so vivid her breath momentarily snagged before she quickly put the hat down alongside the letters.

There were a number of wood carvings, none bigger than her hand—a turtle, a fish, boats of various shapes, and a few crude human figures, one more detailed than the others, of a girl child in a dress, her hair rippling down her back.

"You?" Rogan queried.

She put the figure down among the others. "I don't know." It could have been any anonymous child. Even if it was supposed to be her, he probably hadn't remembered what she looked like.

There was a bundle of maps, most of them brown-stained with age and worn along the folds. She handed them to Rogan to look through.

She found several books. *Twenty Thousand Leagues Under the Sea, Two Years Before the Mast,* navigation manuals, a few dog-eared paperback thrillers. Next came a pile of outdated *National Geographics* and a Boy Scout manual, the edges nibbled by mice or silverfish. Had her father been a Boy Scout once? Or just picked this up somewhere, perhaps for the pages illustrating how to tie knots?

Under that a passport, well-stamped. Briefly Camille studied the photo of a bearded man gazing fiercely at the camera. He was a stranger.

Right at the bottom she found a brown envelope containing unframed snapshots that she peeked at before adding it to the pile on the table, and a large imitation brass cigar tin, rusting at the corners.

Trying to be patient, Rogan watched her lever open the lid of the tin, revealing a magpie collection. Oddly shaped coins from obscure Pacific nations, a gold tiepin—when had Taff ever worn a tie? A pair of mother-of-pearl cuff links, another pair with some kind of dark red stone set in them. Beneath the trinkets and coins some yellowed newspaper cuttings. Camille studied one for a moment before putting it aside. Rogan peered sideways at the announcement of a wedding—Thomas William McIndoe to Mona Violet Hartley. There was a picture of the happy couple, Taff resplendent in a suit and tie, fair hair waving onto his shoulders, looking young and pleased with himself, and his bride in white frills and a cloudy veil, smiling adoringly at him.

The other clipping was a birth notice. *McIndoe: To Mona and Thomas, a darling daughter.*

Camille was carefully unfolding a larger piece of paper. He saw her eyes dilate momentarily, and her hands trembled. Then with a fierce, unexpected movement she crumpled the paper into her hand, her mouth tight and eyes bright and angry.

"What is it?" Rogan queried.

"Nothing. Just rubbish." She dropped the screwed-up ball into a wastebasket near the table and began tipping the other things back into the tin. "If there's anything else you want from this lot—" she waved at the cluttered tabletop "—take your pick."

Taff had been bluffly kind to Barney's boys. Rogan picked out the wooden turtle, that just fitted in his palm. "I'll take this for my brother." Maybe Granger could use it for a paperweight or something.

"What about you?"

"I move around a lot." He traveled light and didn't burden himself with sentimental possessions.

Camille began gathering up the other carvings and dropping them back in the box.

"What are you going to do with them?" he asked.

"Probably burn them. They're not good enough to sell."

They weren't works of art, but Taff had spent hours happily carving them. Rogan and Granger had once had small wooden outrigger canoes with miniature sails that they'd watched him make for them. Rogan didn't recall what had happened to them.

As she reached for the figure of the little girl he said, "I'll have that."

It was an impulse that surprised him almost as much as it evidently had her. She looked disconcerted, and he said swiftly, "Unless you want it after all."

Decisively she shook her head. "You're welcome to it."

He picked it up, the wood cool in his hand. "There isn't anything inside those books is there? Papers?"

She went through them one by one, holding them spine upward and letting the pages fall open. "Nothing." She began returning them to the box.

"I wouldn't mind looking through the navigation tables."

She cast him a rather mocking glance. "They're all yours. Do you want the *National Geographics* too?"

"Sure." He didn't want to miss anything.

She stood up and tossed more things into the box, leaving the cigar tin and the two large photos, then picked up the brown envelope and hesitated before throwing it on top of the rest. A few photographs spilled from it. "You haven't even looked at them," he said.

"I don't want to." Her voice was tight.

"There are photos of my dad there. D'you mind...?"

Camille shrugged, and wrapped her arms defensively about her body. "Help yourself." Her eyes were fixed on the window with its view of the hillside. "Then I'll dispose of the rest. I suppose they have an incinerator here."

Rogan made a decision. "I'll take care of it for you. You should get the stuff in the tin valued, maybe."

"I doubt if anything's worth much." She sounded indifferent. A small pause, then a rather grudging, "Thank you for getting rid of that for me." She nodded at the box.

He finished repacking it and hoisted it into his arms. "Are you all right?"

"Of course." She smiled at him, brilliantly, then said in a brisk tone, "Now that's done I can concentrate on my research." She was already walking to the door, apparently eager to get rid of him. On a note of subtle mockery she said, "Good luck with your treasure hunt."

James was in the foyer when Camille came down.

After driving inland to a tiny settlement surrounding an abandoned dairy factory, he stopped at a modest villa with an impeccable garden where lavender and roses and deep blue forget-me-nots flourished under kowhai and totara trees.

Selwyn Trubshaw looked younger than the seventy-nine years he deprecatingly admitted to; a fit, erect man with cropped gray hair, his brown eyes alert behind rimless spectacles. His library in a large converted bedroom was stacked from floor to ceiling with books and neatly labeled files and boxes, while an impressive old oak desk held a computer and scanner.

Invited to inspect the shelves, reading book titles and the labels on file boxes, Camille experienced a tingling along her spine, lifting the fine hair at her nape, an intuition that she had learned to respect.

Three and a half hours later she was poring over an old diary, scanning the meticulous copperplate writing.

"Given to me by an elderly neighbor," Mr. Trubshaw said. "It was her grandmother's, and she was afraid her children would burn it after she died."

James rested a casual hand on Camille's shoulder. He smelled of cologne, probably expensive but slightly sharp. "Interesting?" he queried.

"Wonderful! This is what you don't get enough of in travel books written by men—the everyday life of the past."

Mr. Trubshaw looked pleased. "You're welcome to come back anytime," he said.

Guiltily Camille realized how late it was, and that he seemed a little tired. He'd been eagerly showing her his treasures, but he wasn't a young man. "I'd love to," she assured him warmly. "James, you've been very patient."

On the way back to the hotel she said, "He has a marvelous collection, and just the sort of thing I'm looking for. I'm very grateful to you."

"Grateful enough to have dinner with me again?"

"Only if you let me pay. I owe you, after all."

He shook his head, but she was adamant, and he graciously gave in.

Chapter 5

Rogan was hot, unable to sleep. He'd sorted through the photographs in the box, and put aside several of Taff. They sat in a neat pile next to the little wooden girl he'd placed on the table after returning to his room.

The maps had yielded nothing of immediate interest; they were old and hadn't been opened for years, he guessed. The nautical tables had some scribbled notes on the pages, but none that looked like directions to any hidden treasure.

Well, what had he expected—X marks the spot?

Dressed only in shorts, he got up and without switching on a light padded to the window, pushed the old-fashioned sash up high to encourage a breeze, and stood looking out beyond the ghostly shapes of the boats in the marina to the sea, or at least what he could discern of it in the darkness. Which wasn't much more than an occasional glimpse of restless white or a glint of silver, but the smell of it rose to the window and wrapped him in its welcome, familiar aroma.

The stars were dimmed in patches by ghostly clouds, and the moon was a luminous half-egg. A car passed, its headlights sweeping the road ahead. The glow of a streetlight was a target for moths and beetles swooping and diving about it.

Was he an idiot, thinking his father might have finally found his life's dream? And what chance did he have of uncovering the secret now?

Granger thought he was nuts. So did Camille, obviously. They could be right.

Something nagged at a corner of his mind, some half-formed thought that had first wormed its way into his brain on board the ketch, only to sink back into his subconscious. Trying to tease it out, he was distracted when a car came into view and glided to a halt outside the hotel.

He recognized the man who climbed out and went to open the passenger door. And then Camille emerged.

They were awfully close. The man said something and bent his head, and she didn't move away. Rogan closed his hands over the cool paint of the windowsill.

Now the guy had both hands on Camille's shoulders and was kissing her. Two seconds, and Rogan couldn't tell who broke off the clinch. He heard the low murmur of her voice, and the man's indistinct reply. Then they both moved out of sight into the doorway.

Hell, had she invited him up to her room? Rogan dived away from the window and was halfway into his jeans before he realized he was about to make a fool of himself, waiting in the hallway to see if Camille arrived with a man in tow.

None of his damn business.

He shucked off the jeans and switched on the bedside

lamp. Immediately a large, whirring bug shot through the open window and batted itself against the pink satin shade. Rogan swore and flicked the switch again, hoping the huhu would return to the open air. Instead it flung itself about the room, blundering frantically into the walls.

He certainly wasn't going to be able to sleep with that in here. For ten minutes he chased it about, swearing under his breath, trying to guide the stupid creature toward freedom with the help of a folded newspaper, tempted to just swat the thing and be done with it.

At last, with a final frenzied propeller-whirr, the beetle discovered the open square of freedom and hurried off into the night. Ready to slam down the window, Rogan paused. The car was gone. Good, he thought, carefully not analyzing his relief.

It wasn't until half an hour later, on the brink of sleep, that it occurred to him the guy might have simply moved his vehicle to a less conspicuous place. The hotel car park, or around the corner into a secluded street.

He hadn't heard anyone come upstairs or the sound of a door closing, but he'd been busy with the blasted huhu and it made enough noise to cover almost anything.

Having run out of excuses, Camille called home the next morning. As she'd expected, Mona told her to burn the letters and photographs, expressing acid surprise that Taff had bothered to keep them. When Camille asked her to make copies of her marriage certificate and Camille's birth certificate, it was too much to hope not to have to tell her why.

"That old tub?" Mona laughed scornfully. "The thing was practically a wreck when I last saw it, over twenty years ago. It can't be worth much."

"Granger said some classic boats have sold for a hundred thousand or even more."

"I don't believe it! Well, at least you'll get something out of that good-for-nothing father of yours."

Camille said, "I don't want the money. You're entitled to anything that he left."

"Darling, that's very sweet of you! I won't say I couldn't do with it, and God knows that man owes me something, but you said one of the Broderick boys is a lawyer? He'll find some way of keeping it all."

"I don't think they're like that, either of them. I wouldn't have known about the will if they hadn't told me."

"Well, I'll send the papers, but I wouldn't count on seeing a cent."

Camille hadn't expected to see Rogan in the dining room at breakfast time.

When he looked up from his plate and waved the knife in his hand, indicating the empty seat across from him, she hesitated only a moment before joining him. "I thought you were checking out yesterday," she said.

Rogan swallowed a mouthful of sausage and egg. "Granger booked me through last night, and they do a good breakfast." He removed a piece of toast from a rack before him and began liberally spreading it with butter.

A waitress appeared and Camille accepted a glass of orange juice and ordered toast, with coffee to follow. Rogan shot her a disparaging look but didn't comment. Instead he said, "Are you checking out?"

Camille fiddled with a spoon, picking it up and glancing at her distorted reflection in the bowl before replacing it on the red cloth. "I have to leave the hotel. They're booked solid now until after New Year."

He sawed off a piece of sausage but didn't eat it. "Are you still planning to move to Kerikeri?"

"Well, I've met this man here—"

"Ah." Rogan sat back.

She said impatiently, "He's nearly eighty."

"Didn't look like it last night."

Camille stared back at him. Last night?

He looked away, then hastily shoveled a piece of sausage into his mouth and chewed. "Different bloke," he mumbled when he'd disposed of the sausage, "I guess."

"You weren't *spying* on me?"

"Why would I want to do that?" He sounded indignant. "I happened to be looking out the window when you came home."

Infuriatingly, she felt her cheeks color. So he'd seen James kissing her good-night. Nothing to be embarrassed about—it had scarcely been more than a peck. Well, a warm peck. A bit longer, perhaps, than your average, but when James would have carried it further she'd pulled back a little and he'd immediately drawn away. As any enlightened man would. Then he'd courteously escorted her through the hotel doorway and left with a promise to see her tomorrow.

Today.

Rogan said, "So who is he?"

Who is who? she wondered. And decided to play safe. "Mr. Trubshaw is an amateur historian," she answered. "A retired teacher. He has a lot of interesting material I'd like the time to study properly."

A flash of annoyance crossed Rogan's face. He grabbed his coffee and gulped some down before attacking his breakfast again. "And he's eighty."

"Just about."

"So has he invited you to stay?"

"No." James had, when she'd told him that she must move out of the hotel and that the receptionist had canvassed the motels and bed-and-breakfast places for her with no success. Camille had declined the offer, afraid he might have thought she was fishing, and unwilling to take more favors. He'd seemed disappointed, but had accepted her refusal without argument.

Rogan asked, "Why not take that berth on the *Sea-Rogue?*"

Camille shook her head. "I don't think so."

"You'd be safe," he assured her quite seriously. "My brother's a lawyer, remember. Ultra-respectable, and he'll vouch for me if you like."

She could hardly tell him that it wasn't a crude attack she feared, rather the effect he had on her.

Her toast arrived, and he watched her spread butter and marmalade, then he quickly finished his own meal as she ate. The waitress immediately scooped up his plate, asking if he wanted anything else, and he gave her his multimegawatt smile and said he'd have more coffee when the lady had hers.

"You needn't wait for me," Camille protested.

"I'm in no hurry. I'll just sit here and admire the view." He glanced out the window at the yachts riding their anchors, but then his gaze returned to her, the afterglow of the smile lurking in his eyes. Camille concentrated on cutting a piece of toast in two.

Admittedly it would make sense to live on board the boat. Cheaper, and she needn't feel obligated since apparently she had a right. Mr. Trubshaw's library was an unexpected gold mine. On the face of it she'd be foolish not to take advantage of a free bed, even if she had to share living space with the most unsettling man she'd ever met.

She thought about the kiss they'd shared, and pushed it

firmly from her mind. It had been nice, but a casual kiss didn't necessarily lead to other intimacies. Rogan Broderick had probably lost count of the number of women he'd kissed. He was so good at it—the very fact that she'd thoroughly enjoyed it was a warning.

Surely she could cope with an inconvenient sexual attraction. She'd had plenty of practice at saying no to men, even men who were quite attractive.

Their coffee came and she drank hers in thoughtful silence. When she put down her cup and began to get up Rogan gulped the remainder of his own coffee and hurried to pull her chair out. For a moment he was close and she caught the aroma of soap and freshly washed cotton, warmed by his body heat. Her arm brushed his sleeve before he stepped back, and she felt his breath on her temple.

He was just too much man, she thought. She'd be mad to even contemplate living in close proximity to him. But now he'd moved away and was regarding her nonchalantly, one thumb hooked in the belt of his jeans.

She breathed again, annoyed with herself. This was akin to a teenage crush, a simple physiological reflex, and she was too old and too experienced to let it affect her actions. If she left today she'd have forgotten all about Rogan Broderick within a week.

The receptionist appeared in the dining room doorway and headed toward her. "There's a call for you, Miss Hartley. Shall I tell him to hold until you get to your room?"

"Thanks," she said, then left and raced up the stairs, arriving breathless to pick up the receiver.

James said, "I didn't mean to interrupt your breakfast."

"I'd just finished."

"I had a thought after leaving you last night. If you're determined to be independent, why don't you claim your right of inheritance and use the boat?"

It seemed almost a conspiracy. "Rogan did offer…"

"Offer?" He sounded amused. "You're entitled, surely. It wouldn't hurt to assert your ownership in case there's any problem later. Nine-tenths of the law, you know…"

"Rogan's moving aboard today," she said.

There was a pause before James said slowly, "All the more reason to stake *your* claim, I should think. There *is* more than one cabin…isn't there? Are there locks?"

There had been one on the door of the master's stateroom, she recalled. "I'm sure I won't need one." If Rogan wanted sex there were any number of holiday-makers around who would probably be happy to oblige. "And I don't think he and Granger will try to bilk me out of my share."

"Still, you can't be too careful. Will I see you later? We could have lunch."

"All right," she agreed. That would give her time to make up her mind and check out of the hotel.

She was tucking her father's cigar tin into a corner of her suitcase when a tap on the door sent her to open it to Rogan, a bulging pack slung over one shoulder and several photographs in his hand.

He said, "These pictures are of your father. I thought you should have them."

Camille recoiled, automatically taking a step back and, apparently assuming it was an invitation, he followed her into the room.

"I don't want them," she said.

Apparently perplexed, he said, "Your mother might."

Camille shook her head.

"You don't know that," he persisted.

"I know my own mother!"

"Yeah, I guess." He looked down at the photographs,

and impatiently she took them and tossed them at the wastebasket.

He gave her a searching look, then noticed the open suitcase beside her laptop on the bed and said, "I could carry that for you if you're coming aboard the *Sea-Rogue*."

Time she made up her mind. It *would* be convenient to be based in Mokohina. Why was she dithering, simply because Rogan upset her sexual equilibrium?

Living with him would very likely cure her. He'd probably leave smelly socks and used underwear lying about, and never clean the toilet—the "head," she remembered it was called. And emerge from his cabin in the mornings with a scruffy overnight growth of stubble, yawning and scratching his chest.

Even that picture had its attraction. His teeth were in perfect order, white and strong, and she'd seen his chest—a splendid, manly sight…

"You can have the master's stateroom," he offered. "It's bigger than the others, with a desk. And a lock on the door."

"It's your father's!"

He gave her a lopsided smile. "He's not using it anymore."

"No, but…you should have it."

"I don't need the space. I'm not doing research."

She remembered the roomy cabin with its bookshelves and sturdy desk. "What are you going to do?"

"My contract in the Gulf only had a few weeks to run and they'd phoned for a replacement even before I left. I guess I'm free for a while."

So he wasn't leaving for "a while" anyway. Camille had harbored some hope his stay would be a short one. She shouldn't be feeling a leap of pleasure that it wouldn't be.

"If you don't like it," he said, "you can change your mind anytime. Is that all your luggage?"

"I've got some things in the bathroom." She hesitated a moment longer, then summoned all the pragmatism she'd worked on since childhood. "I'll get them."

Rogan watched her half close the door to the bathroom, and wandered toward the window. One of the photos had fallen on the floor beside the wastebasket. He stooped to pick it up, paused, and tucked it into the breast pocket of his sleeveless denim jacket. The others were fanned in the basket, along with a crumpled paper cup, some pencil shavings, and a scrunched-up ball of paper.

He glanced toward the bathroom, where he could hear a subdued clatter, then a brief rush of running water. Quickly hunkering down, he extracted the paper ball, and was straightening when Camille emerged carrying a toilet bag. He closed his fist over the paper, and while she was making room for the toilet bag and zipping the case closed he surreptitiously shoved the page into a back pocket before crossing to take the case from Camille.

"I can manage," she said, but he just looked at her and she grudged out, "Thank you."

She picked up the laptop, took her jacket and followed him. He wondered if she noticed the curious look the receptionist cast at them as they checked out and left together. Not that it bothered him.

"We might as well take my car," Camille said. "There is parking near the boat, isn't there?"

"Plenty." The wide tar-sealed area where the road ended was seldom filled.

When they'd made the short journey he took her things on board and opened the door of the bigger cabin. "All yours."

"Are you sure…?"

"You're welcome." He swung the suitcase onto the berth. The built-in cupboard was already empty of Barney's clothes, but Rogan found a carton and packed into it everything they'd previously returned to the desk drawers. When he looked at the books they'd neatly replaced in their railed shelves above the bed Camille noticed his tight expression, and as he took a stack of them to stow in another box she said swiftly, "Leave the rest if you like." Removing them would strip the cabin of every trace of his father. "I won't be needing all the shelves."

A flicker of relief crossed his face. "Okay," he said nonchalantly. "Maybe you'll find some of them interesting." About to leave her, he paused at the door, looking at a framed photograph fixed above it.

"Your mother?" she asked curiously. The picture showed a pretty, dark-haired young woman with a wistful smile.

"Yes. Do you want me to take it down?"

"Of course not!"

He gave her an odd little smile and said, "Let me know if there's anything you need."

In drawers under the bed she found a couple of threadbare blankets but no sheets. Apparently a sleeping bag had been sufficient for Barney.

The cushion on the chair looked flattened and hard, thinned in the middle, and sitting on it confirmed its appearance. She wandered into the main cabin as Rogan emerged from one of the others.

He smiled at her. "All settled in?"

"Yes, but I thought I'd walk into town and buy some sheets." A sleeping bag might have been practical but they made her feel suffocated. "And do you mind if I replace the cushion on your father's chair?"

"Fine. I'll come too if that's okay. We should get in some supplies, unless you plan to eat out all the time?"

Whoever had ransacked the boat had left a few tinned goods but not much else. "I have a lunch date today, but—"

"Your Mr. Trubshaw?"

"No." To stop him probing further, she said, "You're right, we'll need groceries."

She bought a pale green linen set of sheets and a cushion patterned with blue and green dolphins before they visited a minimarket for groceries. By the time they'd returned to the boat the tide had lowered and Camille was taken aback at the difference in levels between the wharf and the deck.

Rogan leaped down, dumped the bags he carried and turned back to Camille to collect her bags as she swung them across.

Then he held out his arms. "Jump."

Camille cast a look at the narrow iron ladder attached to one of the slimy wharf piles, where the gap between the boat and the wharf looked rather alarmingly wide.

Rogan said, "It's safer this way."

He was probably right. She stepped into nothingness and was caught and held against a warm, hard chest for a second before he let her go, only retaining a light grip on her arms as he said, "Okay?"

"Yes." But she felt almost winded. "Thanks."

"No problem." He stooped to pick up the groceries.

By the time the food had been packed away Camille had barely time to tidy herself, deciding not to change from her cotton pants and top before going to meet James.

Rogan was lounging on one of the narrow seats in the

wheel well that he called the cockpit, a bulging hamburger bun in one hand, a beer can in the other.

Eyeing the difference between the deck and the wharf, Camille hesitantly approached the ladder, and Rogan said, "Need some help?"

He was there anyway, his strong hand on her elbow as he hoisted her up to the railing, the other reaching out to grasp a rung of the ladder. "You'll be okay."

"I know." But getting both feet on the slippery rungs from the gently rocking boat was a tricky operation, and it was nice to know that if she made a mistake Rogan was there to ensure she didn't fall very far.

When she'd made it to the top and turned to thank him, he was standing with his hands on his hips, grinning appreciatively.

"No problem," he said. "I enjoyed the view."

Torn between indignation and amusement at the blatant comment, Camille retreated in dignified silence.

Watching her go, Rogan shoved his hands into the back pockets of his jeans. As he turned away his fingers encountered paper, and he pulled the crumpled page out. He'd forgotten about the burst of curiosity that had led him to rescue it from Camille's wastebasket at the hotel. For a moment he hesitated, then he carefully opened it out, arguing to himself that even if Camille thought it unimportant, there was a faint chance this could hold some clue to the mystery of his father's supposed treasure.

It was a child's crayon drawing on lined paper. A woman with long yellow hair held the hand of a child who wore a red dress and had large fat blue tears falling from her eyes to the ground in two evenly spaced rows. Across green-crayoned water, a large man in bright blue trousers stood on a tiny sailboat. Along the bottom of the picture in uneven and painstaking letters, with the ''ss'' back to front, was printed *I Miss You Dady*.

Guilt crawled up Rogan's spine, mingled with an empty, sad feeling that he thought he'd left behind in his own childhood, swiftly followed by a hot, sudden anger. He screwed the paper into a ball again, walked to the bow and hurled the drawing into the water below. His hands gripped the rail and he watched the paper bob on the small swells, floating jauntily away until it was indistinguishable from the lace caps of foam on the restive wavelets.

When Camille entered the antique shop only one customer was browsing some old glass and crystal displayed on a kauri dresser, while a young man with an earnest air stood patiently behind the counter.

The brass bell fixed to the door summoned James from the back of the shop. With a word to the assistant, he swept her out between buttoned chairs and dark-varnished nineteenth-century furniture, to the bright sunshine. ''I thought we'd try the Seagull restaurant just around the corner,'' he said. ''It's new and the food is supposed to be good.''

The tables were black-and-white marble, the chairs black leather slung on chrome, and the combination of slate tiles on the floor, an unlined beamed ceiling and pop music blaring from several speakers made the place noisy. The food came in artistic piles and tasted superb with the expensive wine James ordered, but after one attempt at conversation, telling him she'd moved onto the *Sea-Rogue,* Camille gave up shouting across the table.

As they left James said, ''At least it's possible to get a decent meal and good wine here now. When I was growing up Mokohina was a total backwater.''

''You stayed, though?''

''I left as soon as I could. But after my father retired I

took over the business.'' He shrugged. ''Call me sentimental…''

''What did you do when you left?''

''Took a business degree, and started off in an import-export firm where I was a cog in a very big wheel. I prefer working for myself. But enough about me—what did the police detectives have to say about the burglary?''

''They don't seem to be connecting it to Mr. Broderick's death.''

''I'm sure they're right. From what I hear that was some drunken street fracas.'' James gave a light laugh. ''The elder Broderick's lifestyle seems to have been more than a bit rough-edged. I'll walk you back to the boat.''

''Thank you,'' she said, ''but I'd like to look at the books in your shop again.''

After finishing his lunch, Rogan had visited the Imperial, hoping to find some of Barney's cronies in the bar, but although it was filled with hopeful fishers and their hangers-on who had converged for the tournament, the only person he recalled from the funeral was a seedy type sitting alone in a corner, and already so far gone he could hardly slur out two words. Most of the others were off fishing, Rogan guessed, or avoiding the influx of visitors. The little harbor was chock-full.

He bought a local paper and sat on deck, half concentrating while a bothersome thought struggled from the back of his mind, until it hit him right between the eyes.

Letting out a single explosive word, he shot down the companionway to the cabin, where he swept a searchlight glance about the bookshelves, cupboards and storage lockers that filled every available space.

Chapter 6

Rogan was hauling stuff from the locker under one of the seats in the saloon when Camille came down. She was faintly flushed, her hair ruffled by the breeze outside, or by...he didn't want to think about other possibilities. Her eyes were clear and shining when she smiled at him. Her lunch date had made her look that happy?

"If you'd called," he said, "I'd have helped you down."

"I have to learn to do it on my own."

She was carrying a small parcel. "Books?" he queried.

"Local histories from James's shop."

"James." The guy who'd been kissing her last night?

"He owns the Treasure Chest antique store and he's been very helpful."

"I thought that belonged to old Drummond."

"It belongs to young Drummond now."

Rogan thought hazily there had been a Drummond kid, several years older than Granger and himself, sent off to some boarding school in Auckland. "How long have you known him?"

"Just a few days. I walked into the shop the day I arrived, and…we got talking."

She'd been aimlessly walking after learning of Barney Broderick's sudden death, and a window display of Victorian china and sepia photographs had drawn her inside out of habit, to look for a book section.

James had asked if she was after anything in particular, and when she mentioned her current project he'd inquired casually if her sole reason for coming to Mokohina was historical research. Camille, still shocked at her abortive visit to the *Sea-Rogue,* blurted out that she had planned to meet Barney Broderick but had just been told he'd died in what appeared to be suspicious circumstances.

It seemed insensitive to tell Rogan that. Instead she said, "He introduced me to the local historian I told you about." From the start he'd been concerned and helpful, inquiring if Barney had been a relative, ready to express his condolences until she explained she'd never even met the man, but that her father had sailed with him. Not in the habit of confiding in strangers, she'd found herself drawn to do so by James's kindness and empathy.

"Talking of books," Rogan said, "have you seen the log?"

"The log?"

"The ship's log—the record the master always keeps."

"I know what a ship's log is." She'd pored over dozens of them in the course of research. "*Should* I have seen it?"

"It wasn't in Dad's desk with the boat's papers. I should have realized sooner it was missing."

"Your brother doesn't have it?"

Rogan shook his head. "He'd have told me."

"Do you know what it looked like?"

"Dad generally used one about the size of a desk diary. It's not in his cabin?"

"I don't think so." But they looked anyway, before Rogan turned to the saloon cupboards, peering into corners, pulling out drawers, then to the lockers that held sailing gear and tackle, while Camille volunteered to search the spare cabin that had been Taff's.

"You're okay with that?" he inquired.

"Of course." Her father's things were gone anyway.

Rogan was hauling fishing lines and nets from another locker when she came back to report, "Nothing, I'm afraid."

From outside a man's voice called, "Ahoy there!"

"It sounds like James," Camille said as Rogan went to the companionway.

"Down here," he called.

A thump on the deck, and then James gingerly descended to the cabin. "It was Camille I wanted to see, actually."

Rogan waited for the other man to reach the bottom of the narrow stair, then quickly climbed up.

"I hope you don't mind," James said to Camille. "But I don't have a phone number for you."

"I'll give you one," she promised, reminding herself to retrieve her cell phone from the car and bring it on board.

Extracting a yellowed piece of paper from an envelope, James queried, "I think this is within your period?"

It was a letter, headed with a date in 1837 and beginning, "My dear one," and signed in flourishing curlicues, "Ever, Your Alice."

Mingled excitement and melancholy made her skin tingle, as it often did when she handled personal belongings of long-forgotten people, tenuous links with past lives. "Where did you get it?"

"It was tucked inside a book that came in a box I bought

at auction. I was sorting through them after you left and thought you might like to have it.''

"It's good of you to take the trouble," she said.

He smiled at her, and looked around the cabin. "I admit I was curious about your legacy. It's a rather neglected old boat, isn't it? Nice panel work though.''

"Do you sail?"

James shook his head. "Dry land for me. I get seasick." He studied a ship in a bottle that had survived the carnage of the burglars. "You said the old man left you half the contents along with the boat?"

"Apparently."

"Feel free to consult me if you have doubts about the value of anything. I'll make sure you're not cheated.''

"Thank you. But I don't think there's anything particularly precious. How much do you want for this letter?" Camille asked.

"It's a curiosity, of no intrinsic value. Call it a discount on the books you've bought." He smiled. "Is everything all right? Any problems?" He looked at the piled gear that Rogan had left on the floor during his search.

Not sure what kind of problems he meant, she explained, "The log's missing."

"Missing?" James frowned. His voice was thoughtful. "Well," he shrugged, "whoever trashed the boat probably threw it overboard.''

"Why would anyone do that?"

"Why do vandals do anything? It would break your heart, the ruined treasures I've seen when I'm asked to conduct valuations for insurance claims.''

Another thump from the deck reminded Camille that Rogan was keeping out of the way while she talked with her guest. James looked up. "I suppose I should be getting back.''

She followed him up on deck. Rogan was leaning against the mainmast with his arms folded. His eyes flicked from James to Camille, and she paused to introduce the men.

Rogan gave a curt nod, and James said pleasantly, "I'm sorry if I disturbed you."

"No problem," Rogan grunted.

James lingered, glancing up at the soaring metal masts and then around. "Is the boat seaworthy?" Skeptically he surveyed the weathered wood and stained, folded sails.

"Absolutely."

"How much do you think it'll fetch?"

Camille saw Rogan stiffen. "She's not for sale."

James looked at him with interest. "What do you plan to do with…her?"

"I plan to keep her."

"Really?" James seemed to hesitate for a moment, then nodded and smiled, said goodbye to Camille and cautiously ascended the ladder to the wharf.

Rogan asked, "Is he going to be a regular visitor?"

"I don't think so. Would you object?"

It was a moment before he said, "Why should I object?"

"You sound grumpy."

"I'm not grumpy," Rogan denied, sounding even more so.

"He came to bring me an old letter he'd found, for my research. And he was curious about the boat."

"The *boat?*"

"He's interested in old things."

"And young women."

Camille shrugged. "He's a man."

Rogan's eyes gleamed, and a dark brow lifted just slightly. "So am I."

As if she didn't know it. As if anyone who laid eyes on

him wouldn't. "While we're living tog—living on board, we're going to need some ground rules."

"You needn't worry," he said. "I don't go where I'm not wanted. Of course, if you're interested…" He cocked his head inquiringly, a grin curving his mouth.

Shaking her head, she said, "I'm not."

Rogan looked rueful but hardly shattered. "Too bad."

Obviously he wasn't going to lose any sleep over it. For some reason that roused her anger, but she swallowed it, saying frostily, "I have work to do," and made to go below.

"You're not sleeping with Drummond, then?"

At the top of the companionway, Camille turned and stared at him.

"Sorry, out of order."

"Definitely." She continued on her way.

Dumb ass, Rogan called himself, watching her disappear. What sort of stupid question was that? The woman had class—she didn't jump into bed with men she'd just met, and that included James Drummond as well as himself. Besides, if she was that close to the guy she'd have moved in with him, not Rogan.

The thought lifted his mood and he followed her down, but she'd already closed the door to her cabin.

He began stowing stuff back in the locker, but kept a fishing line out and went topside with it. There, he baited the hook with a limpet prized from the wharf piles and scraped from its shell, and hung the line over the side.

When Camille emerged into the saloon Rogan was coming down again, two good-size kahawai dangling from one hand.

"Fresh fish," he said. "You want yours whole or filleted?"

A peace offering, perhaps. "Filleted, please." She hoped he'd take care of it.

They'd bought carrots, greens and new potatoes on their shopping expedition, and Camille prepared them while he took charge of the fish. In the tiny galley area they inevitably worked close to each other. Her arm brushing against his once or twice sent an electric tingle along her skin, but Rogan didn't seem to notice.

The fish was perfectly moist and firm and almost melted on her tongue. "This is delicious," Camille said sincerely, forking up another piece. "James said whoever vandalized the boat might have thrown the log overboard."

Rogan's mouth tightened. He scowled at a defenseless baby potato and speared it with his fork.

"Is it so important?" she asked.

When he'd swallowed the potato he said, "Someone might have thought it was."

"Do you really believe your father was on the track of lost treasure? Your brother doesn't."

"Whether I believe it or not isn't the point. If Dad had— or thought he had—something valuable, then whoever did the boat over probably beat him up. And I want them."

He looked so grim and dangerous that Camille shivered. "The police don't think that," she reminded him, "do they?"

"They said they'd keep an open mind, but they obviously don't buy the theory."

And they were the experts. She kept that thought to herself. "I didn't know you and Granger intended keeping the boat," she said. And when he looked rather blank she prodded, "You told James…"

"Uh…yeah, well…"

"Didn't you mean it?"

"'Course I meant it." He looked away, then back at her almost belligerently. "The old girl's a good sound craft."

"So, do you want to buy my half?"

Rogan looked startled. "Buy you out?"

"Wouldn't you prefer that to me selling it to someone else? I'm giving you first refusal."

Rogan would have preferred it all right, but he certainly couldn't afford to. He pretty much spent his deservedly high wages as he earned them. Granger was always telling him he should save, invest, think of the future.

But in his job you were never sure how much future you had.

Hopefully he said, "You might change your mind." He hadn't even thought about what was to happen to the *Sea-Rogue* until James Drummond asked. He was more concerned with what had happened to his father and who was responsible, content to leave Granger to sort things out on the legal front.

He'd taken a mild though irrational dislike to Drummond at their first distant and wordless encounter in the bar at the Imperial, and the faint air of disparagement in the man's appraisal of the old ketch had raised his hackles and woken a dormant sense of possessiveness that led him to make a split-second decision to keep the boat.

Maybe he should have listened to his brother. Until now it had made sense to enjoy the fruits of his labor while he could. He had no dependents, no long-term commitments—except one that was blessedly intermittent, to the dive school he sponsored for island kids—and no intention of acquiring any. He'd never figured on having any large assets either. Camille's suggestion that he and Granger buy her out had brought him up with a round thump.

"I won't change my mind," Camille said. "Are you interested?"

"I'll talk to Granger."

As they left the table he pulled two shiny keys from his pocket and handed one to her. "You'd better have this—it's for the new lock. We should lock up if we're out."

"Thank you." She picked up her empty plate and his.

When she told him she intended to phone Mr. Trubshaw and then work in her cabin he said, "I'll go to the pub." In the evening there would be more chance of meeting up with some of the men who'd known Barney.

The carefully unjudging way Camille accepted his plan got under Rogan's skin, and he didn't elaborate. Anyway, with her skepticism about the old man's treasure hunt she'd have poured cold water on his reasons if he'd given them.

So it was a choice between letting her think him a crazy romantic or a man who couldn't keep off the booze. Either way, damned if he cared.

There were a few familiar faces at the bar, but Rogan's cautious questioning elicited nothing more than the rumors that had circulated at the funeral.

"No one took it seriously." A balding man with a beer belly straining at a dingy T-shirt above low-slung jeans quaffed his drink and shoved the glass suggestively under Rogan's nose. "Not until the old guy died that way."

Rogan signaled the barman. "Could some stranger have heard him talking and thought there was something in it?"

A burly Maori man with sleeves rolled up from tattooed arms interrupted. "Who was that young fella at Taff's wake? Not much to say for hisself."

Beer-belly turned. "What young fella?"

"Bought Barney a drink or two—fair enough, considering old Barney'd been shouting at everyone all night."

"I paid for my share of rounds," Beer-belly said offendedly.

"Yeah, yeah, but this guy only got a couple in for Barney, eh."

"Can you describe him?" Rogan asked.

"'Bout your age, brown hair. Not fat, but not skinny either. Bit shorter than you. Looked like a sailor," the man said helpfully.

That would pinpoint roughly half the male population of Mokohina in the summer season. "You don't know his name?"

"I've seen him around, but he's not from here. Don't know where he stays."

The whiskered old salt who'd bailed up Rogan at Barney's wake arrived, squeezing Rogan's shoulder with a horny hand. "Now, young Rogue. How's it going, eh?"

Rogan got him a beer, and asked, "Do you remember if my father left Taff's wake alone?"

Webby touched a match to a carefully rolled cigarette, inhaled and blew two streams of smoke through his nose. "Didden notice, myself. Must've dropped off. I'm not as young as I was."

Rogan hid a grin. The old fellow had probably been dead drunk. "Did you notice a young guy who bought a drink or two for my dad?"

Webby shook his head, then raised an arm. "Hey, Doll! Over here!"

Rogan saw the fiery thistle-head moving through the crowd, before the man broke free and approached them.

Webby told him, "Rogue here reckons some young fella that turned up at Taff's wake was buying Barney drinks."

"Yeah, that's right. Barney had his arm around the bloke for a while." Doll grinned. "Well, by that time ol' Barn needed something to hold on to so he could stay upright. Said the boy reminded him of his sons.''

Rogan asked, ''Did you know the guy?''

''Seen him in the pub a coupla times. Barry? Gary? Yeah, Gary. He's off one a them fancy hire boats that take the tourists out fishing. Can't remember the name.''

Webby leaned confidentially toward Rogan. ''You reckon he's the one that clobbered poor old Barney?''

''I don't know,'' Rogan replied. ''No one seems to have seen Dad leave, or know when he did.''

''Prob'ly,'' Doll guessed, ''not till the publican chucked us all out. Barney wouldn't leave a good booze-up early.''

About fifty people must have been in the bar that night, drinking hard, and they'd very likely milled about outside before dispersing. None of them had noticed the old man wandering off into the darkness—or they weren't saying so.

Any of the fifty might have followed him—perhaps under the guise of helping him find his uncertain way to the *Sea-Rogue*—and then attacked him in the alley.

Rogan arrived back on board lighter in his pocket and heavier on his feet after buying several rounds of drinks and in turn being shouted by Barney's friends. It hadn't resulted in any more information.

In the dark he stumbled noisily on the last step of the companionway, cursed, then cautiously made his way to his cabin. If Camille heard him she'd probably write him off as a useless drunk.

Next day, having been invited to lunch with Mr. Trub-shaw, Camille took along a fresh loaf of bread from a bakery on the shore, and chose a bottle of wine to go with the promised asparagus and tomatoes from his garden. Lunch was leisurely, and after spending a few hours in his library she arrived back at the *Sea-Rogue* to find it apparently deserted. The tide was high and she was able to step onto the boat quite easily.

Leaving her bag and notes in her cabin, she went up on deck, telling herself she needed some fresh air. She was uncertainly surveying the harbor when a faint splashing sent her to look over the rail.

A large black shape emerged and a hand grabbed at the ladder fastened to the hull. Camille stepped back as the man, encased in a shiny wet diving suit, climbed over the rail, and the mask was raised to reveal Rogan's face.

"Your boyfriend was wrong," he said. "There's nothing down there but fish, mud and junk, and I don't think any of it came from here." He ran a hand through his hair and began unzipping the enveloping suit.

Stripped to a minimal pair of swim briefs, he washed down his suit with a hose on the wharf before descending to the cabin.

He reappeared dressed in clean jeans and a gray T-shirt, his hair still damp. "I'm having a beer," he told her from the doorway. "Do you want anything?"

She asked for a fizzy lemon, and a few minutes later he came back on deck with a can for himself and a glass for her.

He sat opposite her in the wheel well, looking gloomy. "How was your day?" he asked her.

"I've got plenty of material to write up."

"Good."

He moved restlessly, frowning, and she said, "I'm sorry you didn't find the log."

Rogan hunched a shoulder and drank some more beer.

Camille indicated the murky green water around them. "It can't be the most pleasant place to dive."

"It's not too bad compared with some of the places I've

worked, but I've done more interesting dives, like the Poor Knights just up the coast. And around the Mediterranean, New Mexico, the Solomons—have you done any scuba?''

"Only a bit of holiday snorkeling now and then. I've thought about learning to scuba dive. I saw a TV documentary recently about the Poor Knights reserve and it looked wonderful underwater.''

"One of the best dive sites on earth,'' Rogan said. "It's a different world down there.''

His world.

He said, "I've got an instructor's certificate. I could teach you.''

Her heart gave an extra beat. "It would take too much time,'' she objected.

"You don't need that much to learn the basics. Get them right, and it's a matter of practice and sticking to the safety rules—staying within your ability, and diving with someone more experienced until you're proficient yourself. Since you know how to use a snorkel you're partway there.''

If anyone else had offered she'd have jumped at it. Staving off temptation, she said, "I don't know if I can afford it.''

"It's free, no strings. Take it or leave it.''

Camille hadn't meant money so much as time. She hadn't expected to be in Mokohina more than a couple of days, but she was still finding new gems in Mr. Trubshaw's collections.

And she had no immediate commitments to get back to. Within a few days her mother was due to fly to Australia to spend Christmas and New Year with Camille's aunt, who was celebrating twenty-five years of marriage in January and had sent her sister a ticket. Camille had been invited but, while appreciating the courtesy gesture, had declined on the grounds of having research to complete. She barely knew her Australian cousins and, to her secret guilt, was glad to have some time away on her own.

She loved her mother and there were advantages to living with her. She understood Mona's fear of abandonment, but sometimes she wished her mother was less dependent. Despite Mona's brave avowals that Camille must do anything she wanted without regard to *her* feelings, any suggestion that the daughter she'd devoted her life to might want to move out from under her wing obviously upset her.

But she was safe and well and for the next several weeks would be enjoying her own holiday. There was no reason Camille couldn't stay on in Mokohina to pursue her research…and learn to scuba dive. Maybe this was too good a chance to pass up.

"You'd have to let me repay you somehow," she said.

"When I think of something I'll let you know."

"Maybe I could start by cooking dinner tonight."

"I could go for that."

She made a meat loaf and salad, and Rogan had two helpings. Afterward he said, "I can give you a lesson now."

Camille glanced at the dimming light outside. "Now?"

"Things you need to know before you get in the water."

He gave her a handbook and said, "Learn that, especially the hand signals." Then he dragged out his own wet suit and equipment, and explained the basic principles of scuba as well as the physiology of diving. He made her handle the jacket-like buoyancy compensator with its harness for the air tank, and encouraged her to practice dealing with the fastenings and the weight belt. "You don't want to be fiddling about underwater when you need to get rid of weight and reach the surface in a hurry."

"Isn't it dangerous to surface too quickly?"

"Damn right, if you're below ten meters. You can burst your lungs, cripple yourself and worse. But we'll go through all the drills before I let you anywhere near that depth."

After she'd detailed the uses of the valves and gauges attached to the gear, he handed her a large, business-like serrated knife. "Get familiar with this."

Camille's eyes widened, and he said, "If you're trapped in weed or a fishing net you'll need it."

She handled it gingerly, then slipped it back into its rubber sheath attached to a leg strap.

They ran through some hand signals before he said, "That's enough for a first lesson."

"Thanks. I'd better sort some of my notes."

"Wait," he said, taking a key ring from a nearby hook. "I should have given you this last night." He twisted a key from the ring. "For your cabin."

Camille took it, reflecting that last night it hadn't even crossed her mind to lock her door. She'd crawled between her crisp new sheets and been lulled to sleep by the soft whispering and gurgling of the wavelets against the boat's sides, and the faint movement as it shifted on the tide. Something had half wakened her later and she'd heard Rogan's voice give vent to a violent, muffled exclamation, followed by silence until his cabin door quietly opened and shut. Moments afterward, feeling pleasantly safe and snug, she'd fallen back into sleep.

Later Rogan eased his own new key onto his father's ring that Granger had handed over to him, and removed the old one belonging to the damaged door.

There were keys on the ring to the deck hatches and lockers, and a smaller one with the brand name of a well-known safe-maker on it. He stared at it for a while, then looked around, searching for something it might fit.

The main cabin yielded nothing and he had no better luck in the small side cabins or the cargo space, even when he lifted the hatch giving access to the bilge and shone a light around the dank spaces below between the bulkheads.

That left Camille's cabin—his father's. Maybe he should have bagged it for himself after all. Frustrated and edgy, he went toward the door, and was contemplating knocking on it when she emerged, carrying a toilet bag and towel, starting when she saw him.

"Am I that scary?" he asked.

"I just didn't expect to see you there," she said.

"There's a mystery key here," he said, holding up the ring and stepping back as she made to open the door to the head.

"What?"

"A mystery key that doesn't seem to fit anything. Do you mind if I look in your cabin?"

"Help yourself," Camille invited. "But I'm sure there's nothing there."

He went in while she closeted herself in the head where Barney had rigged a primitive shower. Rogan heard the pump start, then the brief rush of water, and tried not to imagine Camille standing naked with water cascading over her lovely body, instead concentrating his mind on cupboards, drawers—anything that might be lockable.

One of the desk drawers had a tiny lock with the old-fashioned key still in it, but there was nothing else. And he knew they'd emptied every storage place in here.

Set into the floor in the knee-hole of the desk was a small locker where Barney had stored navigation manuals and charts. The vandals had emptied it, and Rogan had collected up the scattered contents and taken them away to study them.

He opened the now empty compartment, felt around it, and finally got up to find a flashlight that allowed him to see much better.

The space looked shallower than his memory of it. Peering carefully he could see the bottom boards were cut to fit to the sides. He got a screwdriver and levered at a narrow slit until the false bottom lifted out.

When Camille came out of the shower and paused in the doorway he was still kneeling, staring down at a square of metal set into the space.

"What's that?" Camille said.

Rogan saw first her feet, slim and pink-toed, and then a satisfying length of leg, before the tantalizing view was frustrated by the hem of a dark red satin robe that she'd tied firmly about her waist. Quickly he raised his gaze to her face. "It's a safe," he said. With a keyhole the size of the key in his hand.

"Don't they have combination locks these days?"

"Salt corrodes them. This kind's common on boats."

"Aren't you going to open it?"

He'd been wondering if she had anything on under the robe, and then been distracted by the fact that when she leaned forward to inspect the safe the lapels gaped, showing fairly conclusively that she wasn't wearing a bra, anyway.

"Yeah," he said hastily, inserting the key into the lock. It fitted perfectly and turned with hardly a sound.

A flattened ring was set into a groove, and he lifted the lid, the weight of it surprising him.

It wasn't a large safe, not much bigger than a bread box, and it didn't need a second glance to deduce that it was empty.

Chapter 7

Next day Rogan phoned his brother. "Did you know Dad had a safe on board?"

"Where?" Granger asked.

Rogan explained. "And it looks new. Why would he have suddenly put in a safe?"

"Times have changed since he began sailing. Maybe the boat had been burgled before, or he might have just decided he should be more security conscious. He used to get quite large cash payments for carrying cargo."

"There was no cash in it. Nothing."

"The burglars could have cleaned it out."

"No," Rogan said. "It was pretty well hidden and it hadn't been forced. And Dad had the key with him. It was on the ring you gave me, that the police took from his body."

"It would be just like him to buy a safe on impulse and never get round to using it. Money ran through his hands like water anyway. Or he might have bought it in simple hope that one day he'd find something worth putting into it.''

Rogan didn't bother arguing with either theory. Sometimes Granger was annoyingly logical. ''Another thing,'' he said. ''The log's missing. When I found the safe I thought that must be where he'd hidden it.''

''Why would he hide the log?'' Granger asked.

''Exactly. Or why would someone want to steal it?''

Granger said, ''Rogue, give it up before you become as obsessed as the old man. Even if it was stolen, all it means is someone might have taken his wild stories seriously.''

His brother was right, of course. As usual.

Rogan changed the subject. ''Remember James Drummond?''

''His father ran the antique shop. I don't really know him. Why?''

''He runs it now. He came visiting the first night.''

''Why was he visiting you?''

''Not me…Camille.''

''She's still around?''

''Sleeping in Dad's cabin.''

There was a moment's silence, then, ''Aah-huh.''

''She's doing research here, and the hotel's booked out. She wants to know if we can buy her share of the *Sea-Rogue*.''

Another silence. ''I figured we'd be selling the boat.''

''Dad's boat?!'' He hadn't meant to sound outraged.

Granger said patiently, ''I don't have a use for it. And you're the man who doesn't want to be tied down by possessions…or if not, what have you done with my brother?''

''Yeah, yeah.'' Rogan hesitated. ''Could you afford it?''

''No. The new practice is in debt to the bank for at least the next few years, and I can't take on another mortgage.''

* * *

Later Rogan talked to the constable, who listened politely and promised to pass on the information about the missing log.

"There was a guy called Gary somebody at the pub that night," Rogan added. "Off a hire boat."

"Gary Collier. He's on our list."

"Is he a suspect?"

"No more than anyone else. He's a deckhand, but his boat isn't in port right now. When it comes back we'll interview him. Don't worry, Mr. Broderick, we're onto it." Giving him a rather hard look, the constable added, "I believe you've been talking to a lot of people."

"I've been talking with my father's friends. It's pretty normal after someone dies, isn't it?"

"Of course. And I'm sure you know we'll see that justice is done. You wouldn't want to do anything to prejudice our inquiries."

Mooching back along the wharf, Rogan wondered where Camille had gone—she'd left after her minimal breakfast and told him she would be out for the day. Researching, he supposed. Unless she was with James Drummond.

He recalled Drummond's pale eyes, pale hands, his supercilious way of looking at Rogan. And surely he was a bit old for Camille?

The ketch rocked gently when he boarded, water slapping against the hull.

Sun and sea were hard on the old girl but she was still sound, a sturdy workhorse of a boat that had served his father well. He walked all around, noting every bit of peeling paint, every frayed cable or rusted hinge, and when Camille returned he was applying undercoat to the deckhouse.

She had a small backpack on, and by the time he'd wiped

his hands and crossed to help her down she had already negotiated the ladder and made the leap to the deck. "Painting?" she said. "What color is it going to be?"

He'd bought white for the sides and red for the top, the same as before, but he said, "What color would you like?"

"It doesn't matter what I like. I'm selling my half anyway." She began walking across the deck, sliding the backpack from her shoulders.

"Watch out for wet paint," he said.

In her cabin Camille removed several books from the backpack. She opened a drawer of the desk, then hesitated. Going back on deck, she asked Rogan, "Do you suppose I could use that safe? Mr. Trubshaw loaned me some books and old documents so I don't have to go back and forth every day, and I'd hate anything to happen to them." She'd been surprised and touched that he'd trusted her with them. "I mean, if we were burgled again or something…"

"Sure." He fished in a pocket of his jeans and pulled out the key ring to remove the key. "All yours."

She made a pasta casserole, and then worked on her notes while it cooked.

After dinner Rogan was explaining the importance in deep diving of decompression tables and dive computers when James's voice called from above, "Camille?" Then came a muffled swearword.

Camille raced up the companionway, almost colliding with James at the top. "What's wrong?"

"Paint," he said disgustedly, regarding a whitened palm, and a smear on his dark striped shirt. "Why the hell isn't there a sign or something?"

"I don't suppose Rogan was expecting visitors. I'm sorry about your shirt."

Regaining his usual calm he said, "Not your fault. Is there somewhere I can wash this off my hand?"

She took him down to the cabin and Rogan didn't apologize but produced turpentine and pointed out the head.

When James came out Camille made coffee and after having some he asked Rogan, "Mind if I look around?"

"Why?"

James smiled. "It's an interesting old craft."

"I'll show you," Camille volunteered. "If it's all right with Rogan." She directed a questioning look at him.

He gave her a piercing look back, and shrugged.

She left the door of Rogan's cabin closed and showed him the rest of the boat. On their return Rogan was still nursing his empty cup at the table.

Camille accompanied James up to the deck. "Why did you want to see me?" she asked.

"Do I need a reason?" He smiled at her. "I'm expecting some interesting people at the weekend—business friends. They're sailing up from Auckland and I hope to do a deal or two. Would you join us for dinner on Saturday?"

"Yes," she said. "Thank you."

When she returned to the cabin Rogan said, "Do you want to go on with this lesson? By the way, you'll need a medical check with a dive doctor before we go in the water."

"I'm fine," she assured him. "Very healthy."

He cast a veiled, dispassionate glance over her that nevertheless sent a shower of warm sparks across her skin. "Yeah, but you need a doctor's say-so."

She got a doctor's report the following day. Rogan glanced over the few lines and said, "Right. Let's hire you a suit."

The proprietor of the dive shop he took her to greeted Rogan with a camaraderie that indicated they were old friends. "This is Brodie," Rogan told Camille. "A damn good diver when he's not being a shopkeeper."

Brodie—tall, tanned and with thick, streaked blond hair that suggested a beach lifestyle—flashed a white grin at Camille, very blue eyes showing male appreciation but not too blatantly. "What's a nice girl like you doing hanging out with a guy like Rogue?"

Rogan looked pained. "Thanks for the testimonial."

"Anytime." The grin turned to him. "Is this a social visit, or did you want something?"

"I'm teaching Camille to dive." Ignoring Brodie's lifted brows and the wickedly knowing spark that appeared in the sky-blue eyes, Rogan added, "She needs to hire some gear. And then can we use your practice pool?"

"No problem." To Camille he said, "In the water you can trust this guy a hundred and one percent. He saved my life."

Rogan said impatiently, "Oh, shut up, you loon! Find this girl a suit, will you?"

The pool was a saltwater one adjacent to the shop. Half an hour later Camille was entering the water, adjusting her buoyancy and breathing, moving about easily under the surface with the help of the equipment that had seemed so cumbersome on land, and practicing to cope with possible problems like water in her mask or losing her regulator.

The pool was warm and they both wore light, sleeveless suits without hoods, although their legs were encased in close-fitting neoprene. Camille had tied her hair in a ponytail that streamed behind her in the water, and now and then her bare arm brushed against Rogan's slick and muscular one, sending a tiny frisson of awareness all the way to her rubber-finned toes.

When he called a halt after two hours she was surprised the time had passed so quickly.

Over lunch in the Koffee 'n' Kai she asked how long he'd known Brodie.

"Since high school," he told her. "We took our first diving lessons together. After we graduated from dive school we did a stint at a resort hotel in Australia, teaching diving, and worked on a couple of salvage operations. We bump into each other now and then on jobs in different parts of the world."

"So he still dives professionally?"

"Yeah, but he says he wanted a place to come home to—that's why he bought the shop, and a boat. He does some teaching when he's here, and takes recreational divers out for short trips."

"Do you envy him?"

"Hell, no! I guess it suits Brodie though."

"He said you saved his life."

"Crap. We had an air supply problem. I did what he would have done for me. That's what the buddy system's for." He'd told her that divers went down in pairs. If one was in trouble the buddy would come to the rescue or, if that wasn't possible, raise the alarm.

"This afternoon," he promised, "I'll teach you about sharing an air supply in an emergency."

It wasn't too difficult when they were kneeling close together on the floor of the pool, except that despite the neoprene covering their legs Camille felt a disconcerting tingle of awareness when his thighs straddled hers as they swapped the breathing apparatus.

Trying to maintain contact while they slowly surfaced with their arms about each other's shoulders, she lost her equilibrium and floated close against him during the ascent, her legs tangling with his. Heat suffusing her body, she loosened her hold and was drifting away, putting a strain on the breathing hose until Rogan grabbed her wrist and hauled her back.

When they broke the surface she panted, "Sorry."

Rogan grinned and pushed up his mask. "We'll do another practice on dry land."

Kneeling by the pool, without their mouthpieces and masks on, he put an arm about her again, taking a grip on the harness that fastened the air tank to her buoyancy compensator. His skin where his arm touched her was wet but warm, and she had to make an effort to breathe properly as she reciprocated.

"Okay," Rogan said. "That feels good. Not that the other didn't."

Startled, Camille turned to face him, finding him very close, his eyes filled with laughter. The laughter died and became a question, her mouth parted in slight shock, and for a moment she was dizzy. She felt his arm tighten, his hand gripping her shoulder. His gaze was on her mouth.

Then abruptly he dropped his arm, his head jerking away, and he wiped the back of his hand across his forehead. "Do you think you can manage that underwater now?"

For the remainder of the lesson Rogan was professional, well-organized, and almost distant.

The following afternoon they spent time again in Brodie's pool, and Rogan seemed totally focused on improving her technique, watching her with a critical, dispassionate eye. Afterward he went into the town and she took out Mr. Trubshaw's books and the small tape recorder she used for quick note-taking.

When Rogan returned he found her sitting in the cockpit with a book in her lap, and stifling a yawn.

"Oh," she said, looking up as he leaped to the deck. "I'll start dinner."

"You're tired," he said. "I'll buy you dinner in town tonight."

"I ought to pay for you!" she protested. Providing him with meals had been part of the deal.

He overrode her objection. "A reward for coming top of the class."

They dined at the Imperial—despite the brash new cafés in town it still had the most elegant restaurant. "Unless you'd prefer somewhere else?" Rogan had offered.

"No. I love the old Imperial—all that lovely kauri paneling and carving."

"Yeah," Rogan replied. He was glad the new proprietors hadn't modernized the old building too thoroughly.

Over dinner he described places where he'd dived and the people he'd dived with. Camille was a good listener, and he was glad to see her wariness melt slightly.

"Taff was a pretty good diver," he told her, cutting into a carpetbag steak.

"Was he."

The flatness of her tone made him look up. Her expression was closed off, cold.

"Taught me a lot." He watched her, trying to think of something to erase that look from her face. "He was a good bloke, specially to Granger and me when we were kids."

"Really." Her voice was positively arctic.

Damn. That hadn't been the most tactful thing to say. "Not that we saw a lot of him really."

"More than I did."

Feeling clumsy and insensitive, Rogan said, "I'm sorry."

Camille gave him a deliberately blank look, and a brittle little laugh, a shade too high. "I'm not heartbroken. I told you, I didn't even know the man."

There were more ways than one to be heartbroken, Ro-

gan thought. Especially for a little kid. When he was young
his own father had been an almost mythical figure, breezing
in at erratic intervals and disrupting the family routine with
exotic presents, and tall tales of adventures at sea and
strange places he'd visited—and promises that one day he
would discover undersea treasure and make them all rich.

Rogan's mother would smile sadly and shake her head,
and gradually it dawned on him and Granger that "one
day" was never going to happen.

And if it finally had, for Barney it was too late.

Camille said, "This pasta is good. How's your steak?"

"Fine." Obviously she didn't want to discuss her father.
He wanted to hear more about her life, but she evaded his
attempts to draw her out, only giving minimal information
about her school and university years.

Walking home along the waterfront in the fading light,
Rogan would have liked to put an arm about her, pull her
close to his side, feel her warmth, perhaps rub his cheek
against her hair.

Not a good idea. At the pool the first day, when her legs
had tangled with his, even though their wet suits had ensured there was no skin-to-skin contact his body had reacted, his mind filling with images of a bed instead of a
swimming pool, of naked flesh instead of layers of neoprene. And he should never have made that suggestive re-
mark.

Learning to dive was serious business; divers couldn't
afford distractions—it might mean the difference between
life and death. Sex definitely came under the heading of a
distraction.

Working at dive schools, he'd had good-looking women
in his classes. Some turned up in minimal swimwear, tiny
triangles of fabric, and not a few came on to the instructor
from day one. He'd learned to ignore his libido and direct

all his attention—and theirs—to the business of diving, and diving safely. It had never been so difficult before.

A large boat was cruising slowly into the harbor, several fishing rods ranked along the top of its high deckhouse. Rogan said, "Can you see the name on that boat?"

Camille followed his gaze. "No." Darkness was creeping over the harbor and the boat was moving. "Why?"

"A deckhand on a hire boat that's been away from port was seen with my father the night he died."

"Have you been doing some detective work?"

Irritably he said, "I've been warned off. The police don't want me to 'prejudice their inquiries.'"

Camille regarded him curiously. "You loved him, didn't you—your father?"

Rogan shot her a sharp glance. "Yeah, I guess."

"But he was hardly ever home!"

"He wasn't your ideal father," Rogan admitted. "Basically my mother brought us up on her own. But when he was in port it was great. He let us wag school, sleep on board the *Sea-Rogue,* use the dinghy to row about the harbor. And if Mum let him, he'd take us for an overnight sail."

"What did your mother think of it all?"

"She scolded us—even Dad—but he'd always bring her round. He was one of those people who could charm the hind leg off a donkey and then have the donkey eat out of his hand. I think she was always conscious of how short his visits would be, and she didn't want to spoil them for any of us."

His mother must have been a monumentally tolerant person, Camille reflected. Or very much in love.

Her own mother, she guessed, would say Mrs. Broderick had been a fool—a doormat for a selfish, feckless man. And she'd probably have been right.

But seen through her son's eyes Rogan's mother didn't sound like a doormat. She sounded like a nice person, and a strong one, with a generous heart.

Not many women would have put up with a sometime husband like Barney.

Chapter 8

The *Sea-Rogue*'s deck was nearly level with the wharf, but Camille accepted Rogan's proffered hand.

Although he immediately released her, by some kind of tacit agreement they went to lean on the taffrail at the stern and watch the occasional glint of moonlight on the water, the sudden silver of a fish twisting and leaping on the surface.

After a while Camille moved her palm on the rail, preparing to go below, and paused as she felt an anomaly in the smoothness of the wood. She looked down.

"Granger and I did that," Rogan said. "When we were kids."

"What is it?" It was too dark to see.

His hand came over hers, extending her index finger and guiding it slowly over the grooves. His initials.

She said, "You wanted to make your mark on her."

"Right." His fingers were still warm on hers. His palm

flattened her hand over the carved RB. "We knew we shouldn't do it, but we couldn't resist the temptation."

Her heart was thumping. She ought to pull her hand away, he wouldn't hold her against her will. Only her will wasn't awfully strong right now.

His other hand touched her cheek, turned her head toward him. When she didn't protest he bent his head, and then he was kissing her, sweet and gentle but confident.

It was even better than the first time. Longer, deeper, and very, very sexy.

When she finally made the effort to draw away, and he let her, she felt a pang of regret. She should never have allowed it, of course. But it did make a lovely end to a really nice evening. She sighed, and tugged at her hand.

He lifted it to his face, and pressed her palm briefly to his cheek, turning his lips for a quick kiss in the hollow before letting her go.

Camille dug her teeth into her lower lip, trying to kill the weakening sensation that shivered right through to her toes. "Good night," she said, and climbed down to the cockpit and the door.

"It's locked," Rogan reminded her, and while she fumbled in her shoulder bag for her key he joined her in the small space and used his.

She could smell his skin-scent and the seductive muskiness of male arousal. Her own skin was extra-sensitive, his arm brushing against hers sending a warm shiver over it.

Then he stood back. "Good night, Camille. Be careful on the companionway."

Relief and disappointment warred as she made her way down to the cabin, which seemed stuffy and over-warm.

It was only a good-night kiss, she told herself when she lay in her bed, rocked by a passing motorboat that stirred the water. A casual gesture, just like James's light kisses.

But James's kisses, pleasant and quite expert in their undemanding way, didn't leave her feverish and tense, her untrustworthy body longing for more.

Rogan was so brisk and aloof during her lesson next day that the kiss might never have happened, and she decided it was best to pretend that it never had. He looked a bit put out when she told him she was having dinner with James, but waved aside her offer to cook for him before she left, and when she appeared on deck in her green dress and carrying high-heeled shoes, proffered her his help to get on shore.

He placed her shoes on the wharf first, then leaped up himself and took her hands, hauling her after him.

"Thanks," she said, landing only inches from him.

For a moment he didn't let go his firm grasp, a smile lighting his eyes and lifting a corner of his mouth as he gazed down at her. "No problem," he drawled.

She wriggled her fingers and he let go, then knelt and picked up one of her shoes. "Give us your foot, Cinderella."

She would have managed on her own, but he had grasped her ankle and instinctively she put a hand on his shoulder to steady herself so he could slide the shoe on for her.

When both shoes were on he straightened and she said, "That wasn't necessary."

"You might have lost your balance trying to do it on your own. And—" he stepped back and ran a rapid glance of scarcely veiled masculine appreciation over her "—you don't want to spoil that pretty dress."

The boards of the old wharf were striated and uneven, and he was probably right. "Well, thanks," she said.

"If you need help when you come back, yell."

"I may be late."

His gaze sharpened. "Thinking of staying the night?"

"No!"

"Good." Rogan's momentarily rigid stance slackened. "And don't drink too much..." She blinked indignantly and he went on. "...if you want to dive tomorrow."

He'd promised she could try out her scuba skills in the sea the next day.

"I never drink a lot," she told him.

James's friends were three couples, expensively dressed and so interchangeable she had trouble sorting out who was with whom for most of the evening. The men were fortyish, two of the women considerably younger. Once they'd discovered with some surprise that Camille didn't have a favorite fashion designer and knew none of the high-flyers in business and entertainment whose names they casually dropped, the women seemed to run out of conversation.

After dinner James brought out a small collection of antique jewelry he had recently acquired. While the other women clamored to try on some of the pieces, Camille slipped out into the cool air on the veranda, where a few minutes later James found her.

"There you are, Camille!" He put his hand in his pocket and drew out something that glittered in the outdoor lighting. "What do you think of this?"

It was a bracelet of wrought silver, studded with small, sparkling gems. "It's beautiful," she said. "Are the stones real?"

"Of course. Put it on."

"I don't think..."

But he had lifted her hand and was sliding the silver circlet onto her wrist. "The other girls have all tried something. I want to see how this looks on you." His grip was surprisingly strong, overriding her resistance.

"Perfect," he said, turning her wrist so the stones shot flashes of colored light. He raised her hand in his and dropped a kiss on it. "Keep it."

"No," Camille said. "Thank you, but no."

He caught both her hands as she made to remove the bracelet. "Don't you like it?"

"I can't take anything as valuable as this as a present, and I'm sure I couldn't afford to buy it."

"What a sweet old-fashioned view!" he said lightly. "It's a mere bauble, though a particularly pretty one. It deserves the right setting."

"I'm sorry," Camille said. "I can't accept it, James."

For a moment he looked annoyed. Then he smiled, although his eyes remained cool. "Well, at least wear it for the rest of the evening," he coaxed, "to please me?"

Against her instinct, Camille capitulated. "All right."

When she left and he was walking her to her car, she slipped the bracelet off and handed it to him.

"You're sure?" he queried, reluctantly accepting it.

"Quite sure. Thank you for letting me wear it."

He stopped her as she made to get into the car, and pressed a kiss on her lips. "Thank you for coming. Could I persuade you to have lunch with us tomorrow?"

"Rogan's taking me scuba diving."

"Oh?" James looked suddenly intent.

The roar of an engine interrupted and a car swung into the drive, blocking the exit.

James frowned. "Excuse me, Camille."

He strode to the other car as a man opened the door and got out, and they engaged in a short, low-voiced conversation. The newcomer seemed agitated, thrusting his head forward and talking rapidly, and Camille caught the odd vehement swearword.

"I have guests," she heard James say tersely. "I tell you, there's nothing to worry about. Now get out."

He returned to Camille as the man reversed the car out of the drive and sped off the way he'd come.

"Is everything all right?" Camille asked, noting his grim air of preoccupation.

He smiled then. "Perfectly. A disgruntled employee actually. I think he's been drinking. I'll sort him out on Monday."

As she made to turn toward her car he said, "Have the Brodericks done anything about having the boat valued?"

"Not that I know of. Since I'm the one who wants to sell, I suppose it's up to me."

"I can recommend someone, if you like. Do you think they're serious about not selling?"

"Rogan is."

"You might be able to influence him to change his mind."

"Me? I don't think so."

"Don't underestimate yourself." He smiled again. He had a very nice smile, and she wondered why its obvious charm didn't affect her the way Rogan's raffish grin did. "Even the tough Mr. Broderick might melt for an attractive woman."

Camille said coolly, "What are you suggesting?"

James didn't answer for a second. Then he said, "I beg your pardon. It occurred to me that the boat would sell more readily if you could offer a whole rather than a half share. You'd probably get a better price, and more quickly. I spoke without thinking. Of course I didn't mean…what you thought. I'm…interested, myself."

"In buying the *Sea-Rogue?* I thought you didn't like sailing."

"I don't, but I already own a boat—quite a nice little

earner, taking tourists out for game and spear-fishing cruises. That was the skipper, just now.'' Fleetingly a grim look crossed his face.

''Would the *Sea-Rogue* be suitable for that?'' she asked, surprised.

''Probably not, but I'm thinking of a different clientele. Holiday charters and small-ship cruises are a growth area, and classic wooden boats appeal to the romanticism in a lot of people. It would need a good deal of work, but it's a shame to see a beautiful old craft reduced to a seagoing tramp.''

A loud burst of laughter came from the house, and Camille said, ''I'll let you get back to your guests. Thank you for inviting me.''

For her first real dive they drove in Camille's car to a small, deserted cove some miles away. Rogan made sure they checked each other's equipment and reminded her to clear her ears after submerging. They shuffled backward into the water and when it was deep enough turned and began to swim.

The burden of the air tank and weights seemed to disappear. Blue and orange starfish studded the pale surface of the downward slope, and crabs walked daintily over it. A school of tiny fish shot by in silver flashes, disrupting the stream of air bubbles rising from the divers.

Rogan took Camille's gloved hand to guide her to a rock outcrop, limpet-encrusted and bristling with spiny kina like small hedgehogs. He pointed to a narrow opening, touched a finger to what appeared to be a part of the rock, and she discerned a moving tentacle. Rogan put his hand into the crevice and gently eased the little octopus out. No bigger than half a meter long, it turned an indignant crimson, then enraged purple, and as he released it, shot away like a rocket, leaving a cloud of black ink hanging in the water.

The sea life they encountered amazed Camille, and when Rogan gave the signal to surface she couldn't believe they'd been under so long.

After they had removed their breathing tubes and masks, Rogan grinned at her. "Congratulations. You came through with flying colors."

They picnicked on the beach, dived again until their air tanks were getting low, and lazed on the sand for a while. Facedown on her towel, Camille was enjoying the sun on her back where her bathing suit dipped to below her waist, when something cold landed on her spine, and she jumped.

Rogan said, "Sorry, I should have warned you. You'll get burned if you don't have sun lotion on."

"I wasn't intending to sunbathe for long."

"It only takes ten minutes to burn."

His hand was quickly, efficiently spreading the lotion on her skin. And despite the impersonal manner in which he did it, she felt herself going warm all over, the pleasant lethargy induced by the sun laced with new and disturbing sensations. She was glad he couldn't see her face.

He put more lotion on her shoulders and arms, and then said, "Shall I do your legs for you?"

"No." Reluctantly she sat up, creamed her legs from the bottle he handed to her, and passed it back to him. "Do you use it?" She'd thought he'd be too macho to bother.

"Yep. Skin cancer's no joke. I've lost a couple of friends. Want to do my back?"

She could hardly refuse after his ministrations. Kneeling behind him, she poured lotion into her hand and began smoothing it over his warm, sand-dusted skin. She felt the muscle and bone beneath her fingers and the slight move- ment when he breathed. His hair was growing longer already, curling at his nape as it dried in the sun. When she began stroking the stuff across his shoulders he said, ''I'll finish it, thanks,'' and grabbed the bottle from her.

Thankfully Camille resumed her facedown position. She'd wanted to keep running her hands over the tantalizing texture of his skin, trace the outline of his shoulder blades, explore the groove of his spine…

She had never felt this way about a man, never wanted so much to touch, even tease, and be touched in return.

Of course, she'd seldom been so close to such a superb physical specimen. The men she met tended to be academics, more interested in developing their brains than their muscles, spending most of their time in lecture rooms and libraries, or hunched over books or computers.

Any normal woman would be biologically attuned to respond to a man who looked like Rogan Broderick.

And no doubt he was used to it. Just as she was used to being stared at and propositioned in various ways, from the obvious to the subtly sophisticated.

The difference was that her usual instinct was to ward off advances, while Rogan gave every sign of welcoming them. If she'd given in to temptation he wouldn't have rebuffed her. Yet he was keeping his promise that she'd be safe with him, not pressing her to follow through on the kisses they'd shared. He was either a perfect gentleman—she couldn't help a small grin at the thought—or not all that interested.

That possibility should not have disheartened her.

She was almost asleep when he roused her, commenting that they'd better get back. Together they packed up and returned to the *Sea-Rogue*. When their gear was stowed away Rogan produced a bottle of sparkling wine he said he'd been saving to celebrate Camille's first sea dive, and they drank it on deck, teamed with fresh fish bought from a boat that had chugged in late in the afternoon and tied up nearby.

"I should do some work," Camille said, leaning back with a half-full glass in her hand.

"It's Sunday," Rogan reminded her. "Day of rest."

"We didn't go to church."

"Do you?" he quizzed, looking at her quite seriously.

"Sometimes. Are you a believer?"

"It's kind of hard not to be, when you see stuff like we saw today. I mean, some intelligence out there that's bigger than us surely must be responsible for..." he waved a hand "...everything."

She looked down at her glass, watching the bubbles rise, remembering the undersea bubbles from her own breath and Rogan's mingling in the clear depths of the sea. "So do you think your father...and mine...are in heaven now?"

"About that," Rogan said, "I wouldn't like to guess. They were no angels, either of them, but they don't deserve being sent to hell."

And Barney hadn't deserved to be murdered. The anger that was never far from the surface of Rogan's mind tightened his hand on the glass as he gulped the remains of his wine.

He was tempted to hurl the empty glass into the sea, simply to satisfy his need for some violent action. But littering the ocean bed was a sin. Instead he reached for the bottle and leaned over to top up Camille's glass before emptying the remaining wine into his own.

"What did your brother say about buying me out?" she asked.

"We're...talking about it," Rogan hedged.

"And he doesn't want to sell his share?"

"We're not selling." He could rely on Granger to back him up, even if he didn't approve.

*   *   *

First thing Monday Rogan was at the police station. If the cops wanted him to keep out of things while they did their job, he'd just make sure they were actually doing it.

He asked if Gary's boat had returned to port and was told it had. "But," the constable said, "the skipper says he didn't turn up on Sunday and the *Catfish* left without him."

"The Sunday my father died?"

"It isn't necessarily significant. Boats and sailors come and go all the time. Don't worry, we're doing everything we can to track down your father's assailant."

But he was the sole officer in Mokohina, the CIB detectives were based miles away in Whangarei, and the department was notoriously short-staffed. Rogan worried.

While Camille went to see her elderly historian, Rogan took the ketch's dinghy and rowed across the harbor to where the *Catfish* was anchored. The skipper was checking fishing gear. Seeming friendly enough, he welcomed Rogan aboard, offering beer and asking if he wanted anything in particular.

"I heard you were short of a deckhand."

"You want a job?" the man inquired.

"I might know someone who does. What happened to the last one?"

The man's glance seemed to sharpen. "Didn't turn up for work when we were picking up a group at Paihia for a deep-sea trip. Probably found a better berth on some fancy yacht. A couple of American big boys' toys have been around lately. It's no use talking to me about the job. The boss likes to pick 'em himself."

"It isn't your boat, then?" Rogan asked.

The man laughed. "I can't afford anything like this."

"So who would my friend have to see?"

"Mr. Drummond at the antique shop."

"James Drummond?"

"You know him?"

"Yeah," Rogan answered, his brain working furiously. "I know him."

James Drummond was nowhere to be seen when Rogan told the helpful young man behind the counter he was just browsing thanks and strolled randomly about the shop, not even sure what he'd hoped to find. Minutes later the owner appeared and said, on a note of curiosity, "Rogan—can I help you?"

"Just looking," Rogan replied. Scanning the nearby bookshelves, his gaze was caught by a copy of Hakluyt's *Voyages,* large and handsomely bound in thick, dark leather with gilt embossing. His father had owned a similar copy, though he didn't recall seeing it recently. He eased the book from its place and opened it up.

Drummond looked almost startled, perhaps not expecting Rogan to be interested in classic books. "Not a first edition of course," he said, coming to stand nearby, "but a nice vintage copy, in good condition. I'll give you a discount, for a friend of Camille's."

"Thanks," Rogan said curtly. "But I don't think so." He slid the book back onto the shelf. He supposed it was churlish, but he didn't want any favors from James Drummond.

Looking slightly amused, Drummond said, "Were you looking for something in particular?"

"No."

"Camille tells me your boat hasn't been valued yet."

Did Camille tell him *everything?* She spent far too much time with him—dinners and lunches, and hanging about his shop. What did she see in this smarmy, soft-handed weasel anyway? "I'm sure she appreciates your interest," Rogan said, a sour taste in his mouth.

"My interest isn't entirely altruistic, I may be interested in buying. And I believe she wants to sell."

The thought of him owning even part of the *Sea-Rogue* made Rogan want to throw up. Fat use it would be to him if Rogan and Granger refused to let go of their half.

Granger could maybe do with the money. He was on a tight budget with his new practice. Guilt gnawed at Rogan's conscience as he turned to leave the shop.

"Nice talking to you," he heard Drummond say smoothly before he reached the door. But the man's voice changed as he called on a sharper note, "Shaun—come here!"

Shaun, Rogan surmised, glancing back to see Drummond reaching up to the shelf where the Hakluyt was, would be the young assistant who was emerging from the rear of the shop, looking defensive.

At dinner Camille said, "I contacted a marine surveyor this afternoon. He's going to inspect the boat and give us an estimate of what it's worth."

Rogan didn't comment. But his sudden scowl was fierce as he scooped up the last bits of his meal.

She gave him a speculative look, and pushed away her empty plate. "What's making you so bad-tempered?"

"I'm not bad-tempered!" He picked up the can of beer at his side and took a swig, then stared down at the can as if it were a crystal ball. "The cops don't seem to have any idea who attacked my father. I suppose an old drunk who got himself beaten up isn't a top priority for them."

"I'm sure they're doing their best."

"Yeah, well…" Morosely he swilled the beer around in the can, and drank some more. "*Somebody* must know something." Struck by a bizarre thought, he said, "You were in Drummond's shop before the burglary, weren't you?"

Camille looked bewildered. "Yes, the day I arrived."

"Did he have an old copy of Hakluyt's *Voyages* then?"

She hesitated, thinking. "I don't remember seeing one, but then it wasn't what I was looking for. Why?"

"He's got one now. Just like one my father had."

Her eyes widened disbelievingly. "You're not suggesting he stole it?"

"I just wondered how long he's had it."

"You could have asked him."

"Didn't occur to me at the time." He'd merely thought that the old volume was remarkably similar to Barney's Hakluyt, the heavy, smooth leather binding with its rounded, decoratively ridged spine fitting familiarly into the curve of his palm. "He could have been receiving stolen goods."

"I'm sure James wouldn't do that. Not deliberately."

"How do you know? You only met him a couple of weeks back."

"Before I met you," she retorted. "If it's your father's book and he knew it was stolen, it would be stupid to display it for sale so soon. James isn't stupid." Gently she added, "Don't you think maybe you're obsessing a bit?"

"Is it obsessive to want to know who caused my father's death?" At least it helped stop him obsessing about *her*—living with her and giving her diving lessons while keeping his distance physically was driving him nuts.

The Silhouette Reader Service™ — Here's how it works:

Accepting your 2 free books and mystery gift places you under no obligation to buy anything. You may keep the books and gift and return the shipping statement marked "cancel." If you do not cancel, about a month later we'll send you 6 additional books and bill you just $3.99 each in the U.S., or $4.74 each in Canada, plus 25¢ shipping & handling per book and applicable taxes if any.* That's the complete price and — compared to cover prices of $4.75 each in the U.S. and $5.75 each in Canada — it's quite a bargain! You may cancel at any time, but if you choose to continue, every month we'll send you 6 more books, which you may either purchase at the discount price or return to us and cancel your subscription.

*Terms and prices subject to change without notice. Sales tax applicable in N.Y. Canadian residents will be charged applicable provincial taxes and GST. Credit or Debit balances in a customer's account(s) may be offset by any other outstanding balance owed by or to the customer.

BUSINESS REPLY MAIL

FIRST-CLASS MAIL   PERMIT NO. 717-003   BUFFALO, NY

POSTAGE WILL BE PAID BY ADDRESSEE

SILHOUETTE READER SERVICE
3010 WALDEN AVE
PO BOX 1867
BUFFALO NY 14240-9952

NO POSTAGE
NECESSARY
IF MAILED
IN THE
UNITED STATES

Chapter 9

Next day Camille visited the Treasure Chest again. James was busy with other customers, but as they left he came to her side. "Not much that's new, I'm afraid," he said.

"Rogan said you had a copy of Hakluyt's *Voyages.*"

"Ah…" he said. "I'm sorry, it's been sold."

"He wondered where you'd got it from," she told him.

James rubbed a finger over his chin. "It came in an auction lot. I'm afraid my inventory's a bit behind lately. My assistant unearthed the Hakluyt the other day."

"Rogan thought it might have been his father's."

James's brows lifted. Then he laughed. "Did he send you to investigate?"

"No! He mentioned it, and I was curious."

The assistant entered from the back of the premises, carrying a carton of books. "Is it okay to shelve these?" he asked James. "Or are they going to the Auckland store? I don't want to make another mistake."

Looking faintly annoyed at the interruption, James swept a cursory glance at the books. "Yes, go ahead."

"I've arranged for a survey of the boat," Camille said.

"Ah! At last. When you set a price I hope you'll allow me first refusal."

"I promised that to Rogan and Granger."

A momentary frown creased his forehead. "Then I'd like a chance to better whatever they offer. You don't want to take less than you can get for it."

That was sensible, she supposed. And only fair to her mother, the person she felt the money rightfully belonged to. Mona deserved to get the best price possible.

"I'll be meeting friends in Auckland for Christmas dinner," James said. "Would you care to join me? He's the managing director of United Chemical Products, and his wife—quite a connoisseur—has bought several things from my Auckland shop. There'll be other interesting people..."

While she found James's knowledge of his wares and their provenance fascinating, spending Christmas with a crowd of strangers appealed to her even less than spending it alone. "Thank you, but I don't really fancy traveling all that way." And if he meant to stay overnight things could become awkward. "I'll be fine here."

He looked disappointed. "Can I persuade you to come to my place for drinks and cake on Christmas Eve, then? After eight?"

"That sounds nice." Having turned down one invitation, it would be almost rude to refuse that too.

The surveyor gave the boat a thorough inspection and promised a formal written valuation by the end of the week.

Later Rogan phoned his brother.

"Sorry, Rogue." Granger's voice crackled through the telephone receiver. "When she asked me point-blank I had to tell her. Camille's free to sell now to anyone she pleases. And before you ask, the answer's still no, I can't help you in a buyout. I'm not even sure it's a good idea. I'd hate to see you go the same way as the old man. Are you sure you're not just being a dog in the manger?''

"Huh?"

"You've taken a dislike to James Drummond because he's interested in Camille. If you're serious about her you should think about how much you want the *Sea-Rogue*— and why. And how much you want the woman.''

Rogan said huffily, "Don't jump to conclusions.'' He'd scarcely mentioned Camille to his brother—not how he felt about her, anyway. Of course he wanted her—in the most basic way. And he liked her. A lot. It didn't mean he wanted to *marry* her. Or anyone.

Marriage wasn't in his life plan. He had Barney's genes, and he'd seen what that had done to his mother. She'd struggled to bring up two boys and get them a decent education between Barney's occasional visits and with his erratic financial contributions. If she needed emotional support there was no one to give it to her.

Rogan had no intention of doing that to any woman. His conscience wouldn't stand it.

Presuming it wasn't much use asking Granger to guarantee a loan since he disapproved of the whole idea, Rogan visited the local branch of the bank that had been the recipient of his latest hefty check, and emerged decidedly disgruntled after fifteen minutes with the manager.

He knew Brodie would help him out if he could, but although Rogan had no problem asking his friend for the odd favor, borrowing money from him went against the grain. He'd never borrowed so much as a fiver in his life, from anyone.

* * *

He told Camille, "I want to check how the *Sea-Rogue*'s running, and you're ready for a deep dive. Brodie's free on Sunday, and I've asked him to be our safety guy."

Brodie boarded on Sunday morning, and they motored out of the port on still water that became choppy when the boat hit the open sea. Once they picked up a breeze Rogan cut the motor and the men hoisted sail.

Rogan said, "There's something I have to do," and took a small box from his pack on the deck.

Standing at the stern, he opened the box and Camille realized with a faint chill that what he'd had to do was scatter his father's ashes on the sea.

She glanced at Brodie, who also looked a bit shocked. They both watched Rogan's rigid back until he turned, catching their expressions, and said, "The old man didn't want any ceremony about this. We did all that the day of the funeral."

Brodie nodded, and Camille quelled an impulse to give Rogan a hug. His remote expression signaled it wouldn't be welcome.

He took the wheel, and after a while called Camille from her post in the bow where the breeze blew her hair and cooled her face, and showed her how to keep the boat parallel to the shore as they headed north, passing sheer cliffs where seabirds wheeled and dived, and deserted sandy coves.

Standing behind her, he put his hands over hers on the smooth turned spokes of the wooden wheel. Achingly conscious of his roughened palms and the warmth emanating from his body, clad only in light jeans with no shirt, a tantalizing inch or two away, she had to fight an urge to lean back and feel the strength of it against her. She wondered if he was making an excuse to be close to someone—perhaps anyone—after carrying out his sad task.

After a while he moved away, letting her steer the boat herself while he kept an eye on how she was doing. She found it surprisingly exhilarating.

When the boat drew close to the Poor Knights islands, their granite cliffs rising stark and sheer from the blue-green of the sea but softened by tenacious clinging plants, Rogan took back the wheel. He steered to a tranquil cove with a sandy bottom, where there was little danger of their anchor damaging a reef.

Not far away another boat dipped its sail into the wind, and disappeared around a rocky point. A catamaran went past a few minutes later, its wash rocking the *Sea-Rogue* and sending waves curling up the cliffs.

Rogan went into the diamond-clear water first to fix a safety line with a bright orange, flagged buoy to signal there were divers down. Then Camille followed while Brodie, suited up in case of an emergency, remained on board.

Trying to suppress a nervous excitement, Camille concentrated on controlling the amount of air in her buoyancy compensator so that she'd neither sink like a stone nor bob to the surface. Alongside the line, they finned easily in the clear depths. Below, a school of brilliant blue fish streamed through a forest of lazily waving grass-green kelp. Rogan guided Camille to a clearing in the seaweed.

A golden-yellow fish banded with blue fluttered by. Rogan pointed to a stingray the size of a dining table gracefully undulating giant wings overhead, its pale underside with space-alien eyes and mouth clearly visible. Tiny orange cleaner fish wriggled busily out of the kelp forest and back again to its shelter, and baby angelfish fussed about among the green fronds. One swam up to Camille's mask, kissing the glass.

Rogan led her over part of the reef, carefully not close enough for their rubber fins to damage its delicate structure.

She resisted the desire to reach out and feel the weird plants and animals; touching was strictly forbidden within the reserve.

Too soon it was time to go up. Rogan ensured they made a decompression stop before surfacing, and Brodie helped her climb back on board and undo her harness while Rogan slipped his own off.

"Okay?" Rogan quizzed Camille.

"Fantastic!" She was only disappointed they couldn't have stayed longer in the magical, dreamlike world underwater.

He smiled at her. Then, indicating a white motor cruiser lazily riding on the waves in the distance he asked Brodie, "When did that arrive?"

"Soon after us," Brodie answered. "Fishing, I guess—it's outside the reserve."

Something on the other boat caught the sun, making Camille blink at the blinding flash. Rogan raised a hand and peered across the water before turning away.

After lunching on deck while a faint breeze shivered through the clinging plants on the cliffs, and seabirds soared above, Rogan allowed Camille one more dive.

The little cove was still calm, and when they surfaced again Rogan said, "Will you mind if we leave you for a while? You'll be safe here, and Brodie deserves a dive."

"Don't you need an experienced diver on board?" she asked, knowing she didn't fit the bill.

Brodie assured her, "The Knights are practically home to us, and it's a perfect sea. We wouldn't dive if it wasn't safe."

After donning their gear, the two of them stepped straight off the side of the ketch, splashing in together before giving her and each other an Okay sign and disappearing below the marker buoy.

Camille relaxed under an awning the men had rigged, rocked by the gentle movement of the ketch, half dreaming of what she'd seen, flashes of color swimming behind her closed lids, anemones opening their waving petals, seaweed wafting in the faint current...

She saw Rogan arrowing toward her, not in mask and fins, but bare-chested, bareheaded, his hair streaming in sunlit, crystal water. He took her hand as she stretched out a pale, naked arm to him, and she realized they were both quite nude. He smiled at her and pulled her close, their legs entangling as once they had in the practice pool, but without the barrier of neoprene, flesh meeting flesh. A soft, melting heat rose from her thighs. Rogan's body was warm and slick, and he drew her inexorably against him, in slow motion because of the water. He found her mouth and kissed her as they weightlessly drifted. She wrapped her arms about his neck and kissed him back, her heart beginning to thud, while air bubbles surrounded them, bursting with increasingly loud popping sounds...

Her eyes snapped open. The sun had shifted and was heating her body—or the dream had. The thudding and pop-popping sounds resolved into the chug of a motor.

Shaking her head to banish the disturbingly erotic images that lingered all too vividly in her mind, she got up. The sun dazzled her, and black spots floated before her eyes before they cleared and she was able to see properly.

Another boat had entered the cove. A gray rubber dinghy powered by an outboard motor. A man dressed in a wet suit with a hood that framed his face, giving it an anonymous blandness, waved to her as the engine died, and she raised her hand in return. He secured the boat and donned a mask, and an air tank. Rogan and Brodie would shortly have company.

Farther out to sea the big cruiser still rode on the blue water beyond the reserve.

Camille looked at her watch. She'd been dozing for only a few minutes. Descending to the cabin, she got herself a drink, and pulled a book from one of the shelves. *Les Trois Mousquetaires*. A nice, leather-bound copy.

She was reading on deck when the boat rocked and Brodie and Rogan climbed back over the side.

They weighed anchor and ran back down the coast to Mokohina. Sharing take-away fish and chips for three on deck, Rogan noticed the book she'd placed beside her.

"You're reading that?"

"You don't mind, do you?"

"No problem."

A large cruiser came into sight, its wash thumping the *Sea-Rogue* against the bulwarks of the wharf as it crossed the water on the way to the anchorage, and Brodie said, "She's the one that was at the Knights. Is that where the guy with the dinghy came from?" he asked Camille. "We saw him come down."

"I don't know. I was asleep when it arrived." Remembering her dream, she avoided looking at Rogan. "I thought you were always supposed to have two divers."

Brodie chose a fat potato chip from the opened paper parcel in front of them. "Some people prefer solo diving—they'd rather rely on their own resources than trust anyone at all, or have to ask for help and risk someone else's life. It's okay if you know what you're doing, I guess."

Rogan conceded, "Yeah, well...I'd rather dive alone than with some idiot who'd get us both into trouble. But Camille isn't experienced enough for that yet."

When Brodie crumpled up the empty paper and declared he had to get on home, Rogan accompanied him to the wharf and strolled beside him for a little way. "The old girl sailed well today," he said casually.

"Yep," Brodie agreed. "She's a grand old lady."

"There could be a half share up for grabs if you're interested."

Brodie looked surprised, and Rogan said, "I just thought you might like to come in as a partner. If you don't want to...that's fine." He wasn't going to take advantage of Brodie's absurd idea that he owed Rogan because of a routine emergency procedure that was all in a day's work for a professional diver.

Brodie thought for a while. "I already own a dive boat," he said, "and it's expensive to run. If you plan to sail cargo about the islands like your dad, I don't see much profit in it, frankly."

"Suppose there's the chance of a huge profit?"

Brodie laughed. "You're not going after your father's treasure ship, are you?"

"What do you know about it?"

"Nothing. Rumors. I figured that's all they are." Curiously, Brodie asked, "Do you have some evidence?"

Rogan shook his head. Non-evidence, more like. A missing log, an empty safe, a sailor who'd gone AWOL. "No. The police seem short of it too." And like everyone else they didn't believe Barney had actually located treasure.

Rogan was strolling back along the wharf when a voice hailed him, and Doll came hurrying to catch up with him.

"How're you doing, young Rogue?" the man asked. "I hear you're gonna carry on your father's old business?"

"Maybe." Desperate, he said, "I don't suppose you'd be interested in buying a half share?"

Doll shook his head sorrowfully. "Don't have that kind of money, mate. Don't have any, to tell the truth. Gonna miss your dad," he said sentimentally as they reached the *Sea-Rogue*'s berth. "We had some good times when the old Rogue was in port. Sinking a few beers, catching up…" He shook his head again. "Can almost see him there now, sayin', 'Come aboard, me old mate. We'll crack open a bottle and have a yarn.'" A gusty sigh followed.

Faced with such a weighty hint, Rogan capitulated.

When he led Doll down to the saloon it was spick and span and the door of Camille's cabin was ajar. He tapped on the door and peeked around it, seeing her at the desk, a tape recorder lying beside an open book. "I have a visitor, an old friend of my dad's—and yours I guess. You're welcome to join us."

"Thanks," she said, politely distant, "but I need to work. Perhaps you could close the door?"

Apparently she had no interest in friends of her father. Rogan went to pour the expectant Doll a beer.

Several bottles and a number of rambling anecdotes later, Doll showed no sign of budging from his seat at the table.

"Doll," Rogan said when he could get a word in, "do you know of any special hiding place my father might have used to keep something safe?"

Doll looked blank. "Keep what safe?"

Rogan hesitated. "I can't find the log." He'd tapped panels, examined floorboards, climbed into the bilge…

Doll said, "Have you talked to Mollie?"

"Who's Mollie?"

Suddenly shifty-eyed, Doll muttered, "Um…friend of Barney's. Ol' Barn saw a fair bit of her when he was in port, the last few years."

"A *lady friend?*" Rogan swallowed unwarranted outrage. His mother had been dead for over ten years. As far as he knew, despite their long separations and unlikely though it seemed, Barney had been faithful to her until she died. If he'd found solace in another woman's arms since, who was Rogan to judge? "Mollie who?"

"Edwards. Works at Denny's Bakery. Got another beer?"

"No," Rogan told him ruthlessly. "Time to go home, mate, sorry." Any more and Doll would wind up sleeping right where he was. Rogan didn't fancy waking up to that in the morning, and didn't think Camille would appreciate it either.

He saw the man safely to the wharf and on his slightly unsteady way back to town, and then went to the nearby phone booth and squinted at the curly-cornered phonebook, looking for Edwards. There were several and he wasn't sure which was the right one. Besides it was getting a bit late to be phoning a lone woman—which he supposed Mollie Edwards was.

Next morning Rogan was on the doorstep of Denny's Bakery when it opened. A large bearded man wearing a white apron let him in and indicated the rows of loaves behind the counter emanating the rich, warm smell of new-baked bread. "Can I help you?"

"I'm looking for Mollie Edwards. She was a friend of my father's," Rogan explained.

"Mollie's off work—had a nasty fall coupla weeks or so back. She's only just out of hospital. Makes you think what can happen to you just walking down your own back steps, eh?" The man shook his head. "Mind you, she likes a bit of a tipple and she'd been to a funeral that day, she was a bit upset. Apparently she was carrying empties down to the bin when she fell."

"That would have been my father's funeral, I guess. Can you give me her address?"

"Your father was Barney Broderick?" When Rogan

confirmed it, he said, "Bad business, that. Bella Vista Road—fourteen I think. Garden's full of driftwood and stuff. Even an old dinghy. A great one for her garden, Mollie."

The dinghy was painted yellow and filled with flowering plants. More flowers spilled from used tires cut into the shapes of ships or swans and painted white. Crushed seashells crunched under Rogan's boots as he walked up a path between fragrant bush roses. Dodging a glass fishing float in a net dangling from the ceiling of the tiny porch, Rogan rang a ship's bell on a bracket beside the door.

The woman who opened up was thinner than when he'd seen her at the funeral, and the brassy curls had gone limp. Her cheeks were pink, but Rogan suspected that was artificial, like the bright red on her lips and the blue applied to her eyelids.

"Ms. Edwards?"

"Mrs. Edwards," she corrected him. "And you are…?"

"Rogan Broderick. We met at my father's funeral."

"Oh!" she said softly. "Did we? Poor Barney. Rogan," she repeated. "Well, you'd better come in."

A cluttered little front room was dimmed by pink velvet fringed curtains, the walls were hung with flower paintings, and a shelf thing in one corner held exotic shells, lumps of coral and a ship in a bottle.

"Can I get you a cup of tea?" she offered, after urging him to sit. "Or something stronger? I'm not allowed just now, the doctor said, but I've got beer or gin. And sherry."

"No, thanks," Rogan said, sinking into dented sofa cushions. "I heard about your accident. How are you now?"

"Very tired." She took a winged chair with a deeply buttoned back. "I can't even get out and do my garden."

"I'm sorry. It must be frustrating for you."

"Barney used to help me with the heavy digging. When he was around. He was a bit of a rough diamond, your father, but he had a good heart."

"Yes, you said so at the funeral."

She looked at him blankly. "Did I? I'm sorry, I hit my head when I fell, you see. I know I was there, but it's all a bit hazy." Hesitantly she said, "I spoke to you?"

"You said you'd like to talk to us—me and my brother."

"Oh…I did? Well, I'm glad you found me. I was fond of your father."

"I'm sure he was fond of you too," Rogan said, and was dismayed when her eyes filled with tears. "I don't want to upset you."

She fished in a sort of pocket hanging from the side of the chair and pulled out a tissue to dab at her eyes. "It's all right. It was very sweet of you to come."

Feeling guilty, Rogan said, "Um…I wondered if you could help me, Mrs. Edwards."

She sniffed, and vigorously rubbed the tissue over her nose. "Mollie," she said, straightening. "How can I help?"

"Do you recall if my father said anything about his ship's log?"

Slowly Mollie shook her head. "I remember him coming up the path—I was weeding, and then I heard the gate and there he was." Her face had lit up, a tremulous smile on her painted mouth. "I think that was the day he arrived." She gulped, and for a moment the scarlet lips trembled. Using the tissue again, she wiped her cheeks. Some of the color came off. "They said it's very common with a head injury to have memory gaps. But I would like to be able to remember more about his last visit," she finished wistfully.

Rogan leaned forward. "I think my father might have hidden the ship's log. You don't remember if he said anything about it? Or about finding treasure?"

Mollie smiled. "I'm sure he did." And as Rogan's head jerked up, "He was always talking about treasure!"

Defeatedly, Rogan sat back. "Yeah, I know."

"Why would Barney have hidden his log? Oh, I *wish* I could remember!" Her hands thumped the arms of her chair, and the color in her cheeks was real now. "Half the time I can't even find things that have been in the same place for years! I must have shifted them and forgotten. It's so annoying! Even my house keys—and I always hang them on the same hook at the back door…" She stood up, then put a hand to her head.

Rogan quickly got up too and took her arm. "Are you all right? Can I get you something?" he asked.

"No, I'm fine now."

He'd have to tell Granger about Mollie. Barney would have wanted them to look out for her. "If I can do anything for you…"

"I'm well looked after…the district nurse comes and the neighbors have been good, but they're elderly, and…it's the garden that worries me. I haven't even been able to walk about it all and see what needs doing. Would you mind…if you let me lean on your arm…?"

They began at the front, where she inspected the flowers in their crammed beds and containers, tut-tutting at the determined weed or three that Rogan obligingly pulled out. Along the side of the house narrow beds of daisies and fuchsias and lavender argued for space, and at the back a surprisingly large lawn was shaded by old, spreading fruit trees. Tall hedges screened neighboring properties and sheltered the exuberant shrubs that bordered the lawn.

Mollie stopped at a rosebush with large crimson blooms.

"That's funny! My roses are all in the front garden. What's this one doing here?"

"Maybe you ran out of room. Would you remember every plant you have?"

"Yes! I mean…I did. It must be new, but why did I put it here?" Her brow creased, and her voice trembled.

Rogan touched a petal and a waft of perfume lifted into the air. "It smells good." He plucked a just-opened bloom and handed it to her.

She closed her eyes and inhaled. "Deepest Secret," she said.

"Deepest secret?" Rogan repeated.

Mollie opened her eyes. "That's what it's called—the rose. I remember now, Barney planted it for me!" She looked at him with dawning excitement. "He dug the hole extra deep. We had to put it here because otherwise the neighbors might see…" She faltered.

On the back of Rogan's neck hairs rose. "See what?"

"I—I'm not sure. I remember him preparing the hole."

Rogan stared at the prickly bush, and the recently turned earth it sat in. "Mollie," he said, "do you mind if I dig up your rose?"

Chapter 10

Camille had spent the morning with Mr. Trubshaw, and made a light lunch for them both before leaving with another pile of books.

Descending to the cabin, she found Rogan at the table, his head bent.

"Hi," she said. "What are you doing?"

He looked up, his eyes more brilliant than ever, his face taut with suppressed excitement. "Reading the log."

Now she saw the book that had been hidden by his arms enclosing it on the table. "You found it! Where?"

"It's a long story," he said. "And look." He reached for a cigar tin similar to the one that had been in the box of her father's belongings. It was just big enough to have held the log. He took something from it, extending his palm.

"A sovereign."

"An 1852 sovereign. It was inside the logbook. They were buried in my father's...uh...lady friend's garden."

She glanced at him, then down at the coin in his hand. Unable to suppress a small thrill, she said cautiously, "It doesn't prove anything, does it? It's only one coin." Probably worth a couple of hundred dollars at most, according to what James had told her when he'd shown her his small coin collection.

"If this is a sample from a hoard," Rogan said, "who knows how many more there are? Dad certainly thought he was onto something."

But his father had been—according to general opinion— deluded, or at the very least wildly overoptimistic. She said carefully, "He could have got it anywhere—even been conned into buying it." It must have been general knowledge throughout the islands frequented by the *Sea-Rogue* that Barney Broderick was a sucker for a treasure story. There were probably plenty of single old coins able to be picked up for a song.

Rogan's jaw jutted. A flicker of doubt entered his eyes.

Camille said, "Is there anything in the log about it?"

"I haven't been through it all yet. But he certainly had *something* he didn't want anyone finding. What's more—" he frowned, his eyes momentarily glazing "—Mollie had a convenient accident the day after Dad's funeral."

"*Convenient?* Mollie's the lady friend?"

"Right. She was found by a neighbor, unconscious at the bottom of her back steps. They're concrete and everyone assumed she fell and banged her head on them. She's been in hospital since Dad's funeral."

"You're not suggesting someone hit her?"

"It just sounds too coincidental to me."

"Coincidences happen all the time."

Rogan sat back, scowling at the low ceiling. "Yeah, I know," he said wearily. "All circumstantial. Anyway—"

he lowered his eyes and gave her a piercing look "—I don't want anyone else to know I've got the log, okay?"

"I won't tell anyone."

"Including your friend Drummond."

"All right." If it made him happy...

He said, "Mollie invited us to Christmas lunch."

"Us?" Camille queried. "She doesn't know me."

"I told her I won't leave you here on your own unless you have a better offer, and she said to bring you along. She's got no children and all her neighbors have families to share Christmas with."

Mr. Trubshaw too was spending Christmas with his family in Whangarei, probably staying overnight.

"It's very kind of her," Camille said doubtfully.

"Seems she was hoping Dad would be sharing it with her. She'd already made a plum pudding and put a mini-turkey in the freezer before her accident. Says she doesn't want them wasted. She's lonely. I think she wants company."

"All right," Camille agreed. "I'll come. We should take her some flowers or chocolates or something."

"Better still, a plant," Rogan suggested.

Next day, Christmas Eve, Brodie spent a couple of hours fruitlessly canvassing increasingly desperate options for a loan. Later he and Camille visited the town's sole nursery and Rogan found a potted miniature rose labeled Golden Coin and already Christmas-wrapped. Camille slanted him a dry look but had to admit the compact but perfect buttercup-yellow flowers were charming, their subtle scent an added attraction.

He also bought a tiny pine tree in a pot, and a packet of Christmas decorations. Back on board Rogan placed the tree in the bow and enlisted Camille's help to decorate it.

"I might go to Brodie's and buy some dive gear," Camille said. "A sort of Christmas present to myself."

"I'll come with you," Rogan offered, and she accepted, grateful to have his expert advice.

He asked Brodie for a dive certificate, filled it out there and then, and gave it to Camille. "Your official graduation document. You need to present it when you're hiring or buying dive gear."

Brodie also had a couple of shelves of diving and boating books. Rogan bought one on New Zealand dive sites and handed it to her, saying, "Call it a Christmas gift."

When she insisted on reciprocating, he allowed her to buy him a book on wreck diving.

Brodie grinned as he rang up the sale, and said he was taking a couple of American divers out in his boat later, and would Camille and Rogan like to join them?

They spent a few hours on board and in the water, and raced a summer storm back to port. Leaving the heavy air tanks with Brodie, they were almost at the *Sea-Rogue* when the threatened downpour began, a typical Northland deluge of fat, heavy droplets that steamed on the pavement.

Camille's T-shirt and shorts were quickly soaked and raindrops were streaming down her bare legs when they reached the deck. The Christmas tree fixed to the bow still sparkled, remarkably perky, the ornaments shinier than ever.

Grinning at her, Rogan dumped the pack containing their wet suits and thrust water-slicked hair from his forehead. A flash of lightning momentarily lit his face, accentuating its clean, strong lines, and seconds later thunder rumbled overhead. The rain hitting the deck hissed about her ankles. She raised a hand to push bedraggled tresses from her eyes. One stubborn strand remained, and Rogan carefully lifted it away, tucking it in with the rest behind her ear.

His hand lingered, a finger tracing the outline of her ear, following the shallow groove below to the curve of her chin, then lifting her face to him. His eyes asked an explicit question, and for the space of a breath she stared back at him, then with an effort of will she took a step backward, and his hand fell away.

He slanted her a wryly understanding smile and said, "We'd better dry off."

Camille bolted to her cabin, vigorously toweled her hair, and emerged dressed in her loose blue cotton pants and a primrose T-shirt.

Rogan joined her as she was preparing their evening meal. Declining help, she kept herself busy until it was time to eat. Rogan had seated himself at the table with the log, but a couple of times when she looked up from her self-imposed chore he was studying her instead of the book.

Maybe it was the close atmosphere created by the rain that made her more aware of him than ever. With the door shut the saloon was warm, the air seeming thick, almost claustrophobic, while piled black clouds outside darkened the cabin.

The boat kept bumping dully against the wharf. The storm was sending bigger than normal waves into the harbor, and through the portholes Camille caught glimpses of bare masts nearby dipping and swaying. She had to concentrate to keep her feet.

"Are you okay?" Rogan queried as she carefully lifted a pot over the safety rail on the small kerosene stove that swung on its gimbal.

"Yes."

"You don't get seasick?"

"Not so far," she said. "I haven't spent any time on boats until now." She hadn't been sick on either of their sea trips, but the weather had been clear, the water calm, and even today the choppy waves preceding the storm hadn't bothered her.

When she placed two filled plates on the table Rogan put aside the log, closing it.

"Have you found anything in there?" she asked him.

"I know where Dad and Taff were sailing."

"Does it say they found treasure?"

"No," he admitted. "But they seem to have spent some time around a group of uninhabited atolls before sailing for Rarotonga. They can't have been delivering cargo."

"Couldn't it have been because my father was ill and couldn't help sail the boat? Barney might have been waiting for him to get better, and then when he realized he wasn't going to, headed for a hospital."

"Or they might have had another reason." He dug his fork into a piece of lamb and lifted it to his mouth.

Camille began on her own meal. "Are you going to buy the boat?"

Savagely Rogan stabbed another piece of meat. "What's the hurry?"

"My mother can do with the money." All Camille's life Mona had bemoaned her lack of a decent income, comparing her straitened circumstances with her sister's comfortable lifestyle, financed by a husband with a good steady income from a good steady job. Generous presents that arrived every birthday and Christmas from Australia only served to sharpen her envy and sense of unfairness.

"Your mother?" Rogan queried.

"She's had a hard life. It's time something good happened to her."

"Weren't you something good?"

"A nice thought, but I was a mixed blessing."

Rogan couldn't argue with that. He knew what hard

times his own mother had experienced, despite her gallant and unswerving love for his father. "Were you unhappy?"

Camille looked faintly startled. "Not specially. My mother loved me and did her best, even helped me get through university. That wasn't easy."

His mother had done the same for Granger before she died, with a little help from Barney and from Rogan himself, meticulously repaid despite his protests. "It can't have been easy for you either."

"I've done what I wanted to do."

Like her father, he thought, but as a child she'd been Taff's responsibility, which apparently he'd shucked off. Hard to believe that the man who'd seemed fond of "Barney's boys" and spent hours teaching them seamanship and carving toys for them had been so cavalier about his own family. But then, neither he nor Barney had been exactly constant fathers or husbands. He asked, "Where did you grow up?"

"In Auckland until I was seven. We moved around a bit before I started university."

"Did Taff know where you were, when you and your mother were shifting about?"

"I don't think he cared."

"He might have."

"Your father found us easily enough. Presumably mine could have done the same."

"Didn't he ever visit?"

"Not since my sixth birthday. I never heard a word from him after that." She failed to hide the bitterness in her voice.

"Maybe," Rogan said thoughtfully, "Dad knew where to find you because Taff had kept tabs on where you were."

She gave him a look of patent disbelief, and he dropped the subject.

* * *

After they'd eaten, the rain was still pounding on the deck and the darkness increased. Rogan switched on the cabin lights, sat down and pulled the logbook toward him again.

"Haven't you read it all yet?" Camille asked curiously.

"My father's writing isn't the easiest to read, and he used a kind of personal shorthand sometimes. Some bits I can't work out. Makes me wonder why he bothered to hide the log at all…" he finished gloomily.

"I'm accustomed to deciphering handwriting in old documents," she offered.

He looked hopefully at her. "See what you make of this," he suggested, pointing out a phrase as she slid into the seat beside him. "'Shoals of Queens?' But there are no such shoals on any of the charts."

"It could be shoals…or shadow? Shades," she said. "Shades of…Demons?"

"Demons?" Doubtfully, he leaned closer to her. "I thought it was Queens."

"I think that's a D, not a Q. Demons or…Dumas!"

"Dumas?"

"Well…maybe that came to mind because I've been reading *Les Trois Mousquetaires.*"

"I think you're right, though." He scowled at the words, then looked at her sharply. "Are there any marked passages or anything in that book?"

"None that I've seen. No treasure map either."

He acknowledged the small gibe with a glint in his eye and a faint twist to his mouth before turning back to the page.

She said, "Of course that's not the only book Dumas wrote. And there was the younger Dumas, his son."

"Who wrote the book your name came from, yeah."

She wondered if he'd read *La Dame aux Camelias* in French. "Did your father own any other Dumas's?"

"Not that I recall. *The Three Musketeers* is the best known."

"Maybe you should look for a group of three islands."

"Or two—a big one and a small one, for the father and son. I'll have to study the charts again. And can you get me that book—just in case there's something you might have missed?"

Camille went to her cabin and reached on tiptoe to pull the book from the shelf over her bed, but as she straightened the boat gave a heave, thumping against the wharf, and she lost her balance. The book in her hand, she fell against the wooden frame of the berth and sprawled on the floor with a small cry.

Instantly Rogan was in the doorway. "What happened?" He crouched beside her as she struggled to sit up.

"The book," she said, still clutching it. "Take it, will you?"

He took it and put it aside, then turned to her. She was ruefully regarding a nasty little scrape just below her elbow.

Rogan gave a low exclamation. "How did you do that?"

"On the edge of the bed," she said. "It's nothing."

He helped her up. "Let's see."

The skin was raw and pink, and blood oozed from it. He pushed her onto her berth and said, "Sit down. I'll get the first-aid kit."

He was back quickly and, sitting beside her, gently dabbed disinfectant on the wound and dried it with gauze before applying a dressing. "There you are," he said, firming the edges into place.

Camille lowered her arm, letting her hand fall into her lap, and raised her eyes, finding him closer than she'd realized, his eyes darkened, the pupils enlarged against the arresting blue of the irises. A strand or two of dark hair had strayed onto his forehead, and she noticed a faint sheen of sweat on his hairline. The rain hadn't really cooled the air, only made it more humid. She wanted to wipe away the dampness with a finger, but stopped herself, curling her hands together instead as she murmured, "Thank you."

His smile was taut. "No problem." He closed the few inches between them to drop a light kiss on her lips.

Every nerve in her body reacted to it like tinder to flame. When he lifted his head she knew her eyes had dilated. The skin of her face grew tight over the bones, cheeks flaring. Her mouth tingled and she felt her lips involuntarily part as she drew an unsteady breath, trying to control the tremor that shook her.

She saw Rogan's eyes go more brilliant than ever, and for a second she could clearly hear the rain thudding on the boards above them, the waves slapping against the hull, but not as clearly as she heard his quickened breathing.

The light flickered and the boat lurched. Rogan lifted a hand to steady her, his fingers closing about her arm. She sucked in another breath of warm, thick air, and he muttered, "Oh, what the hell…" and pulled her into his arms.

It was heaven, it was where she needed to be. He held her to him and his mouth unerringly found her parted lips, taking her on an erotic foray into unknown territory. She hadn't known a man's scent could intoxicate, his kiss be more darkly potent than wine. That a mere trailing of his fingers down her arm could awake sensations that stormed over her skin from head to toe, a brushing of knuckles over her cheek could set her on fire, his hand raking into her hair, cradling her head with a combination of tenderness and strength, could melt something deep inside her as he furthered the kiss into an intimacy she had never before experienced. Had never allowed.

Now she wanted it, craved it, craved *him* and all he could give of himself. Her hands touched him—his hair, springy and soft against her fingers, his neck, taut and smooth and warm, and his shoulders, broad and muscular beneath the cotton of his shirt.

One of his hands slid inside her shirt at the waist, and she shuddered with pleasure as he caressed her bare skin, a finger tracing the groove of her spine.

The boat swayed again, tumbling them onto the berth that was wide for one but hardly big enough for two. Momentarily removing his mouth from hers, Rogan hitched them both farther onto the mattress and rolled her under him, his body hard and hot on hers as he kissed her again.

But the small break had sent a shaft of sanity into her mind, and despite her body's clamor to ignore it, the cool wind of caution grew stronger.

It was a while before Rogan realized that she was trying to extricate herself. When he lifted his head he looked dazed, his eyelids heavy, his cheeks flushed under the tanned skin. Voice slurred, he asked, "What's wrong, honey?"

"This," Camille panted. "I'm sorry...I shouldn't have...please stop!"

He blinked, his eyes clearing incredulously. "Stop?"

Her hands flattened against his chest, shoving at him. "Get off!" she said sharply.

For a moment his stubborn, immovable look appeared, and her heart thudded as she realized what a vulnerable position she was in. If he decided to carry on regardless she wouldn't have a chance, trapped under his extremely fit body.

A fleeting shock crossed his face. He rolled off her, onto his back, hitched himself on one elbow and demanded, "Why, Camille?"

It was a fair question. She had actively encouraged him, before freezing. "I'm sorry," she said again. He deserved an apology for her about-face.

"Not half as sorry as I am, sweetheart." As she sat up he remained where he was, regarding her broodingly. "I always carry necessary supplies," he said, "in case that's worrying you."

She supposed it was illogical that the assurance only strengthened her resolve. "That's not it," she said, adding stiffly, "And I'm not your sweetheart," trying to tidy her tousled hair, and sliding off the bed.

Rogan didn't follow suit, instead making himself comfortable against the pillows, clasping his hands behind his head. "Can't we talk about it?"

"I made a mistake. So did you."

"You mean you're not that kind of girl? Hell, I know already you don't fall into bed with just anyone. But I know too that you want me—have for a while, just as I want you. We're both adults, and as far as I know fancy free."

"*You* might be."

"You're not in love with that Drummond guy," he stated on a note of disgust. "And if you have another boyfriend why isn't he here with you?"

"I don't have a boyfriend. And when I do it'll be someone prepared to stick around for the long haul, not a fly-by-night Lothario with a girl in every port."

Rogan sat up, dropping his hands. "Yee-owch!" he said, wincing theatrically. "That's what you think I am?" He laughed and hauled himself off the berth, his feet hitting the floor, then he was looming over her.

Refusing to give way, Camille glared at him. "If the cap fits."

Rogan seemed to think about it. "Not *every* port," he murmured finally, a glint of humor lighting his eyes. Then more seriously he said, "I don't set out to lay every woman who crosses my path, Camille. I like you, you're beautiful and sexy and nice, and yeah, I've wanted to take you to bed ever since I first saw you. But I guess you're right," he conceded. "If you want a nine-to-five guy, the cottage with roses round the door, I can't give you that." He paused. "Only I don't think you'll get what you need from James Drummond. He's a cold fish, and you're definitely not."

Camille flushed. "I don't think you can make judgments on what I need. And my relationship with James or anyone else is none of your business."

Rogan tipped his head. "I'd just hate to see all that lovely passion thrown away."

"Passion passes," Camille argued. "Other things are more important."

"Like what?"

"Loyalty, reliability, trustworthiness."

"Yeah," he said derisively. "All fine and admirable. But without passion, a bit dull, don't you think?"

"Passion without them is a flash in the pan, an illusion with no substance."

His eyes intent, he said, "You're speaking from experience?"

"I don't suppose my experience is nearly as extensive as yours," she retorted. "And I'm not going to swap stories."

"That wasn't what I meant. Did some man hurt you?"

"Yes," Camille said flatly. "My father. Now if you don't mind, I'd like to be left alone."

Chapter 11

Camille thought Rogan wasn't going to move, his eyes piercing, his shoulders hunched aggressively forward, fingers thrust into his belt. Then he shifted his shoulders in what might have been a shrug, and stepped away from her. "Okay," he said. "I'll be around if you need me."

She wasn't sure if she was supposed to read a hidden meaning into that, and didn't answer as he left, only moving to close the door behind him.

The rain had stopped without her noticing. An eerie yellow light seeped through the saloon windows and now that the storm had passed she realized it wasn't yet dark outside.

Remembering James's invitation to pre-Christmas drinks, she considered canceling, the prospect of socialising not alluring, but the excuse to get away from the close atmosphere of the boat seemed like a godsend.

Thank heaven she hadn't succumbed to the madness of the moment. James had promised to pick her up at the boat and send her home in a taxi, and the thought of being interrupted by him while making love to Rogan made her hot all over.

She changed into her dark pants and her favorite knitted top, then grabbed a jacket, pulled it on, and picked up her coin purse.

Opening the door, she scarcely glanced at Rogan, seated again at the table.

"I'm going out," she said as she passed him. "I may be late back."

"Running away?" he said. "There's no need. If you didn't believe me before, what happened just now must have proved I don't impose myself on unwilling women."

"I'm not running away. I have a date."

"Drummond?"

"James."

He gave her a knifelike look. "Have a good time." His tone implied, *I hope you both get food poisoning.* But perhaps he was trying to be gracious, despite the dour expression on his face. She supposed any man was entitled to look like that in the circumstances. She had never been so tardy calling a halt with an obviously aroused male.

"Do you need any help up there?" he asked as she headed for the deck.

"No, thanks."

"Please yourself."

She would, Camille thought, climbing to the wharf. She certainly hadn't been put on this earth to please Rogan Broderick. Or to accept pleasure from him.

Used to the ladder now, she easily negotiated it and quickly walked away from the boat, from temptation, breathing in the wet, metallic after-rain air, dodging droplets from overhanging trees and buildings.

Clouds still hung over the hill, hiding the houses on the brow, but the rest of the town looked newly washed and almost deserted, most people still sheltering indoors, some with lights glowing softly through their windows. Looking back, she saw light shining from the portholes of the *Sea-Rogue* as it rocked on the ever-restless water.

She ought to find herself another place to stay. Mr. Trubshaw might take her in—but he was elderly and frailer than he looked, with a familiar routine that a boarder would disrupt, and so courteous he wouldn't refuse her even if it were inconvenient. She'd feel guilty about asking him.

James's invitation was presumably still open, yet she was reluctant to take it up. He might read too much into her belated acceptance.

The water was leaden and the waves high, tossing the anchored boats about and racing to the little beach with foam flying from their white peaks. James's car swept up and he opened the door for her, saying reprovingly, "I said I'd pick you up at the wharf."

"I needed fresh air," she said, after climbing in beside him. "It's stuffy on the boat."

Perhaps because he was doing a U-turn, he didn't reply, not taking the opportunity to renew his invitation for her to stay with him.

Despite her misgivings, she might have been persuaded to accept, but Rogan's gibe about running away rankled. She was torn between removing herself from clear and present danger, and proving to herself—and him—that she was still fully in control of her emotions, and her body…

With her mother's experience an object lesson in the risks of entrusting her heart to another's careless keeping, Camille had no intention of getting involved with a man who was more interested in chasing rainbows than establishing a relationship.

James had several other guests, but as they left he quietly

asked Camille to stay a little longer, saying, "I want to talk to you privately."

They sat looking out over the darkened harbor, sipping coffee and liqueurs. "No progress on the missing log?" he asked.

Camille hesitated, not accustomed to lying. "The police haven't found it," she said uncomfortably.

James sat back, putting down the spoon he'd used to stir his coffee. His voice lightly mocking, he said, "And is Rogan still looking for clues to his father's imaginary treasure ship?"

Unreasonably nettled at his tone, she said, "He doesn't think it's imaginary."

"Does he have any evidence at all?"

"Um...I don't think so," she muttered. "Not really."

"And have he and his brother made you an offer on the boat?"

"No. I believe he's been talking to banks."

James seemed restless, the wicker chair creaking a little as he shifted his feet and hooked one knee over the other, a slight frown on his brow. As if coming to a decision, he said, "If he was going to raise a loan it should have materialized by now. I'm afraid I can't wait forever. Of course I'd have no objection to you remaining on board while you finish your research, but I'd like to make you a formal offer." He took a piece of paper from his pocket, unfolded it and placed it on the glass-topped table between them. "I've drawn up a sale document. If the Brodericks can top this—" he shrugged "—I hope you'll allow me to consider raising it. Although I think my price is fair."

It was more than fair, she thought, leaning forward to read it. When she'd got her breath back, she promised to think about it, but said, "Don't you want to get a valuation of your own?"

"I know what it's ostensibly worth," he told her. "To me its antique value makes the boat special. Call it a rescue operation." For a moment his eyes rested on her with warmth, and he added, "For you and the *Sea-Rogue*. I know you're keen to get rid of your unwanted legacy, and I do hate to see beautiful craftsmanship unappreciated and allowed to deteriorate."

"I don't think Rogan would allow it to deteriorate," Camille demurred. "He loves the *Sea-Rogue*."

"I'm sure he's sentimentally attached to it. But if he means to knock about the islands the way his father did I doubt he'll maintain her as I would. Broderick Senior seems to have had no idea of her historical attraction, and I doubt if his son is any more aware what could be made of it. It would be simpler, of course, if I could purchase the entire boat, in which case I'd be willing to pay an even better price per half. Perhaps if you mention that they may change their minds about selling to me."

When Camille arrived back on board there was no sign of Rogan. Maybe he was at the pub again. Considering his mood when she'd left him, he might have felt like a drink or two.

She picked up her cell phone and dialed her aunt's number in Australia. With the time difference it would still be early evening there.

Her mother sounded happier than she had in a long time. "I'll miss you on Christmas Day, though," she said. "We're all disappointed you refused to come with me, but I know how important your moldy old books and papers are to you." Her laugh held a familiar shrill note that combined indulgence with a faint air of accusation. "I hate to think of you all on your own for Christmas," she added fretfully.

"I won't be," Camille assured her. "Rogan and I are having lunch with an old friend of his father's."

"What sort of friend?" Mona queried suspiciously. "Who is he?"

"She," Camille explained. "Mrs. Edwards."

"Barney's girlfriend?" Mona snorted.

"Do you know her?"

"No, but he probably had one in every port."

Tempted to defend him, with no evidence whatsoever, Camille bit her tongue. She'd accused Rogan of the same thing, she recalled uncomfortably, with as little reason.

Mona said, "You're not getting too close to this Rogan, I hope? I tell you, Camille, the Brodericks are bad news."

"We're not close," Camille assured her, conscious of a sharp tug of regret. "We both just happen to be at a loose end on Christmas Day, and Mrs. Edwards took pity on us."

On Christmas morning Camille attended a service in the seamen's chapel before joining Rogan for the walk up the hill to Bella Vista Road.

Mollie welcomed them both literally with open arms, giving Rogan a hug and then enveloping Camille in a similar embrace and a wave of violet scent. She let Camille help her in the kitchen, while Rogan opened a bottle of sparkling wine and later took on the task of carving the turkey.

Mollie's pleasure in sharing her festive meal was touching, and the single tear she wiped away when she spoke of having prepared all this for Barney made Camille's own eyes prickle in sympathy. Rogan proposed a toast to his father's memory, and while they ate he gently teased Mollie into a mood of flushed and slightly giddy enjoyment.

After lunch Mollie rested in her favorite armchair and

her guests tackled the dishes. When they returned to the sitting room she was fast asleep.

Rogan said quietly, "Shall we take a walk in the garden?"

He took Camille's hand in his and led her to the back door, quietly closing it behind them as they stepped onto the lawn. Passing under an old plum tree, he picked a luscious dark-red fruit and offered it to her, but she shook her head. "I've eaten too much already."

Rogan bit into the plum himself and soon finished it, tossing the pip onto the garden as they admired the flowers. "This is where my father buried his log," he said, indicating a rosebush with deep crimson blooms.

It didn't look any the worse for having been disturbed. He plucked a perfect flower, just opening up, carefully removed a couple of thorns, and handed it to her. "Merry Christmas," he said. "I'm sure Mollie won't mind."

"Thank you." She inhaled the wonderful heady scent.

Rogan looked around. "Pity there's no mistletoe." His hand fractionally tightened on hers, a smiling question in his eyes.

He was almost irresistible in this mood, enough to make any woman's heart melt, her knees crumble.

"It's Christmas," he reminded her hopefully.

Steeling herself, Camille pulled her hand from his. "Don't push your luck."

He laughed at her pungent tone, and led the way back to the house. Opening the door for her, he paused. "You've made Mollie's day, and I haven't enjoyed Christmas so much for years."

Neither had she, Camille realized with considerable shock. Christmas with her mother, ever since she could remember, had been an exchange of presents in the morning followed by church, then a simple cold lunch, a lazy afternoon, and dinner at a restaurant in the evening, because Mona didn't see any point in going to the trouble of preparing a special meal for two, and a day off from cooking was a treat.

Sometimes friends had invited Camille and her mother to join them, but Mona always said she wouldn't impose on someone else's family, and didn't want anyone's charity. Of course if Camille wanted to go…

But that would mean leaving her mother alone, so Camille had regretfully turned down the invitations.

When Camille and Rogan reentered the sitting room Mollie opened her eyes. Brushing her newly gold-rinsed curls from her eyes, she said, "Oh, I fell asleep—so rude!"

"Not at all," Camille assured her.

Rogan said, "We filled in the time very nicely. I've been showing Camille your garden."

"It's beautiful," Camille told her.

"Thank you. Rogan was such a help when I came home from the hospital."

Camille cast him a look of surprise. "I didn't know you were a gardener."

He laughed. "Not me. I just did what Mollie told me."

After returning to the *Sea-Rogue,* Rogan and Camille snacked on leftovers that Mollie had pressed upon them, then sat on the seats flanking the *Sea-Rogue*'s wheel, both with their feet up and shoulders resting against the bulkhead. Camille was still reading *Les Trois Mousquetaires,* and Rogan frowned over one of Barney's navigation tables, looking from it to the pages of the log.

Camille finished the story just as the light was fading too much for her to see the rather small print. She closed the book and went down to the saloon. When Rogan joined her a little later she was making coffee, and he accepted a cup, taking a seat beside her at the table.

"James has made an offer for my half of the boat," she told him. "A very good offer. I'd be stupid to turn it down. But I'd like to give you the chance to match it."

"Thanks," he said, tight-lipped. "How much?"

She told him, adding, "He said he'd raise the price if you and Granger wanted to sell too."

"Why?"

"He wants to restore the boat to its former glory and charter it to people who will appreciate its character."

"I appreciate the old girl just the way she is and without any tarting up, thanks. And Granger and I aren't selling at any damn price. Doesn't it seem strange to you that he's so dead keen to own her?"

"He's an antiquarian. The boat's a classic."

Rogan said abruptly, "Did you know his deckhand disappeared the day after my father was attacked?"

Blinking, Camille said, "What?"

"The deckhand from his boat, the *Catfish*. He'd been talking to my dad at the pub the night before, buying him drinks. Hasn't been seen since. And I'm sure the *Catfish* followed us out when we went to the Poor Knights."

"Followed us?"

"Remember the boat that was anchored just outside the reserve—where we could be watched the whole time?"

"It wasn't the only boat out there. And why would it have followed us?"

"Maybe the boss told them to keep an eye on the *Sea-Rogue* in case we were on the trail of…something. Suppose Drummond has reason to believe Dad found treasure?"

"What reason?" Camille asked, exasperated. "I don't think he ever met your father."

"The deckhand!" Rogan said impatiently. "He took

something from Dad that proved the treasure was real—something Dad had in his pocket that night. Or maybe he beat the old man to force information from him. Then he went to his boss with it and...mysteriously disappeared. Drummond—or someone in his pay—ransacked the boat looking for the log or maybe some other clue, and didn't find it. So now he wants to buy the *Sea-Rogue* because *he knows there's something on board that will tell him where the treasure is.*"

Desperately he looked about the saloon as if he could make it yield up its supposed secret.

Camille closed her gaping mouth. "You can't believe such a preposterous theory!"

He gave her his stubborn look. "I don't believe Drummond is that desperate to get hold of the boat because of some philanthropic desire to restore her. He's not getting his hands on her if I can help it."

The Christmas break ran into the weekend; the banks and most businesses were closed for four days, and Camille found herself tense and edgy. Living with Rogan was becoming more and more difficult for her. There wasn't a great deal of room on the boat, and it was inevitable that now and then they would accidentally brush up against each other, or encounter each other coming in or out of the cramped head—Camille with a robe pulled around her, Rogan wearing only hastily pulled-on jeans or a pair of shorts or just a towel tucked about his waist.

She was continually conscious of his very masculine presence, the tug of his casual attraction that he made no effort to either exploit or inhibit. It was just there.

In a strange way Camille knew in her bones she could trust him. Her emotions were chaotic and irrational—an odd mixture of rock-solid security and a knife-edge tension that seemed to grow more palpable every day.

They couldn't continue this way—she couldn't.

She had thoroughly explored Mr. Trubshaw's library, and returned the last books and documents she'd borrowed, with warm thanks for his help and a parting present of a rather rare but modestly priced volume from James's shop. So now she didn't have the excuse of research to keep her here.

She broached the subject of the buyout again with Rogan, and he said irritably, "What's the hurry?"

"Can you do it?" she asked abruptly.

"Match Drummond's price? No," he said. "Look, why not wait until we know if there's a treasure or not?"

"What difference would that make?"

"I suppose, none," he admitted slowly. "If my dad and yours found it together, I guess it's half yours anyway."

Camille blinked. "How do you make that out?"

"Taff or his descendants are entitled to half of any profits from their voyages. If they found something it's half yours."

"Half of a chimera," she mocked.

Rogan said, "You own half the boat's contents too."

"There's nothing worth much," she objected, "except the navigation equipment, and that's included in the price of the boat. You're welcome to everything else."

He looked exasperated, pushing a hand through his hair. "Can't you just wait a bit?" he pleaded.

She should say no, not let the intensity of his gaze sway her. "I can't wait much longer."

On Sunday James Drummond unexpectedly turned up on the wharf, hailing Rogue as he sat in the cockpit, the log against his upraised knees.

Hastily closing the book, Rogan stood up with it firmly held at his side. The tide was low and he had to squint upward under a raised hand.

"Interesting book?" Drummond asked easily.

Rogan shrugged. "Camille's below."

He watched Drummond's cautious descent of the narrow ladder, and his clumsy landing. Entering the cockpit, the man nearly knocked Rogan off his feet.

Steadying himself, Rogan lifted the hand clutching the log as Drummond grabbed a line, saying, "I'm not really a boating man. The damned things never stay still." With a smile of apology, he turned and carefully descended the companionway.

His and Camille's voices sounded annoyingly intimate, and Rogan found himself straining to catch the words, possessed of a mad desire to go down and punch Drummond's supercilious nose for him.

He glanced at the book in his hand, then descended to the saloon. His denim jacket lay on the banquette next to Camille. Muttering an apology, he reached across her to snag it, and shrugged it on, shoving the log into a pocket to free his hands as he approached the companionway. No way was he leaving it on board while Drummond was around.

He spent a couple of hours with Brodie, drinking beer and swapping memories, and he was leaving when Brodie said, "Did you hear about the body they found?"

A cold shiver attacked Rogan's spine. "What body— who found?"

"A trawler dredged it up in their net this morning, in deep water offshore. Badly decomposed, I gather. I don't think anyone knows who it was yet."

When Rogan got back there was a note from Camille saying she was having dinner with James. He crumpled it in one hand and threw it in with the galley garbage before making himself a cold meal. Much later he was lying on his bunk trying not think about what she and Drummond might be doing when he heard her come in. Then he rolled over and went to sleep.

In the morning, he went to the police station demanding details of the unknown body and was told formal identification was pending and the constable could tell him nothing else. There would of course be an autopsy, but the man's death was probably an accident. It could possibly be Gary Collier, he allowed reluctantly. Mr. Collier had been known as a heavy drinker.

James had invited her to a New Year celebration at his home. "Bring your friend Rogan along," he'd suggested. "There'll be quite a crowd."

"No, thanks," Rogan said tersely when she relayed the invitation. "Is it your sort of thing?"

It wasn't, really. Although she admired James's home for its elegance and taste, her previous experience of his business friends hardly engendered any eagerness to repeat the experience. She had thanked him for the invitation but been deliberately vague about her plans, letting him infer that she might have other options. "It was nice of him to ask…us," she said, dodging Rogan's question.

"To ask me, you mean." He looked skeptical. "I wonder what he's playing at?"

"He was just being friendly." Rogan had rebuffed James's every attempt at engaging him in pleasant conversation. "And you're being a—" She broke off before adding *dog in the manger*. There were dangerous waters in that direction.

Rogan cocked an inquiring eyebrow, a trick that surely must have taken weeks of practice, yet it never failed to affect her in a way she despised, causing a faint fluttering about her heart, a weakening of her knees. "I'm being a what?" he asked curiously.

"A boor!" she flashed with a rare loss of temper.

Both brows shot up at that. "And Drummond," he suggested, "is a perfect gentleman, I suppose." He laughed— a harsh, cut-off sound. "Does he even know how to kiss a woman properly? He probably makes love like a flatfish!"

"I wouldn't know," she said coldly. "Not having your wide experience of mating habits at sea."

For a moment Rogan just stared at her, then gave a delighted shout of laughter.

Biting her lip, Camille watched him, but couldn't help a self-conscious smile when he caught her eye, his own alight still with humor. "I'm sorry," she said guiltily. "I shouldn't have called you a boor."

Rogan shook his head at her in mock reproof. "You have a nasty tongue on you when you're aroused."

In the afternoon of New Year's Eve Camille went with Rogan to visit Mollie. After coffee and scones, she sat with the older woman on the back porch while Rogan spread mulch from a wheelbarrow over the flower beds, in the hope of preserving some moisture in the soil through the summer. He wore age-softened jeans that molded themselves to his taut haunches, and an old T-shirt, with a battered yachting cap that Mollie had produced, insisting he couldn't work in the sun without something to cover his head. The sleeveless denim jacket he always donned now when he left the *Sea-Rogue* was hung over a spare chair. One of its zipped pockets bulged and hung low with the weight of the ship's log.

Having refilled the barrow, he paused to temporarily remove the cap and dispense with his shirt.

Watching him pull off the garment, resettle the cap and then shovel another heap of mulch from the wheelbarrow, Camille wondered if he'd remembered to apply sunblock before leaving the *Sea-Rogue*. A shivering, warm sensation starting in her midriff spread through her entire body. A sensation that was becoming altogether too familiar.

As if he'd felt her gaze, Rogan looked up, straight into her eyes, and it was almost as though she stood naked before him. Her heart pounded and she couldn't, this time, look away, afraid that her unguarded hunger for him showed all too clearly in her face.

Rogan straightened, his hand tight about the shovel as he rested the blade on the ground. Under the cap his eyes were shadowed, yet she felt his gaze like a rapier, and a quiver of purest, primitive pleasure prickled over her skin.

He pushed the cap back a little, then settled it more firmly, and turned away to resume his task.

Camille could scarcely breathe. Something had happened in that two seconds of eye contact, she wasn't sure what. But it was both thrilling and wickedly dangerous.

Mollie said, "Camille, dear, if you look in the fridge you'll find some beer. I'm sure Rogan would like one."

There was a six-pack there, and Camille removed a can, holding its chill to her hot face for a few seconds before pulling off the top and going outside. She hesitated, then crossed the lawn to hand him the drink. As he took it from her their fingers touched briefly, and she removed hers as though the touch had burned.

Rogan's brows lifted, then something sparked in his eyes, and he raised the can to his lips, thirstily downing the beer. She tried not to watch him, but the movement of his strong throat fascinated her, and in the hollow at the base a trickle of sweat nestled. She had a momentary bizarre fantasy of catching it on her finger and tasting its saltiness with her tongue.

A hidden shudder ran through her. The sun was scorching on her hair, and the intense blue of the sky behind Rogan's head made his eyes seem more deeply aqua than ever as he lowered the can and looked at her.

"Thanks," he said. "I can do with some cooling off."

Camille, not meeting his eyes, gave a tight smile. "It was Mollie's idea. And her beer."

He smiled, and the altered shape of his beautiful mouth hypnotized her. "Thanks all the same." Before she could guess what he intended, he leaned forward and dropped a kiss on her mouth, too quickly for her to react in any way.

She couldn't help looking at him now. Along with the warm taste of his lips, the tang of the beer lingered, cool and bitter, and she ran her tongue over her lips.

Rogan's eyes darkened to near-black, and his expression was suddenly intent, probing, almost ruthless.

Camille recalled her first impression of him, that he was a pirate, a throwback to an earlier time, a danger to law-abiding sailors—and to women. Trying to break the moment, she said, "You ought to have sunblock on."

"Are you offering?" he asked softly.

Recalling the day he'd asked her to apply some to his back, she was assailed by an alarming shaft of desire. Dumbly she shook her head. "I don't have any with me."

A feeble excuse, and he knew it. No doubt Mollie could produce a bottle of the stuff. His mouth curved again, but he only said, "The hottest part of the day's over now, and I've almost finished here."

He took her hand and she jumped. Then he was pressing the still-cold, empty can into her palm, closing her fingers about it. He nodded and went back to his work, and she walked in a daze to the porch, ignoring Mollie's knowing smile and continuing into the kitchen to drop the can in the recycling bin in a corner.

From the window over the sink she could see Rogan carrying on as if nothing untoward had taken place, his stunningly perfect male form bending and straightening to a steady rhythm, the muscles subtly rippling under his skin. She couldn't see his face anymore, but the darkened glance he'd given her lingered in her mind, and her body remembered…

The unthinkable had happened, she realized with a dazed, hollow dismay. Despite all her sensible admonishments to herself—her clear resolve that she would never be carried away by mere physical attraction, her awareness that it would be sheer stupidity to give in to the temptation that Rogan Broderick presented, and her determination to resist it—all that had somehow been cast aside.

She'd fallen in love—hook, line and sinker, heart and soul, head over heels. In every way possible. With a man who would surely break her heart, just as her father had broken her mother's.

Chapter 12

Mollie confessed she hadn't the stamina to see in the new year, but she insisted on their having a meal before they left, saying Rogan deserved it after all that work.

Camille helped her to prepare it, and afterward they lingered for a while, leaving as dusk lowered over the hill.

A band was playing on the green strip across from the Imperial, for an audience of mostly young people. Part of the road was closed to allow revelers to spill onto it, and a buzz of voices arose from the public bar of the hotel. Some patrons sat with their drinks on the top floor veranda, surveying the scene. Aboard the boats people crowded the decks, a few on bigger craft reclining in chairs, but most perched on any vantage point they could find.

Liquor was banned for the night on the street and the beach, and the lone constable had been joined by several other uniformed officers, conspicuously patrolling the area and confiscating bottles and cans. Some of the crowd had rather obviously consumed a fair amount already, but they seemed reasonably good-natured about not being able to carry alcohol into the area. The pub was still open, and a steady stream of customers was evidently keeping the bar busy.

"Want to stay for a while?" Rogan asked Camille as their progress was impeded by the growing, expectant throng.

"Yes, let's." She didn't really want to join James's house party, but it seemed a good idea to put off returning to the boat, in the light of her disturbing new discovery. Safer to spend time with Rogan in a crowd.

Rogan steered her across the roadway as best he could, between knots of dancing, swaying concert-goers, and found a spot under a pohutukawa where they could sit on the soft grass and lean against the shaggy trunk of the tree.

Shoulder to shoulder with him, she discovered a sharp, sweet pleasure in the warmth of his upper arm pressing against hers. She could feel the slight bulkiness of the log book in his jacket pocket. Gradually he seemed to relax, tipping his head back, tapping fingers on his upraised knee in time to the music. It was loud enough to preclude conversation, and she was able to indulge in a dangerous pretence that these precious shared moments might lead to...

Nothing, she reminded herself brutally. There was no way that Rogan was interested in a shared future. And no way she could let herself fall into the same trap that had turned her mother into a bitter, disappointed and lonely woman.

She moved to edge away from the unbearably tempting contact. And Rogan, apparently misinterpreting the action, draped an arm about her shoulders, enclosing her in a loose embrace so that she leaned on him instead of the tree. "That's more comfortable," he said with satisfaction. "Mmm?"

The rhetorical question almost roused her to hysteria. *Comfortable?* It was wonderful—and appallingly risky. With her back against his chest, her head resting just under his chin, his arms cradling her, she was assailed by a confusing mixture of utter contentment and poignant longing. If only this closeness could last she'd be happy forever.

But of course it couldn't. Rogan would sail away without a backward glance whenever the fancy took him, and leave her pining like all the women in all the songs about men like him and his father—and hers.

But tonight, for a little while, for the rest of the year— she smiled to herself sadly, counting the meager hours remaining—she would ignore the future and just enjoy the present. With that thought she relaxed against him, and his arms tightened fractionally in response.

The music belted out and the audience, becoming increasingly dense and raucous, clapped and cheered, danced and jumped about. Then nearby an altercation broke out and escalated into fistcuffs involving several people.

Rogan moved, and pulled Camille to her feet. "Best get you out of here," he said, shielding her with his body as a couple of struggling young men almost collided with them, while others surged toward the fray, whistling and hooting.

Someone bumped her; she was torn from Rogan's hold, heard him call her name and lost him in the crush. Jostled and pushed, only the fact that she cannoned into a large brown-skinned man saved her from sprawling on the ground.

He grabbed at her arms and grinned down at her. "Sorry, love, I'm taken."

A woman at his elbow said, "Shut up, Hemi!" and to Camille, "You all right?"

"Yes, thanks," she gasped as the man released her. The

couple moved on, and she looked about, trying to find Rogan.

Policemen converged on the fight, and she saw someone throw a punch at one of them, knocking his hat from his head before they were both enveloped by seething brawlers.

In a few minutes it seemed it was all over. A police van nosed its way between the dancers, some of whom hadn't even noticed the contretemps behind them, and then she saw, finally, Rogan pushing his way toward the beach, a trickle of blood seeping from a small cut over his cheekbone as he looked about him, his face taut and anxious.

Her heart, which had been jumping all over the place, settled back into something like its normal rhythm as she too fought her way to the sand and met him there.

His expression relaxed. "Thank God you're okay."

"I'm fine, but what happened to you?"

He looked a little surprised at her shrill tone, but gave her a crooked grin and said, "I copped a couple of punches. But I got a few in of my own." He seemed quite pleased with himself, making her want to hit him herself. He raised a knuckle to the cut, and glanced at the blood left on it before dropping his hand to his side. "It's nothing," he said.

She was torn between relief and a strange fury because she'd been worried about him. "That cut needs seeing to," she snapped. Close up she could see a dark swelling about it. "We'd better get back to the boat."

"I told you, it's nothing."

But he fell in beside her as she made her way along the beach, almost tripping over a couple who had made themselves a snug hollow and were oblivious to the entertainment and to the rest of the world.

While Rogan gave a quiet laugh she skirted them and marched on—as best she could in the soft sand. Eventually they regained the path and continued to the wharf in silence. The tide was high and Camille ignored the hand Rogan offered to help her board. In the saloon she got out the first-aid kit and said crisply, ''Wash that cut and I'll put a dressing on it for you.''

He cast her a rueful look before obeying, and came out with a tissue pressed to his cheek, then sat at the table while she efficiently cleaned the wound with disinfectant and stuck a dressing into place.

''Thanks,'' he said, and as she made to close the first-aid box he caught her hand. ''What are you mad about?''

''I'm not mad.''

She tried to tug away but he retained his hold. ''You're angry. I'm sorry about losing you, but some guy jumped me and you were probably safer out of the way.''

''I'm perfectly capable of looking after myself.''

''What, then?'' Rogan seemed genuinely puzzled.

''Nothing, I told you!'' She pulled more strongly and he reluctantly let her go. Her mouth tight, she put away the kit while he stayed at the table, watching her every move.

''You've got blood on your shirt,'' she said when she looked at him again.

Rogan looked down. ''Yeah.'' He stood, his hand going to the pocket of his jacket as if he needed to check the log was still there. ''They nearly ripped this off me.''

''You hear of teenagers beating up other kids for their jackets or shoes.''

''Not in Mokohina. I couldn't see them clearly in the dark and with all the stuff going on, but this was no kid.'' He added slowly, ''And I think, though he was wearing a fishing hat pulled well down, I recognized him. I reckon he was after the log.''

Camille blinked. ''There was a riot going on. You surely

don't imagine it was manufactured just so someone could steal your jacket and take the log?''

"I guess not." But he didn't seem convinced. Slowly he added, "If Drummond knew I had it, they could have been waiting for an opportunity."

"James? You're surely not saying *James* attacked you!"

"I don't suppose he'd dirty his lily-white hands. But I'm pretty sure the thug was the skipper of Drummond's boat."

It sounded like something out of a TV series. He *thought* he'd recognized one of his attackers, and was *pretty sure* it was the skipper of James's boat. He was so hostile to James he'd see the other man's hand in every misfortune that befell him.

The hostility was rooted in his natural grief and anger over his father's death, and he'd fixated his hatred on James simply because he didn't want to sell the *Sea-Rogue* and James had made an innocent offer to buy it. She supposed the boat was some kind of symbol for him.

And there was possibly another reason—Rogan made no secret of the fact that she attracted him; sexual jealousy added to the mix made for a powerful though irrational motivation for his escalating paranoia. But this had gone far enough. "For heaven's sake!" she said, her voice rising as unease grew to real fear—although she wasn't certain what she was so afraid of—and then transmuting into anger. "Drop the conspiracy theories, Rogan. You don't have any proof!"

He regarded her unblinkingly for a second or two, then appeared to give in. "Okay. I need to clean up. We should drink a toast to the new year later."

Bewildered by the sudden capitulation, she took a moment to digest what he'd said, and looked at the saloon clock. There was still an hour or so to go. She turned back to Rogan and remembered she loved this man. It didn't seem right to start the new year angry with him. "Yes," she agreed. "On deck?"

"Okay." He gave her an odd little smile that went straight to her heart, starting a slow fire, and then he headed for the washroom.

Camille went into her cabin, leaning back against the door. What a fool she was, but she couldn't suppress the emotional fire that careless smile had ignited. Despite the despairing knowledge that this could come to nothing, her feelings wouldn't be denied. Was being in love always this terrible mixture of euphoria and dread bordering on panic?

A line came into her head: *Love makes fools of us all.* She didn't know where it was from, but everything she knew about love reinforced the sentiment.

Maybe from the day she'd agreed to move aboard the *Sea-Rogue* she'd been fooling herself, all the good reasons she'd come up with mere smokescreens to mask the fact that already she'd fallen under the perilous spell of his flagrant attraction, wanting to be with him, to know him.

It was too late to stop herself from falling for Rogan, the most unsuitable man she could ever have chosen. But it wasn't too late to do something sensible about it. She couldn't stay here. Already she'd procrastinated long enough about her departure. First thing tomorrow she was out of here, taking herself far away from temptation, from further heartbreak. Because the longer she stayed around the more difficult and traumatic the inevitable parting would be.

She thrust clothes into her suitcase and zipped it up, packed her computer and emptied her things from the desk into her backpack. The sale agreement that James had signed was in the top drawer—two copies folded inside each other. She looked at them for a long time, tempted to tear them across and drop them in the plastic rubbish basket by the desk.

Think, she told herself.

There was one way to make the clean, sure cut that would ensure her emotional survival.

With shaking hands she opened the folds of the agreements, smoothing the document flat against the wooden surface of the desk. The print blurred, but she knew what it said anyway. She stood with a pen poised in her hand for more than a minute, and then, hearing Rogan leave the head and close the door behind him, she bit her lip fiercely and signed her name at the end of both pages.

Backing away, she resisted an urge to retract, take the pages and consign them to the wastebasket.

This wasn't a betrayal—it was a pragmatic action that should have been taken before. Her mother would get the money that was morally hers. James would probably persuade Granger, if not Rogan, that the sensible thing to do was sell their share to him—her conscience twinged uncomfortably but she refused to give in to it. And Rogan...?

Rogan would go back to his profession. Probably the idea of keeping the *Sea-Rogue* had been a mere whim anyway. Camille was doing him a favor. His obsession with the boat and its link to his father's supposed treasure couldn't be healthy. Already he was manufacturing bizarre fantasies about James—a respected businessman—being involved in some kind of skullduggery, even suggesting he might be responsible for Barney's death.

When Rogan rapped on the door she jumped.

"You're not working...now?" He glanced at the pen she still held.

"No." She looked down as though unaware how it had got into her hand. Her brain seemed foggy.

"White wine or red?" he asked. "We still have a bottle of bubbly."

He retreated into the saloon and she followed, putting the pen on the table. "I don't mind."

"I like a woman who's easy to please." He grinned at her. "Bubbly, then. I guess that's appropriate."

He liked all women, she suspected. Easily pleased women probably pleased him easily too…

She was sounding like her mother, soured by experience.

Rogan collected two plastic flutes and led the way to the deck. When she'd settled herself onto one of the cockpit seats he passed her a flute filled with crisp, bubbling wine.

The music came clearly over the water, and most boats were fully lit up. Fairy lights twinkled along the foreshore, and beyond the curve in the shoreline the appreciative crowd about the hotel waved upraised arms in time to the beat. Occasional shouts and squeals of laughter cut into the night air. There were parties going on everywhere.

Yet despite the noise all around, Camille could hear the restless ripple of the waves against the *Sea-Rogue*'s hull, the soft thump as it rode close to the wharf.

She said, "Mollie misses your father."

"Yep."

Odd, she thought, when Barney had only been in port a couple of times each year. "She's very grateful to you for helping her. What will she do when you leave?" Her throat ached.

He turned to look at her. "Granger will make sure she's taken good care of."

And what will I do?

Silly question. She'd be long gone before then. Tomorrow she would hand over the sale agreement. Burn her boats—an appropriate metaphor, she thought wryly—because after that it would be untenable to stay around Rogan.

She was very sure he wouldn't want her then anyway. He would never forgive her. A sharp grief assailed her at that, and she gulped down the remainder of her wine to dispel it.

They were on their second refill when a faint breeze raised bumps on Camille's skin, making her shiver.

Rogan said, "Are you cold? I'll get you a jacket."

"I'll get it…"

They both stood up in the tiny space between the seats, and found themselves not only face-to-face but so close they were touching, her breasts brushing his chest, his hands closing about her arms to steady her.

Their eyes locked, scant inches apart.

Distantly Camille heard a drumroll, and the chant of the crowd onshore counting down the last seconds to midnight, joined by people on the boats bellowing across the water.

Softly, Rogan joined in: "…four…three…two…one…"

Huge cheers and whistles erupted, bells and horns followed, and a rocket whooshed illegally skyward and burst in a shower of stars. The band broke into a strident rendition of "Auld Lang Syne."

Neither Rogan nor Camille took any notice. His eyes dark and fathomless, his expression taut, he said quietly, "Happy new year, Camille."

And then he kissed her.

It was slow and tender and utterly ravishing. He tasted of wine and heat and the sea, and his mouth was a seduction in itself, firm and assured, working an enchantment that she couldn't—didn't want to—resist.

He lifted his head a fraction, and his hands smoothed the goose bumps from her arms. "Oh heck, Camille!" he muttered. Then he shifted his grip, one hand at her waist shaping her body to his, the other about her shoulders, nestling her head into the crook of his arm, and he kissed her again.

Surely, deeply, with an edge of impatient sexual hunger that recognized her tentative, cautious response and sought to break through the restraint she put on it.

She tried to retain some measure of control, even as he gathered her still closer to him, and gently but inexorably coaxed her mouth to open to his erotic invasion, a mind-destroying, insatiable onslaught on her already aroused senses that sent her spinning into a vortex of pure physical delight, crumbling every carefully built defense.

When they surfaced she was dizzy and Rogan's breathing was loud and uneven, his voice gritty when he said, "I want to continue this down below. If it's not what you want too, say so now. Either way, you'd better be sure this time."

The pain that squeezed her heart threatened to break it in two. This was their goodbye, although he didn't know it. Was she going to leave with only the memory of a few kisses to sustain her for the long years without him?

As she hesitated, he gave a moan of frustration, and his hand slid to her breast; his palm closed over the softness of it, as if he held something delicate and precious. "You want me," he said, stating a fact without triumph or surprise. His thumb briefly found the evidence, and Camille drew a sharp breath, her head involuntarily lifting, and a shudder of sheer pleasure shook her.

Rogan dipped his head and his open mouth was hot on the skin of her throat, his tongue buried in the hollow at the base. "You want me," he repeated, raising his head and looking into her eyes. Someone had a searchlight and. the broad light beam swept over the boat, showing his face with the skin of his cheeks taut, his eyes glittering under close-drawn brows, the face of fiercely reined desire. Then it was dark again and she was shivering.

"You're cold," he said. "Let me warm you. I want you

hot under me, on top of me, around me. Naked with me, as close as two people can be. Just this once I want to be inside you, Camille, with your breasts in my hands and my tongue in your mouth, making you come for me, with me. To be with you all night, together in a bed. Tell me you want it too. Please.''

She wasn't cold, she was shivering for a quite different reason, and the eroticism of his words was so powerful she almost melted right there and then in his arms.

He was asking for one night. Starkly honest as always, not declaring undying love, making no empty promises. And what more did she have to lose, when already her heart was lost for ever? At least she'd have one unforgettable memory to keep by her. ''I...I want it,'' she whispered. ''I want you...''

She felt the deep breath that he sucked in and then let out in a sigh of satisfaction. ''You won't be sorry,'' he said. ''I promise.''

Camille couldn't help a wry smile at that. She might regret this step for the rest of her life. But right now it was what she desperately wanted, and although her head might be warning her that she was being rash and perhaps making the biggest mistake of her life, for once she was going to let her heart have its way. Just this once.

Rogan led the way down to the saloon, taking her in his arms the moment she reached the bottom of the companionway to kiss her again as the night wrapped a thick, warm blanket about them. Banishing her rational mind, she slid her arms about his neck and kissed him back with abandon, matching his fierce passion with her own.

The minimal top she wore yielded to his eagerness to remove it, and she lifted her arms, allowing him to haul it off, not caring where it went. He urged her to her cabin where the berth was wider than his own, and they kissed over and over, discarding clothing as they went.

Deliberately Camille cast aside all shyness, all reserve. She didn't have much experience, but had read plenty of books, seen films, heard her friends talk. Even experimented a little, although her wariness of involvement had inhibited her considerably.

This was the only time she was going to have with Rogan, with her one real love, and she didn't mean to waste any of it. There was no point in treating it as an exercise that could be repeated until she got it right. She'd let Rogan lead—at least at first—but she was determined that for him too this would be a night to remember. Not because he'd had to hold back and teach a novice, but because she'd matched him in every way, given him as much as he gave her, been generous and voluptuous and irresistibly sexy.

By the time they reached the bed and fell onto it in a tumble of limbs, they were both nearly undressed. Rogan shucked the rest of his clothes and then devoted himself to doing the same for Camille between a storm of kisses, and finally they were skin to skin, mouth to eager mouth, climbing over each other in a laughing, breathless effort to explore each other's nakedness on the less-than-ample mattress.

The laughter turned to tense anticipation as Rogan adjusted their position, deliberately drawing out the preliminaries, taking his time to find out all about her body, smilingly gauging her reaction to this touch, that caress, inviting her to touch him and letting her know exactly how he felt about her fingers lightly running down his chest, her mouth defining the muscles of his shoulders, her hand discovering the contours of his haunches, and the hard, proud jut of his penis. But he pulled her hand away, saying, ''Not right now. I don't want to jump the gun.''

She smiled and dropped a quick kiss there, making him groan and swear, at which she laughed, and he punished her by gently closing his teeth over her shoulder, nibbling on her fingers, drawing them into his mouth, until she did the same for him, and his eyes darkened and smoldered, and he freed his hand from its imprisonment and kissed her almost roughly, his mouth moving over hers in arrogant possession.

They murmured and stroked and teased, kissed again and again, found other places to kiss, grew steadily more unbearably aroused, until Rogan reached for his jacket and after a few moments finally turned on his back and held her over him. "Is this okay with you?"

"Yes." She was scarcely able to speak. He had her breasts in his hands, just as he'd promised, and she was beginning to feel floaty and golden. Molten. Light and ethereal and yet earthy, sensual, totally conscious of the state of her body—and his.

"Now?" he queried, and she nodded.

"Now…please!"

He made a guttural sound in his throat, like a leopard's purr, and then he slid easily into the slick, satiny depth of her, and his hands settled her against him, snug and close.

She let her sigh of pleasure breathe into his mouth as she bent to meet his kiss. A deep, increasingly excited and exciting kiss, although his hands urged her to stillness as the uncontrollable drive to the ultimate goal grew despite his efforts to delay their climax.

When she flowed around him, her muscles clenching in ecstasy, he finally let go and joined his own pleasure to hers, increasing it so that she thought she would never be able to stop the continued waves of sensation that washed over her, until at last they quieted to lovely, waning ripples.

She lay against him sated, her mind blessedly dormant,

content to wallow in the aftermath, until Rogan stirred and looked for tissues. His jacket lay at the foot of the berth, and when Camille moved she accidentally kicked it off so that it thudded on to the thin rug covering the boards. "Oh," she said guiltily. "The log."

"No harm," Rogan assured her, settling again beside her, sliding an arm under her shoulders.

"You haven't found anything in there, have you?"

"Not that pinpoints their find. There are dozens of scattered islands in the group, over fifty miles, but I can't see a group of three or even a pair that would account for that cryptic note."

Camille said slowly, "There were really four heroes in the book, you know, counting D'Artagnan. Maybe you should be looking for four islands."

He stared at her. "Maybe. If we could narrow it down…"

Gazing into space, he frowned. Over the door he dimly saw his mother's picture smiling down at him. Remembering her love for and loyalty to Barney, he was attacked by a grief he'd thought put behind him long ago.

Something teased at the back of his mind—something he'd noticed after the burglary when replacing the picture on the sturdy hooks his father had secured it to. "Just a minute," he said, easing himself away from Camille. He left the berth and took down the photo.

Coming back to her, he switched on the light over the bed and turned the picture. The cardboard backing was obviously old, yellowed and dusty. But it was fixed with shiny silver staples to the frame. He reached for his jeans and took out a pocketknife.

"What are you doing?" Camille asked.

He didn't answer, lifting the cardboard to reveal the white back of the photograph with numbers pencilled on it.

"No map," Camille said, disappointedly, assuming the numbers were a photographer's code.

"Better than that! It's a GPS coordinate." His father had used the Global Positioning System on board to pinpoint exactly where he'd found his target, and rather than trust it to the log, had recorded it here, cautiously not hiding too many eggs in one basket.

"A what?" Camille asked.

He explained, "Look, this figure is the latitude, and this is longitude."

She stared at the notation. "How exact is it?"

"It's practically a pinpoint direction. X marks the spot. He must have found something there!" Hauling her close, he kissed her triumphantly, and kept on kissing her as he pressed her to the mattress and his hand found her hip, then stroked upward to her breast while the kiss deepened.

When at last he lifted his head and she could get her breath, she said, "Don't get too excited—"

"Oh. Sorry…are you too tired…?"

He began to release her and she said, "Not that. I mean…you still don't have any proof there's a treasure."

"The only way to prove it is to go there and see."

Slightly troubled, she said, "Is it so important?"

Rogan regarded her somberly for a moment. "It was to Dad. Maybe important enough to have indirectly caused his death. Somehow I feel I owe it to him."

Camille, a slight lump in her throat, nodded. She wasn't sure what had inspired such loyalty and love in Barney Broderick's son, but then if he'd been anything like Rogan…

She touched her palm to his face, a small ache in her heart reminding her that she probably had only this one night with him. Her eyes stung, and he said, frowning, "What's the matter?"

''Nothing.'' Determined not to spoil what time they had left, she lifted her other hand and drew him down to her, offering her mouth.

He willingly complied, kissing her with glad passion, wrapping her again in his arms, fanning the embers of desire to a renewed white-hot fire that flared quickly and consumed them in its wild and glorious blaze.

This time she fell properly asleep, and didn't even stir when Rogan eased her down, pulling the sheet over her.

He got up to go to the head and stumbled over his jeans, picked them up and quietly left the cabin.

His T-shirt was in the saloon, he recalled vaguely, along with Camille's light cotton top. Dropped anywhere in their eagerness to get naked with each other.

Camille had been just as impatient as he was, surprising him and increasing his already overwhelming desire for her. Maybe they had both been suffering from frustration, adding an intensity to their lovemaking that he didn't remember experiencing since his first, clumsy encounter with a willing girl. And that had certainly not come up to expectation.

But Camille…she'd more than matched his conviction that they'd be perfect together.

Coming out of the head, he pulled on his jeans and zipped them. A pale blur on the floor of the saloon was Camille's thin cotton top. He lifted it, inhaling her unique, woman scent, neither flowery nor spicy but sweet and aphrodisiacal. Her skin had smelled like that, and it had been smooth and cool, then warm under his hands, with firmness and softness underneath. She had neat, round breasts that fitted into his palms, and a beautifully shaped behind that she liked him to stroke. When he'd run his hands over it, she'd curled her legs up and nestled into him like a contented kitten…

Damn, he was hard again, and she was fast asleep. He switched off the light over the berth, but the glow coming in the portholes clearly showed her dark lashes forming perfect crescents against her cheek, her hair tumbled in unaccustomed disorder. He wondered how she felt about being wakened for sex…

There was a lot he didn't know about her. Well, he'd learned quite a bit last night. And he looked forward to finding out a good deal more.

Stopping by the desk, he hung her flimsy top over the chair. There was a piece of paper lying on the desk, and the searchlight that had found him and Camille earlier on deck swept the boat again. The words "Sale" and "*Sea-Rogue*" in bold letters leaped at him before the light passed. They were still imprinted behind his eyes when it had gone and he blinked, without thought snatching up the paper.

His hand was shaking, his body icy cold.

Turning, he almost stumbled over her suitcase and backpack, stacked beside the desk along with her laptop in its bag. The significance of that took a moment to penetrate.

He looked at Camille, innocent in her sleep. And then back at the paper he held. It had been in full view, not even folded.

He could still feel the imprint of Camille's kisses on his mouth, his body. He could taste her on his tongue. He knew how it felt to be inside her and have her close about him, tight but incredibly soft and warm and silky.

Now he was cold. Despite the summer night, and the stuffiness of the cabin.

He stood irresolute for seconds before heading for the door. The couple of steps seemed like a mile.

Quietly he closed it behind him and switched on the

saloon light, placed the papers on the table and sat down to peruse them.

His chest constricted as he read the words on the first page, then turned to the second.

They were identical. Two copies of a sale agreement for a half share of the ketch *Sea-Rogue,* including chattels and contents as at the date of Barney Broderick's death. Drummond had been thorough, the i's dotted, the t's crossed. Both pages carried his signature—and Camille's. Dated yesterday.

Chapter 13

Camille was having an erotic dream involving her and Rogan in the depths of the ocean, making love on a bed of waving seaweed, the water caressing their limbs as they twined about each other in leisurely abandon...

It was the noise that woke her, a steady chug-chug. The mattress seemed to vibrate beneath her and the cabin swayed. The boat was moving.

Moving?

She threw off the sheet, her feet hitting the floor with a thud. Hastily she pulled on panties and knotted a sarong at her waist. Her top was folded across the back of the chair in front of the empty desk, and she grabbed it and hauled it over her head. On the way to the door she stopped short, her heart plunging, and whipped around to look again at the desk. No pale oblong of paper showed against the dark square.

She'd left the sale agreement there in full view, and Rogan had found it and...

What was he doing?

Flying to the door to wrench it open, she was stunned to find that she couldn't. Foreboding making her hot and cold in waves, she tried again, then fumbled for the lock where the key had always been, confirming her dread suspicion. No key.

This was incredible. No one in his right mind would lock someone into a cabin and then…what?

Sickening panic attacked her. Maybe Rogan *wasn't* in his right mind—hadn't she accused him of being paranoid? Hadn't she worried that he was deluded, obsessed, unbalanced on the subject of his father's death and its relationship to a will-o'-the-wisp treasure?

She banged on the door with her fists and her open hand, yelling Rogan's name, but there was no response.

Anger swamping fear, she kicked at the door, and looked about for something to attack it with, but found nothing that wasn't screwed down or too light to be of any use.

Her cell phone. She'd call the police.

She fumbled in the desk drawer, then hunted through her shoulder bag, knowing it was useless. Rogan had found the phone and removed it.

Going to a porthole, she saw they had cleared the harbor and now a mere one or two lights winked from the shore. The only sound was the inexorable mutter of the engine.

There was nothing to do but return to the berth she had so recently shared with Rogan, sit with her knees hunched up, wrap her arms around them and pray.

When she heard footsteps on the deck her head jerked up, and she scrambled again to the porthole, but could see nothing. The engine stopped, and for a moment her heart leaped in hope. But the boat continued on its way, and the creaking and flapping noises she heard indicated that he'd raised the sails and was saving fuel.

After a long time there was more thumping overhead, a rattle and a splash. The boat didn't seem to be moving anymore and she figured they were at anchor.

A key scraped in the cabin door, and every muscle went bow-string tight, her skin prickling with gooseflesh.

When Rogan's solid figure appeared in the doorway pure instinct took over. She launched herself off the berth and straight at him, in an adrenaline surge of searing rage. Her fists thudded into his chest, and he staggered. She tried to get past him, and even as he grabbed her arm to haul her back from the doorway she raked at his face with her nails. He stopped her with hard fingers on her wrist, and she sank her teeth into his hand.

She heard him suck in a breath of pain, and experienced a primitive stab of satisfaction. Then he had both her wrists, holding her away with infuriating ease. She twisted them out and down, taking him by surprise, and swung a fist at his face, but he blocked it with his arm, numbing hers, and laughed, this time using a different hold to ward her off. She kicked at him, wishing she'd thought to put shoes on.

"Settle down!" he said sharply.

"The hell I will!" She made to bite him again, and he moved, pushing her toward the berth until her knees buckled and she fell, then somehow he turned her so that she was facedown against the pillow, her wrists clipped behind her.

Helpless and more enraged than ever, she wriggled and kicked out as best she could, but now he undoubtedly had the upper hand. "You can't win," he said.

She made a strangled sound of fury, fighting uselessly against his implacable hold, and gasped, "Bastard!"

"Cat," he retaliated succinctly. "I'll be wearing your claw marks for a week."

"Good!"

She made another convulsive effort to free herself, and he said with ominous calm, "If you don't keep still I'll have to tie you up."

"You wouldn't dare!" she panted.

"Think about it," he invited.

Camille didn't want to think about it. She wanted to *kill* him. She felt defenseless and vulnerable and stupidly afraid. It wasn't nice and all of it was his fault. She hated the thought of giving in, but if he carried out the threat she'd be even less able to defend herself. Or escape.

For a few more seconds she lay taut and defiant, the veins in her wrists throbbing in his iron grip. "Let me go," she muttered, letting herself become limp.

"Is it safe?"

Camille gritted her teeth. "I won't attack you again."

At first he retained his hold, then his hands left her, and she twisted to face him, pushing herself up on the pillows as he stood over her.

Dawn was breaking, and in the gray light she could see the raking marks her fingernails had made down his cheek. His gaze was steady and somber on her mutinous face, but his mouth was uncompromising and not at all gentle. She could scarcely believe that it had wooed hers last night with tenderness and passion. He was wearing only jeans, his chest bare, and she had to consciously block out the memory of what it had felt like under her hands, against her breasts...

She wrenched her gaze up to his face, to the accusing eyes and hard cheekbones and jutting jaw darkened with overnight shadow.

He didn't look like a madman. He looked very sane and very determined and very dangerous. It wasn't reassuring.

"What the hell," she demanded, "do you think you're doing?"

"Saving you."

The answer was so unexpected she couldn't believe she'd heard it right. *"What?"* She'd never thought he suffered from a religious mania.

"Although I'm not sure you deserve it," he told her grimly, and reached into the back pocket of his jeans. He tossed the sale agreement at her, to land on her thighs.

Feeling sick, she muttered, "You don't understand."

"Damn right I don't. How much have you told Drummond?" he asked.

"About what?"

"About me finding the log, and the Dumas clue, for starters. Have you been his little pawn all along? Did he put you up to going to bed with me? Maybe he suspected I knew more than I was letting on to you? I hope the pillow talk was satisfactory."

Camille stiffened, her eyes hot. He was calling her a liar. And worse. "Don't you dare accuse me of…" She wasn't sure what to call it, but using sex to get something definitely wasn't anything she'd ever stoop to. As she'd clearly intimated to James, she recalled, her conviction of his probity momentarily shaken.

At her hesitation Rogan's eyes assumed the bleak look she'd first seen when he'd entered the Imperial's dining room with his brother, then they turned cold and hard.

"I wouldn't do that!" she insisted. "And anyway, James thinks you're crazy! I don't know what you think you're doing, but you can turn this boat around and head back to Mokohina right now!"

He looked at her incredulously. "Maybe it's escaped your notice," he said, his tone scathing, "but you're not in a position to give orders, *Milady.*"

Fighting down panic, she said, "This is stupid! You could go to jail for years for kidnapping!"

He didn't flinch. "I guess you could call it that. The thing is, you and I are the only two people in the world who know how to find that wreck. On past evidence, the first thing you'd do tomorrow is run and tell your *friend* everything you know."

"I told you—"

"And I won't risk him or his mate doing to you what they did to my dad—and probably to the *Catfish*'s deckhand—when he has no further use for you."

"Are you telling me," Camille said with conscious sarcasm, "that you're doing this solely for my sake?"

He gave her a crooked grin that almost dented the armor of her anger. "It's not only your skin I'm concerned about. I don't want him finding the *Maiden's Prayer* before I do. Or knocking me off to give him a better chance."

"Give me one good reason to think James is a crook and a murderer! It's ludicrous!!"

"I *gave* you reasons," he argued, his eyes sparking with anger, "and you said you didn't believe me! I've spent a lot of my life working with men of various sorts and of umpteen nationalities and I've learned to trust my gut instinct. When you live in an entirely male community some things get very basic. Your life might depend on one of those guys one day, and you have to know which ones you'd trust, and which will literally knife you in the back if circumstances—in their eyes—warrant it. Like recognizing the difference between a harmless dolphin and a killer whale can mean life or death when you're down at the bottom of the sea. Drummond might never have physically lifted a finger against another human being, but I tell you, at heart he's a killer."

He was so convincing, so matter-of-fact certain, that despite herself Camille was shaken. Surely he couldn't be right? She said, "All you're saying is you have a *feeling* about him!'' But she didn't sound nearly as forceful or scornful as she'd meant to.

"I've never been wrong before."

"You're wrong about me! And if I *were* part of your preposterous plot, why would I sign my share of the boat over to James?"

Apparently he hadn't thought of that. "Maybe," he said slowly, "if you really don't believe in the treasure, you made a deal to ensure you didn't walk away with nothing. So you settled for a bird in the hand, with a little sugar on top. His offer was for way more than the market value."

"I haven't made any deal—at least, only to sell the boat."

His mouth tightened. "Either way, I can't trust you," he said flatly. "And if you're innocent I hate to think what he might do to get you to tell what you know now."

He lifted his head, and she heard what he'd heard, the beat of a motor coming rapidly closer. He turned and left the cabin, closing the door behind him. She heard him cross the saloon, then the motor came close and cut out, and Brodie's voice shouted Rogan's name. As she slid off the berth a bump and a shudder flung her down again.

After struggling back to her feet she went to the door and tried it, finding with some surprise that Rogan hadn't locked it again. She heard Brodie say something and laugh, and Rogan growl an indistinct reply.

She emerged onto the deck to see that the sun was rising and they were anchored just outside an unfamiliar cove where the cliffs rose sheer above the waves that dashed against them. The men had somehow roped the two craft alongside each other, and were manhandling bundles and boxes from the motorboat to the ketch, stowing them in the cargo space.

Rogan ignored her, hefting a couple of air tanks onto the

deck. There was a stack of them waiting to be loaded. Brodie said, "Hi, Camille."

"Has Rogan told you what he's doing?" she demanded.

Shooting a look at his friend, Brodie told her, "Said you're on a trip to the Islands."

"*He* may be! Will you take me back to Mokohina?"

Brodie stopped with another dive tank in his arms, then as Rogan snapped his fingers handed it over.

Looking confused, Brodie said, "Did you have a fight?"

Rogan put the tank down and said, "She's not going anywhere with you."

Camille informed Brodie, "He's abducting me."

Brodie seemed uncertain, and even more puzzled. Looking at the fierce red weals on Rogan's face, he said, "Did she do that?"

Grinning faintly, Rogan touched the backs of his fingers to his cheek. "There's a tigress under that sweet exterior."

Sweet! She'd give him sweet! Camille glared.

Bewilderment showed on Brodie's face. "Um…why?"

"Call it a lovers' quarrel," Rogan said.

"I am not your lover!" Camille stated hotly.

Rogan turned a cocked eyebrow to her, and she flushed. "I'm being held against my will!" Even to herself it sounded melodramatic, unlikely.

Brodie looked from one to the other of them, obviously shocked. "Rogan wouldn't…I mean, he wouldn't…um… against your will…?"

"She was willing enough last night," Rogan said. "Or this morning, rather. Early."

Camille felt her cheeks burn. "You're twisting things! What you've done is a criminal offence!"

Brodie was incredulous. "You're not saying Rogue *attacked* you?"

Rogan said quietly, "Tell him, Camille."

If she said yes Brodie would take her back to Mokohina, she was almost certain. Even if he didn't quite believe her, he was the kind of man who wouldn't leave a woman in the power of an accused rapist.

Both men waited for her answer.

"No," she said. "He hasn't physically hurt me. He locked me in the cabin and sailed off in the night."

Brodie's expression changed to relief, though he was obviously troubled. He turned back to his friend. "I guess you had a reason?"

"Several," Rogan told him. "One of them being she's safer with me."

Camille made a scornful sound, and Brodie frowned. "She's in danger?"

"She may not think so, but yes. Look, I don't have time to go into the whole story. Trust me, Brodie. And keep quiet about all this, okay?"

Ignoring him, Camille said, "Abduction is a serious crime, Brodie. Do you want to be an accessory after the fact? Take me back with you and I promise I won't go to the police. Nothing will happen to Rogan."

Brodie thrust a hand through his unruly hair. "I dunno, Camille. If Rogue says—"

"Oh, for heaven's sake!" Camille burst out. "Is anything *Rogue* says or does okay with you?"

"Rogue wouldn't do this without a damn good reason. Sorry, Camille," he added uncomfortably.

She saw it was useless trying to persuade him. All she could do was seethe until he cast off, and she watched in despair and disbelief as he turned his boat and headed back along the coastline in the morning light.

Rogan replaced the forward hatch and pulled up the anchor. She gauged the distance to the shore, but she had no hope of reaching it before he saw her, and the cliff looked unscaleable. They could be miles from civilization. This might even be an uninhabited island.

The sails snapped open, and Camille huddled in the cockpit and tried not to watch Rogan walking easily about the boat, checking ropes and sails, bending to tighten something, standing and steadying himself with a hand on a mast while he gazed about them at the deepening blue of the sea.

"Breakfast time," he said to Camille at last, the first words they'd spoken since Brodie left.

"I'm not hungry."

"Suit yourself." Rogan shrugged and disappeared into the galley. The smell of frying bacon wafted to her, and she got up and stepped from the cockpit onto the narrow deck, clutching at the nearest rope. Land was still visible, but they were too far out for her to swim for it.

Rogan climbed out onto the deck, a coffee mug in his hand. She turned her head and saw a grim look on his face, changing to something that might have been relief when he saw her. "You're not getting any silly ideas, I hope," he said.

Camille looked away again. "Not me," she said. "That's your specialty."

His laugh was short and sharp. "One day you may thank me for this."

She cast him a glance of disdain. "In your dreams."

"We could be rich," he said, "if my father was right."

"Your father was as crazy as you are. Has it occurred to you that people will wonder where I've got to?"

"Who—Drummond?" His lifted shoulder indicated he didn't give a damn about James.

"My mother. She'll worry if she doesn't hear from me."

He looked pensive, as though that might have given him pause. "You can phone her," he said.

"You took my phone!" she snapped.

"For your own protection." He looked at the sky, which was clouding over. "You can tell her you're on a pleasure cruise."

"Pleasure!"

His grin went awry. "I guess I can't expect any more pleasure like last night's for a while."

"Ever!" she assured him fervently.

He grimaced. "You'd better explain to your mother that once we leave the coast your phone will be out of range. Do you want to call her now?"

Camille thought about it. If she could just get across some message, some idea of her predicament…

Rogan must have been reading her face. "And don't get clever," he said ominously. "I'll be right beside you."

Could she say, "Call the police" before Rogan cut her off?

But how long would it take for the police to come to her rescue? Presuming they took it seriously at all. It might take them ages to check it out, let alone figure out where she might be.

Meantime her mother would be in a state of panic. She would almost certainly cut short her long-awaited holiday and fly home. And her sister's anniversary celebration would be overshadowed by anxiety. Camille wouldn't hear the last of it for years.

Of course none of these were good reasons to hesitate if her life was in danger.

Think it through, she exhorted herself. If Rogan was unhinged it was about one subject—in every other way he was as sane as she was. Although he'd been furious when he found the sale agreement it didn't seem likely that he planned to throw her overboard.

He might be a pirate, and abducting her was certainly

illegal and immoral and it had made her mad as hell, but it wasn't directly life-threatening. A police search would cost time and money and manpower. She'd be asked what her relationship was with her abductor. Even if she said nothing, Brodie would do his best to defend his friend, and she'd tacitly admitted she and Rogan had indulged in consensual sex. The media would love a story like that.

There would be suggestions that she'd simply changed her mind about going off with him. Yet if the police believed her Rogan would probably go to jail.

She discovered with a shock that being infuriated by his actions hadn't stopped her loving him. The thought of Rogan locked up in a cell made her stomach churn.

"It's early," she said aloud. Mona would still be in bed.

Rogan cast her a shrewd look. "Later, then."

The sky was overcast, the morning turning bleak. Gray clouds lowered over the boat and the water became leaden, the swells lifting the boat high before dropping it into the troughs. When rain began to fall Rogan left the cockpit and stayed under cover in the deckhouse.

Going down to the galley, Camille discovered that it wasn't only the strain of the morning's events and the thought of sending Rogan to prison that was making her feel sick. Looking at food made it much worse, and every movement of the boat brought a corresponding heave of her stomach.

When Rogan came down he tapped on the door of Camille's cabin and, since she didn't respond, pushed it open.

She was lying motionless on her berth, and one look told him why. Her face was as almost as green as the pillow she was clutching with one desperate hand while the other held a plastic basin, and her skin had a waxen sheen.

He swore, making her momentarily open her eyes. Then she closed them again, her bloodless mouth clamped tight.

Swiftly he crossed the cabin to hunker down beside her. "Hey," he said, "have you thrown up?"

Her lips barely moved. "About twenty minutes ago."

"I'll get you something. Just stay there."

"Stupid…" she said faintly.

Rogan grinned, not unsympathetic despite his deep, still smoldering fury.

His conscience bugged him as he went to the galley and shook a pill out of a plastic container. But he quelled the small voice, arguing he'd had no choice once he'd discovered Camille's betrayal. It had been stupid to trust her with the secret of the log. She could have been in with Drummond all along. And even if she wasn't, going on past evidence she seemed to tell the damned man everything. A risk Rogan couldn't afford to take now.

He returned to the cabin with the pill and a glass of water, and helped her get it down before she moaned and fell back against the pillow. "I hate you," she whispered.

"I know," Rogan acknowledged equably. "I'll bring you a biscuit."

She shuddered.

"It'll help," he promised. "And then we'll get you up on deck. You need fresh air."

Camille didn't bother to contradict him. There was no way she was moving from this bed. She'd die here if necessary. At the moment that seemed not a bad idea.

Within seconds Rogan was back; even with her eyes closed she sensed his presence. Something touched her lips, and she jerked her head away. A mistake. She moaned, and Rogan pushed the fragment of dry ship's biscuit into her mouth. "It will help," he repeated. "Believe me."

After she'd managed to swallow a few pieces, he gently bullied her to let him help her onto the deck. The rain had stopped, and he wedged himself into the corner of the cockpit and held her against his chest after lifting her feet up to rest on the slats. "Keep your eyes open and look ahead to where the boat's going," he instructed her.

She was angry with this man, he was a pirate and a kidnapper and quite possibly at least mildly insane—and responsible for her being here at all, feeling as she did. It would be what he deserved if she threw up over him.

Only his solid chest was heavenly to rest against, and his arms held her firmly and comfortably as the boat forged its way through the waves that occasionally misted her face with blessedly cooling spray…and actually he was right; she was beginning to feel a little better, breathing in the salty, rain-washed air.

She wasn't sure when she dozed off or how long she slept, but she woke to sunshine and calmer water, and a surprising feeling of hunger.

Rogan hadn't moved. He said, "Feeling better?"

Camille sat up, pulling away from him, irritated with herself. "Yes," she said curtly. "Where are we?"

"Heading for North Cape. If you want to contact your mother it had better be soon, before we lose signal range."

He stood up and stretched his arms, and she thought he must be stiff from holding her while she slept. He pulled her phone from his pocket and sat beside her, an arm along the coaming at her back, silently reminding her that he'd be listening.

"Camille, darling!" Mona's voice was faint, distant. "I tried to ring you but your phone was switched off. I suppose you were buried in your musty old books again. You'd have loved it last night—we went to the opera. Your uncle paid for everything, he insisted! And tomorrow…"

Her voice began to fade in crackling interference, then came back. "...a terrible line! Where are you?"

"On the boat," Camille said. "Sailing. Mum—"

"Sailing?" Mona queried on a higher note, her voice breaking through the static. "I know you're living...that man but...thought it was tied up! You're not...a *trip* in that...? Is it even seaworthy anymore?"

"We're on our way to—"

Rogan pressed a warning hand over Camille's mouth and whispered, "The Islands."

"—the Islands," Camille echoed tightly when he removed his hand, the description so wide that no one would be able to identify which of the many remote islands of the Pacific they were headed for.

"...islands? ...how long?" Mona demanded.

"I don't know. We'll be out of phone range soon." The crackling increased on cue and she raised her voice. "You may not hear from me for a while."

"You're with that Broderick boy, aren't you?" Mona said sharply, loud enough to cut through the increasing noise. "Camille, don't be a fool! You know what sort of man your father was—him and that Barney Broderick, both the same. Like father, like son..." Her voice faded again. "...setting yourself up for heartbreak...I can say..." Her voice shrilled, though static drowned out some words. "...trouble to...away from you all those years to have you...the same...I did."

"What?" Camille pressed the phone to her ear.

"...say I didn't warn you...hope you'll come...senses."

"Mum..." But the noise was so bad now it was useless to persevere. "I love you," Camille said, not knowing if Mona could hear. "I'll be in touch as soon as I can."

Her hands were trembling as she shut off the connection.

Rogan immediately took the phone from her, saying, "You did well."

Camille stood up, all her anger with him resurfacing. "I did what I was told to do," she said coldly. "I hope you're satisfied."

"You *are* feeling better," he said.

Remembering her resolution to talk sense to him, she said, "You can't expect to get away with this. Just take me back to Mokohina and we can forget it ever happened."

"No way," he said flatly. "It ain't gonna happen."

She stared toward the land that looked tantalizingly close, and he said, "It's farther than it looks, and if you didn't drown first or get dashed to piece on the rocks, you could die of exposure before you reached help."

Camille tightened her mouth and turned away, climbing down into the saloon. If she stayed she'd scream or hit him or both. And neither would be very productive.

The instruments by the saloon table were lit, mysterious lines moving across small screens on a couple of them. There must be a radio of some kind. She approached the machines and examined buttons and switches for a clue. A faint crackling sound emanated from one that showed the number 16 steadily on its dial.

There was a microphone attached by a hook. Gingerly she unhooked it. "Hello?" she said quietly. Nothing happened, and she looked at the microphone and found a switch. "Is anyone there?"

After a few seconds a voice asked, "What is your name and position?"

She hadn't a clue what the boat's position was. "I'm Camille Hartley, and—"

"Can you speak up? The boat's name?"

"*Sea-Rogue*. I've been kid—"

A hard hand snatched the microphone from her, even as

another snaked about her, clamping her mouth. Rogan said, "Sorry, false alarm. I've told the kids not to play with the radio. Thanks for responding."

By the time Camille had wrenched herself free he'd cut the contact and the number had disappeared from the screen.

"That's the emergency channel," he said as she twisted to face him, defiance and fury in her eyes. "Only to be used if the boat is in danger of sinking. Nobody would be too pleased if you brought some ship miles off course to rescue you and they found a perfectly seaworthy boat and a woman who just didn't like the company she was in. Try another trick like that and I'll lock you up again."

"You can't do this to me!" she raged.

"Sorry," he said curtly, "but I can. And I am. You can settle down and make the best of it, enjoy the trip. Or spend it sulking in your cabin."

"*Enjoy the trip?* When you've *forced* me to come along with you?"

"You don't seem to have found it too much of a hardship sharing quarters with me in the harbor—even your bed."

She didn't relish the reminder, and fired back at him, "If you think that's going to happen again, you can take a running jump!"

"You slept with me knowing you were going to sell to Drummond!" He looked positively lethal, his cheeks whitening and his mouth taking on an ominous look as his eyes became diamond-hard and glittering. "And that you were leaving!"

What was he so livid about? She didn't understand him. "I'd finished my research. There was no reason to stay."

"So what was that…last night? A farewell present?"

Trying to appear nonchalant, she shrugged. "It just… happened. It seemed a nice idea at the time."

"*Nice?*"

"Well, I'm sorry if you didn't like it!"

"Of course I bloody liked it!" He didn't look any less angry. "I didn't know what you were planning, did I? And I don't have time for this. Someone ought to be keeping watch. Are you coming back on deck or do I lock you in your cabin?"

Wanting to throw something at him, she met his steady gaze with a fulminating one of her own. "I'm hungry!" she said.

A glimmer of humor lightened his expression. "I made you a ham sandwich, without butter. It'll help settle your stomach. You can eat it on deck."

He took it from the kerosene fridge, handed her a small bottle of water, and motioned her ahead of him. The sandwich was good, and the water cold and refreshing. When she'd finished, not wanting to sit in the cockpit with Rogan, she settled for leaning on the stern rail with her back to him, watching the hypnotic surge of the boat's wake stirring the water. Seabirds flew behind them, then veered away to find something else of interest or to land on the bobbing waves, disappearing finally into the distance. A couple of times she saw container ships near the horizon, their low decks laden with cargo. Once she thought she glimpsed the white hull of another boat, rearing from the waves behind, but then it vanished. Maybe she'd been mistaken.

Rogan came to stand beside her, lifting binoculars to his eyes and scanning the sea.

Camille didn't offer to cook, and Rogan found lettuce, tomatoes and more ham, spread fresh sliced bread thinly with margarine, and loaded two plates. Camille supposed foodstuffs had been included in the cargo Brodie brought.

She took her plate without comment, climbed back to the

cockpit when he told her to, and ate in silence. There was every reason not to thank him, not to cooperate with him in any way. But she felt petty and ungracious, remembering he'd nursed her through her bout of seasickness and even provided for when it had passed. After they'd finished she muttered, ''I'll wash up.''

''You'd better have another pill,'' he said. ''In a day or two you'll be okay.''

She took the one he offered, and when the dishes were done retired to her cabin, reaching for the first book that came to hand on the shelf above the bed.

It was about treasure wrecks and recovery efforts. She dipped into three chapters and found descriptions of tragedy followed by murder, mayhem and greed. Incredulously she read that only a few years previously poachers on a wreck site had engaged in deadly undersea battles, going so far as to cut a legitimate salvor's air line and try to blow up his boat. While she knew that even today piracy was rampant in parts of the world, she'd had no idea that people were still committing murderous acts in pursuit of sunken treasure.

The next day began fine and clear, but later the sea became turbulent, the boat tossed on confused waves that seemed to come from all directions. They must have passed North Cape, where the Pacific met the contrary currents of the Tasman Sea between New Zealand and Australia.

As the land diminished behind them she was attacked by a sick alarm. Ahead there was nothing but empty, inky sea meeting the blue bowl of the sky on a blurred line of deep indigo. Out there she would be miles from anywhere and without any means of communication, alone with a man who didn't like or trust her anymore and who might be unhinged.

She should have taken the chance to warn her mother of

her predicament, try to get an urgent plea for help across before Rogan stopped her. The stories she had read the previous night came to mind. Over the centuries the lust for gold had made monsters of men. Had love blinded her to the possibility that she might be in real danger? How stupid to have decided that not spoiling her mother's holiday or her aunt's anniversary party was more important than her own safety, maybe her life!

Rogan had disregarded the law, common sense and the possible consequences for himself when he made off with her. Supposing there really was a treasure, how far would he be prepared to go in order to conceal its location—and perhaps keep it all for himself and his brother?

If she sold half of the boat to James, Rogan and Granger would still be entitled to their own share of any treasure. So why was Rogan so worried?

She hadn't handed over the agreement to James to conclude the contract, and Rogan had her in his power. According to him she could claim half of any profit resulting from the *Sea-Rogue*'s voyages, including the results of any treasure hunt, whereas he would get only a quarter.

If she died, his share would double. Shivering, she clutched at the wooden rail under her hands. Had she been wrong in thinking he wasn't a danger to her?

"Camille?"

She jumped as his hand touched her arm, backing into the curve of the rail, eyes wide and wary.

Rogan scowled at her. "What's the matter with you?"

It was too much. "What do you *think* is the matter?" she yelled at him. "I've been kidnapped, locked in and threatened with being tied up, forcibly prevented from communicating with anyone, and I have no idea what you mean to do with me."

"*Do* with you…?"

He lifted a hand and she screamed, *"Don't touch me!"*

The scowl changed to a look of shocked comprehension. "What do you think I mean to do with you?" he demanded.

"I don't know!" she cried wildly. "But I'll fight you with every breath!"

Rogan laughed suddenly, and she tightened her grip on the rail behind her, facing him with her chin up, her body taut, trying to conceal the stark fear that stretched the skin over her cheekbones and made her breathing uneven.

His laughter abruptly stopped, and he said, "I won't hurt you, Camille, I swear. For God's sake get that idea out of your mind. I didn't mean to scare you silly."

"I'm not scared," she lied valiantly. "I'm *angry!*"

"Sure," he said, patently disbelieving, his tone soothing. "I guess I can't blame you. You look cold. Do you want me to fetch you something warmer to put on?"

Surely if he meant to kill her he wouldn't be concerned about her being cold? Beginning to feel foolish, she shook her head. "I'm all right."

Rogan regarded her for a second, then nodded. "Let me know if you need anything."

Camille had nursed every intention of giving Rogan no cooperation, speaking only when necessary. But unless she skulked in her cabin she couldn't totally avoid him.

The vastness of the ocean all around was awe-inspiring, and its ever-changing colors, from green to turquoise blue to indigo and even purple on the horizon, were hypnotically beautiful. The intense blue of the sky was sometimes cloudless, sometimes held wisps of white or gray, or plump luminous cushions of overflowing cumulus gilded at the edges.

At night the stars spilled their splendor across the vast

sky, so bright and close it was almost possible to believe she could reach out and touch them, while the moon gave a pearly sheen to the restless water.

Her resolution not to share any of these pleasures made them less satisfying. Despite the beauty all around, and the number of books on board that she read for hours at a time, after three days she was close to screaming with boredom.

Rogan was always busy—studying charts, altering the angle of the sails, or scowling over the radar screen, when he wasn't at the wheel. She couldn't help admiring his handling of ropes and sails that looked so complex and confusing. There was a guilty, poignant pleasure in just being with him.

In the saloon she found a sailing manual with diagrams of rigging and equipment, and instructions. She settled down in a corner of the cockpit to learn something about her enforced environment.

When Rogan went below she took the manual and began to walk about the boat, identifying the sails and the sheets—which were ropes, not sails—and the heavy iron cleats for securing them, that were a tripping hazard on the deck.

"What are you doing?"

Her hand on a line, Camille turned to the sound of Rogan's voice. "Trying to find out how this thing works."

"Why?" He came closer, angling his head to see the book in her hand. "If you were thinking of shoving me overboard and sailing her yourself, I'd think again…"

"I'm not that stupid!"

"So," he said, "can you remember what this is?" He pointed to a sail.

"The mizzen?"

"Good girl. Do you know what it does?"

Learning that she could manipulate the boat, make it

obey her, gave her a satisfied sense of accomplishment. That evening she cooked, and they ate on deck while the sunset polished the water with gold and set the few clouds hanging over the horizon on fire. The silence was less hostile. She was too tired, she told herself, to maintain her antagonism.

In the following days they slipped into an edgy truce. The boat was a world of its own, and after ten days Camille lost count of time and dates. She seemed to be living in limbo.

One evening Rogan said, ''You'd better take a seasickness pill before you go to bed. The weather isn't looking good for the next twenty-four hours. And make sure the portholes in your cabin are closed.''

In the night Camille woke to find the boat pitching in a way she'd never before experienced. Waves thumped heavily against the hull, and as she threw back her sheet she saw water spitting at the portholes.

Hurriedly she pulled on cotton shorts and a shirt, then a pair of sneakers, staggering against the alarming movement of the boat, and lurched into the saloon. Rogan must be on deck. She could hear rain, and she donned a slicker from the wet-weather locker under the companionway.

She made her way up to the cockpit and was immediately attacked by driving rain that stung her eyes, so she couldn't at first see Rogan and had to quell a spurt of panic. Suppose he'd been washed overboard? Ghostly white-tipped waves seemed to be coming at them from all directions. Then his voice came loud against the sound of the water hissing over the bow and thumping along the deck. ''Get below!''

She could just make out his dark figure battling with a recalcitrant sail. The boat heeled, more water washing over it in a furious rush, and Rogan bellowed, ''Look out!''

Camille grabbed at the nearest solid object, then quickly

clipped on a safety line before making her way along the madly swaying deck.

"I told you to go below!" A wave foamed over the bow and traversed the entire deck, pulling at their ankles and calves.

"Let me help!" she shouted against the wind's wail and the fierce whack of the water. "Tell me what to do."

Another wave made her stagger and gasp. Rogan cursed, then handed her a line. "Keep that taut, and when I tell you, start tying the sail." Then he turned to work at containing the snapping sail while the boat was thrown about on ill-tempered waves like a giant's toy.

She had never been so scared in her life.

Chapter 14

Once Rogan had accepted that Camille wasn't going to leave him to it, obeying without question every order except to return below where she'd be dry and warm and safe, they faced the waves and the wind together. Her heart leaped in fear each time a wall of dark water threatened to bury them, but somehow Rogan sent the craft soaring over the slavering crests and sliding down the other side. His grim confidence was a reassurance she clung to while they fought to keep the boat afloat and in one piece.

Toward dawn the wind abated and the rain stopped, and gradually the water became calmer under a sheet of gray sky. They were wet and exhausted and Camille's arms and shoulders and back ached. But they had weathered the storm. Now she knew exactly what it meant.

Too wrung out to talk, they watched the increasing glow that warned of the imminent arrival of the sun. Camille didn't remember when she'd been so alive, as if every nerve was alert, every particle of skin newly sensitive. She felt the coolness of the still-brisk wind, tasted the salt tang of blown spray, smelled the ocean and the old wood of the boat and the subtly erotic scent of the man beside her.

"We made it," Rogan said, his arm about her shoulder.

Instinctively she turned, lifting her face, and saw the brief hesitation in his before he lowered his head and their mouths met, damp and salty and cold, but instantly warmed.

He drew her closer, parted her lips under his, and kissed her so superbly she felt floaty and soft and beautiful, despite being soaked to the skin and exhausted. She raised her arms and held him, wanting the kiss to last forever, wanting not to think, only to experience this moment as if it were the rest of her life.

Even when it became an explicit statement of desire, a carnal claim to her mouth, her body, she didn't protest, nor at the possessive caress of his hand over her breast, her rib cage, the curve of her hip and behind.

It was Rogan who broke off the kiss and moved her hands from about his neck, holding them tightly between his own as he muttered, "I have to sail this damned boat. We're on the edge of a hurricane here…"

Coming back to reality was a shock. Camille blinked at him, trying to reestablish some kind of equilibrium. What had she been thinking of?

While they'd been battling the storm together all that mattered was keeping the boat afloat and themselves safe. But the relief and elation at realizing they had come through unscathed had needed some physical expression.

"You'd better go below and dry off," Rogan said. It sounded like an order.

"What about you?" He was just as wet as she was.

"I'll be fine."

She didn't argue. A long hot shower would have been

nice, only at sea the water was strictly rationed. Instead she rubbed herself down vigorously with a towel and put on clean dry clothes from undies to cotton shorts and a T-shirt. Then she scrambled some eggs that had been preserved in petroleum jelly, made coffee, and took them up to Rogan.

He smiled at her somewhat quizzically when she presented them. "Thanks. And thanks for helping out. You were terrific."

"Just looking after my own skin," she told him. "I've no desire to drown at sea."

He grinned. "Back to normal, are we?"

She didn't feel normal, she felt confused and chagrined. For a short time she'd forgotten how they'd come to be here, forgotten his perfidy and her own pride, lost in his arms. Without answering, she turned away.

Rogan gave a sharp sigh. "Okay," he said, "I get the message. Here—you'd better have this."

Reluctantly turning back to him, she saw he was holding out his hand, her cabin key resting on his broad palm. "If it'll make you feel safer," he suggested.

She had never feared being sexually assaulted by him. Even when she'd briefly had nightmare thoughts about possible murder, rape hadn't figured in them.

Gratitude was an inappropriate reaction. He'd had no right to appropriate the key and imprison her in the first place. But the unexpected gesture was oddly warming, and she was horrified to discover a threat of tears pricking at the backs of her eyes. She snatched up the key and fled down the companionway.

After fighting for their lives together, it simply wasn't possible for her to maintain the distrustful distance she'd established between them. In the following days Camille took her turn at keeping watch, and mealtimes were no longer silent. Although there was undeniable tension in the air, when Rogan pointed out a spouting whale not far off Camille couldn't hide her awe and excitement, and when she turned to him he grinned back at her, sharing the moment.

Several days after the storm a blue, cloudy smudge appeared on the horizon, gradually resolving into a tiny island hill, covered in thick, dense green except where gray rocky outcrops refused any foothold for plants. A rim of sun-bleached sand edged part of the island. White frills of foam about a mile from the shore warned of a protective reef surrounding it, but beyond the breakers the water was tranquil and jade-green.

Other islands appeared and disappeared, until the boat approached a ring of small, sandy atolls, no more than a few feet above the water, surrounding a huge lagoon of translucent blue-green like Rogan's eyes.

Slowly they sailed closer, keeping away from the telltale white water. One oval islet held three coconut palms with gracefully bowed trunks and gently moving green leaves, and close by a tiny hump of white sand had room for only one tree rising against the tropical sky.

The three musketeers and the young latecomer, D'Artagnan. Barney's fanciful description had been apt.

Rogan approached with caution, sounding for hidden hazards, and anchored securely well clear of the reef. He shucked the jeans he wore, revealing swim briefs that did nothing to conceal his magnificent masculinity, pulled on a wet suit, and picked up a mask and snorkel.

"You're not using scuba?" Camille asked in surprise.

"Not yet." He adjusted the mask. "Just looking around."

After he'd slipped into the water she soon lost sight of the snorkel, and it seemed a long time before he climbed back on board and stripped again to his briefs. Unwilling to admit how relieved she was to see him, Camille averted her eyes from his damp, near-naked body, despising her predictable and shaming reaction. ''Did you find anything?''

He pushed back his wet hair and wiped salt water from his forehead with the back of his hand. ''Coral and fish and crabs. How would you like fresh crabs for dinner?'' He held out a bag that had half a dozen encased in mesh.

They feasted on the crabs while the setting sun turned the white sands of the atolls pink and the palm trees became silhouettes against the fading sky, their restless leaves stilled when night descended on them and stars spread like gems on velvet over the blackness above.

When she finally roused herself to go to bed, darkness had wrapped about them like a feather quilt, but the moon showed her Rogan's face, starkly lit as he turned his head and said quietly, ''Good night, Camille.''

She had a mad urge to say, *Come with me.* Such a night demanded some kind of homage, a pagan sacrificial offering. The tropical warmth, the subtly scented air, the rhythmic rocking of the boat, the brilliant fecundity of the stars, created a mood of reckless eroticism.

Frightened by the power of her instincts, Camille descended the companionway and locked herself in the cabin—not to keep Rogan out, but to ensure she didn't fling open her door and invite him in when she heard him leave the deck.

In the morning Rogan moved the boat farther round the lagoon and went snorkeling again. This time he emerged with barely concealed triumph in his face as he pulled off his mask. ''There's something down there,'' he said. ''I'll have a bite to eat and then suit up for a dive.''

''I want to come.''

He scarcely glanced at her. ''Wreck diving on a coral

reef isn't for beginners. I'll have enough to do looking after myself. There are all kinds of risks.''

When he had disappeared into the green depths Camille experienced a few minutes of unreasoning fear. If anything happened to him down there, how would she know? She pictured a ghostly ship sitting on the bottom, broken masts ready to snag a harness or tear at a wet suit, tangled cables that would hold a diver in a death grip until he ran out of air or ditched his tank and surfaced too fast, risking the dreaded bends.

If that happened he could die, or be crippled for life.

There were probably sharks in these waters. Though he'd said they seldom bothered divers. She reminded herself that Rogan had years of experience and was certainly not stupid. He wouldn't take unnecessary risks.

Even with the lure of treasure before him?

A strange noise drew her attention to the sky, and she looked up to see an airplane rapidly approaching. It was quite small, a silver-winged intruder that made a pass over the boat, then another before flying off in the direction it had come from, leaving behind silence except for the wind setting the palm leaves clacking, and the insistent boom of the waves against the reef.

The water gleamed and glistened under the blaze of the sun. The *Sea-Rogue* shifted as if trying to escape the anchors that held it. Waves washing over the reef sent a fine misty spray into the air. A single seabird with outstretched wings floated in the air above the deserted lagoon.

Camille had never felt so alone.

The deeper Rogan dived the less time he could spend on the bottom, and the more he'd need to allow for decompression stops on the way up. She had no way of knowing if he was still down or on his way up—or if he'd got into trouble on the bottom.

Her eyes hurt from scanning the sea and watching the buoy marking the shot line that would guide his ascent. She clutched at the rail, feeling under her tense palms the scored marks where he'd showed her his and Granger's initials. When he finally surfaced and clambered to the deck she said tightly, "I thought you'd drowned down there!"

He didn't say anything until he'd lowered his tank gently to the deck and removed his mask. "Would you care?" He began stripping off the suit.

"Of course I'd care!" Her voice was shrill despite her effort to steady it. She'd have been devastated, racked with pain and regret. Afraid she'd betrayed herself, she said, "I can't sail this blasted boat, for one thing!"

Peeling the suit from his legs, Rogan laughed, casting her a glance.

"It's not funny!" she snapped.

The laughter died. "You were worried."

She compressed her lips, so she wouldn't scream at him.

He left his gear on the deck and came close enough to place cool fingers against her cheek, his eyes studying her with a too-concentrated stare. "I'm touched."

She batted his hand aside. "Don't patronize me! And keep your hands to yourself!" It was all too tempting to lie her cheek against his hand, lean on his bare chest and give way to tears of relief and release from tension.

His face went blank for a moment. He said, "I won't leave you all alone, Camille."

But he would, he *would*…if she gave in to her emotions and let him take her heart, her life, in his hands. "You're like my father," she whispered. "And yours. All they cared about was their damned treasure hunt."

The brilliant aqua gaze didn't waver. "I care about you, Camille. And your father did too."

Her chin lifted. "How do you make that out?"

''Why else did he keep pictures of you…and the letter you wrote him when you were a little girl?''

''What letter?'' Sickeningly, she knew. Stupid, perhaps, to be embarrassed by something she'd done when she was five years old. But the small, cold lump of lonely hurt she'd felt then had never entirely left her—it was still hiding away in a locked corner of her heart.

''You should talk to your mother,'' he said. ''Ask her if Taff didn't try to get in touch with you.''

She recalled the last time she'd spoken with Mona. The static had made nonsense of what she was trying to say, and Camille had been too stressed at the time to analyze it, torn between reassuring her mother and wondering if she ought instead to be screaming for help.

But now that she thought it through she realized she could make sense of it. *I didn't take the trouble to keep him away from you all those years, only to have you go through the same thing I did.*

''No!'' she said aloud, her eyes fixed on Rogan almost accusingly. Surely her mother wouldn't have been so cruel? She thought of the many times she'd asked when her father was coming back, only to be told on an acrid note she had been too young to understand that he was too busy to bother with them. Or, with a bitter laugh, that maybe he'd remember their existence someday. And finally that he'd forgotten them and she might as well stop asking and forget him too. ''You're not the only child in the world without a father,'' Mona had reminded her in exasperation. ''We can get along quite well without him.''

Of course she'd been right on both counts, but Camille had been ten years old before she could make herself believe that she would never see her father again. It wasn't as though he was dead, like the father of one of her friends. Other children at school had divorced parents but still saw their fathers on regular or special occasions, even holidaying with them.

"Ask her," Rogan reiterated.

He turned away to pick up his gear, and she said jerkily, "Did you find anything?"

"Brass fittings, a few pieces of wood, broken china. I can't do another deep dive today. I'll map what I saw and try again tomorrow. All I need this trip is enough to prove the wreck is the *Maiden's Prayer* and that the cargo is still there and worth salvaging. Any major salvage has to be done carefully, with regard to the archeological value of the wreck, and everything should be recorded."

She was glad to hear that, knowing what valuable historical data might be hidden down there. Her reading had revealed that in the past wrecks had been blown apart by divers intent on recovering valuable cargo, and poachers had never been particularly scrupulous. It wasn't in their interests to record details of where they'd found their ill-gotten gains.

When Rogan was suiting up the next day she said, "I want to come with you."

"I told you—"

"You said you wouldn't leave me again." Any danger she faced underwater would be better than the nightmare of apprehension she'd suffered yesterday. "Surely I'm entitled, as a part owner. You've seen the site, and it doesn't sound dangerous. So it's deeper than I've dived before, but you know I can do it. You taught me yourself."

"This isn't a teaching exercise!"

"I know. I won't hinder you, I promise."

About to strap his dive computer to his arm, he stood with it in his hand, regarding her dubiously. "You'll do everything I tell you," he growled finally. "No arguments."

"Haven't I always," she said, "underwater?"

"Stick close unless I signal otherwise. Let me know immediately if you have a problem. Surface when I say so, no matter what, take it slowly and remember the decompression stops are absolutely vital on the way up."

Camille nodded. "I'll get my gear."

Remembering Rogan's instruction to stick by him, as they swam down the shot line she tore her gaze from the coral wall of the reef, fans of bright orange against a backdrop of white studded with blue and red, pink and purple, and farther on, huge formations like acres of giant green petals. A great, grumpy-looking, fat-lipped head poked from a hole in the reef and her heart skipped a beat. Large grouper were theoretically capable of swallowing a diver, but Rogan had assured her that had never been known to happen.

Brilliant fish—butter-yellow, cerise, electric blue, deep orange, many striped or spotted, sometimes both—darted by in hundreds, dazzling and disorienting her.

Rogan grabbed her hand, signaled Okay? She returned the signal, and he nodded.

The seafloor was strewn with shells and lumps of coral. Rogan pointed to what seemed just another coral outcrop, until she made out the shape of it. An empty porthole lying on the seabed, encrusted with coral and other sea creatures, the brass frame dulled with verdigris.

Soon they swam alongside something long and slightly curved—and with a clutch of excitement she recognized the timber outline of the upper part of a ship's side, amazingly almost intact, most of it buried under the sand, the ghostly remains of a long-ago tragedy. Touching the heavily encrusted wood, she was engulfed by the same bittersweet emotion that always assailed her when she handled mementos of people who had once lived and breathed and now were gone.

Rogan stopped and turned a lump of coral, and another, then picked up a third and paused to examine it. When he held it up for her she could just discern a series of small half-round shapes like a stack of…coins!

Silver coins, stuck together by verdigris and a hundred and fifty years of coral growth. Rogan placed the lump into the mesh bag at his waist, and gently fanned an area of sand with his hand, stirring it up and away from the sea-floor.

Camille tentatively did some fanning of her own, and after several minutes of trying in various spots she saw the unmistakable gleam of gold. Pushing aside the concealing sand, she scooped up the object and nearly lost her mouthpiece, choking back a cry of sheer astonishment. It was unmistakably a sovereign, twin to the one Barney had buried with the logbook. Rogan came to her side and held out the bag for her to place the piece inside it. He had several more things in the bag, that looked like coral lumps to her, but she caught a gleam of gold, a glimpse of color.

Burrowing into the sand, she felt something round and small, and found a gold ring with some kind of stone, and triumphantly held it up. Rogan gave a thumbs-up, then pointed to his dive computer, signaling that they were to surface.

Reluctantly she followed him to the shot line, finning up toward the light. They were pausing for their last decompression stop when a disturbance sent fish darting in all directions, and a throbbing noise assailed her ears, becoming so loud and close it was frightening.

Rogan's head jerked up, and she too peered anxiously toward the surface. The hull of the *Sea-Rogue* was a dark shape some distance away. Now another shape joined it, and the noise abruptly stopped.

Rogan looked at the computer on his wrist. She sensed his impatience, but he counted down the minutes until it was safe to ascend before signaling her upward.

They broke into the dazzle of sunlight together, and it was seconds before Camille's eyes could make out the *Sea-Rogue* and beside her another boat—a high, white, seagoing motor cruiser. The *Catfish*.

Chapter 15

Rogan's fist tightened on the shot line he still held. Inwardly he cursed. Drummond—or his henchman—had tracked them down. The *Catfish* probably had the latest radar-tracking gear known to humankind, able to spot even a wooden-hulled boat from miles away. Maybe the metal masts had given them away. Once or twice he'd thought the *Sea-Rogue* was being followed but he'd hoped the storm had taken care of it.

He'd been right on the first count, wrong on the second. And he and Camille couldn't stay in the water forever.

When he hoisted himself onto the *Sea-Rogue*'s deck he wasn't surprised to see Drummond waiting for them, dressed like an ad for casual menswear in a knit cream shirt, beige cotton trousers and boat shoes, his face more pasty white than ever. And beside him, the *Catfish*'s skipper.

Ignoring them, Rogan turned to help Camille, knowing how heavy the air tank would feel out of the water.

"James!" Camille said. "What are you doing here?"

"You cheated me," he said. "Disappearing with this…pirate."

Rogan said, "She didn't come willingly." He was helping Camille get her harness off before removing his own.

Drummond stared at Camille. "Not willingly? What did he do to you?"

"Nothing. I'm all right." She moved closer to Rogan.

Drummond's cold gaze moved with her, then went to the buoy some distance away that marked the wreck. "You found the sunken ship?"

Rogan said, "A wreck. The reef's probably caught hundreds of vessels over the years."

"But you've got something there you thought worth recovering." James's eyes lighted on the bag at Rogan's waist. "May I see?"

"No." Rogan gave him a steady stare, readying every muscle for Drummond's next move, conscious of Camille's soft, unsteady breathing beside him. He wouldn't give a fig for their lives once Drummond was sure he'd located the treasure.

Drummond laughed quietly, and jerked his head at the *Catfish*'s skipper. "Evan?"

The man snaked a hand behind his back and it reappeared holding a very business-like black pistol. Camille gasped.

"May I see now?" Drummond asked, a polite mockery.

Rogan stood his ground, calculating how far away the gunman was. Drummond he was sure he could deal with, so long as the slimy bastard didn't produce a gun too, but it was hard to see where he'd conceal one in his perfectly-fitting outfit. Rogan's hunch was he'd keep his own nose clean and let his skipper do the dirty work. But Evan handled the gun as though he knew how to use it—perhaps had used it. Maybe forced his deckhand to choose between being shot or going overboard in the deep ocean.

"Camille signed that agreement," he said. "I gave it to a friend for safekeeping." He hoped like hell Camille wasn't showing surprise at that untrue statement. "If she doesn't come back from this trip you have no legal claim to the *Sea-Rogue* or anything we found."

"You think that matters now?"

It had been a forlorn hope at best. At a guess, Drummond had wanted the boat because he believed Barney had hidden the log or something equally important on board. Now he didn't need it. "My father owned the salvage rights," Rogan said. "You'd have trouble disposing of anything you find."

Contemptuously Drummond said, "I've been disposing of…difficult items from New Zealand for years. It's not a problem when you have the right contacts."

The hairs on the back of Rogan's neck prickled. That was close to an admission of illegal trading. It would be easy enough to smuggle stuff out on the *Catfish* when the boat didn't have passengers, to rendezvous with yachts— even bigger foreign trawlers or commercial vessels—on their way to Asia, Europe or America, and transfer stolen antiques or prohibited cultural items. Like historic carved wooden or jade ornaments and weapons, treasured by Maori and rarely available now to collectors.

"I'm not here to explain my business to you," Drummond said impatiently. "Give me the bag. Or…Camille, perhaps you might do it for him." His eyes dared Rogan to resist.

Camille hesitated, then went to Rogan and, sending him a glance that held a message he couldn't read, unclipped the bag from his waist.

She turned quickly, the bag swinging in her hand, and flung it straight at Evan's head.

Rogan pitched himself after it as the gun went off and he felt a searing heat in his left arm. Then he had the man on the deck and grabbed his wrist, bringing it down hard on the nearest iron cleat.

He heard the man's yelp of pain and the gun spun away and splashed overboard.

Where was Camille? Was she all right? What was Drummond doing?

Evan's fist caught him on the side of the head, and he saw stars. Blindly clenching his own fist and scarcely feeling the further blows that Evan landed, he pounded at the man's face like a maniac until he felt him go slack.

Scrambling to his feet, he swung round with his heart in his mouth, then almost laughed. Drummond was backed up against the mainmast, his face the same sickly color as his shirt, and Camille had her diving knife at his throat.

"You wouldn't," Drummond was saying. "Camille…"

Camille said, "I *will* if you don't call off your dog." She moved the knife until it pricked the skin under his jaw, a trickle of blood flowing down his neck.

Rogan said, "No need, honey. I'm okay."

Her rigid shoulders relaxed a trifle. She said, "We'd better tie them up. You're good at knots…"

Rogan did it efficiently. He noted with detached relief that Evan was coming round. The man winced and moaned when the rope went about his bruised wrist, but Rogan hardened his heart and made sure the knot was secure. He lashed both men back to back with the mainmast between them and straightened, feeling strangely light-headed.

Camille was pale too, struggling out of her wet suit. "You're bleeding!" she said.

Blood was seeping down the arm of his suit and onto

his hand. A ragged tear in the sleeve showed a raw wound that throbbed now. "I don't think it's serious," he said. "I've had coral cuts deeper than this. Bring the first-aid kit up here. We don't want blood all over the saloon."

He stripped off his suit and Camille cleansed the wound. The bullet must have glanced by, but she said, "You ought to see a doctor. If that plane came back maybe we could signal them."

"Plane?"

"There was one yesterday when you were underwater. It circled a couple of times and then went away."

Rogan grunted. "Probably belonged to our friends over there," he said. Evan had drawn his knees up and was resting his head on them. Drummond sat with his legs outstretched, looking furious and white-faced. "My guess is Drummond sent Evan chasing after us when they saw the *Sea-Rogue* was gone, but they lost us in the storm. So then he hired a plane, and when they found us Evan picked him up from some island with an airstrip and they homed in."

Catching Rogan's eyes on him as Camille began to bandage the wounded arm, Drummond spat, "You can't do this! You'll never get away with it."

Rogan's brows lifted. "You came on board my boat and threatened me with a gun."

"I was worried about Camille—you admit you kidnapped her. I came to help her."

Rogan gave a crack of laughter. "Some white knight!"

"Camille…?" Drummond appealed to her. "You know I wouldn't harm you," he coaxed, and when she didn't respond he said on a higher note, "If you die, the Brodericks get the lot, don't they? Do you think he'll resist that temptation? It's a small step from kidnapping to murder."

Rogan said, "Maybe you'd know." Camille was con-

centrating on fastening the bandage, her mouth tight, her
cheeks very pale. She ignored Drummond.

He raised his voice further. "You can't trust him, Camille. You'd be safer with me. Don't let them cheat you of
your legacy…it's worth a fortune, and I have the money to
help you recover it."

Camille took the first-aid box and still without looking
at him went below.

When Rogan followed she was sitting on the banquette,
her hands tightly clamped in front of her as if she were
praying—or trying to hold herself together.

"Are you okay?" he asked.

"Yes." Her voice was barely audible. "Shouldn't we
radio the police or something? And you need medical attention. Evan might too. He doesn't look good."

Anything Evan got he deserved, in Rogan's opinion.
Still, things could get awkward if the man died. It was all
very well in films and TV programs for people to get
knocked out and be up and running about in ten minutes.
But concussion could be serious—and Rogan had been so
intent on quickly finishing off the fight and making sure
Camille wasn't hurt he hadn't been exactly careful of how
much injury he was inflicting on the man. Self-defense, but
he didn't fancy having to prove it in court.

"I suppose," he said, looking at her worriedly. Was she
in shock? Not surprising after what they'd been through.

She seemed remote, detached. He wanted to comfort her,
but instinct told him she would repudiate that. Feeling helpless and angry, he went to the VHF and called up the nearest authorities, several hundred kilometers away.

It wasn't easy explaining, but eventually he got a promise to send a naval vessel that was more or less in the area
to assess the situation.

When Rogan had thanked the operator and signed off,

Camille said quietly, "I was wrong about James. I'm sorry I didn't believe you."

Rogan shrugged. "I suppose it sounded pretty weird." He flexed his arm, finding it painful but not unusable. "I'll get those two onto their own boat where they'll be out of the way."

"I'll help." She resolutely got up.

"I don't need help." He guessed she didn't want to have to touch either of them. "They're trussed like chickens, it shouldn't be a problem." Especially since their unwelcome visitors had thoughtfully roped the boats together.

Drummond was positively green now, his forehead beaded with sweat. When Rogan unhitched him from the mast and hoisted him up he said, "What are you doing?" his voice high with fear, and Rogan was tempted to say, *Throwing you overboard.*

That gave him an idea. He turned his head and called, "Camille? Bring your tape recorder here, will you?"

He hauled his prisoner to the taffrail and pushed him back against it, precariously balanced. "I'm going to ask you a few questions."

Drummond's eyes rolled back. "I'm about to be sick!" he muttered, and Rogan twisted him round just in time to avoid being sprayed with vomit.

By the time Drummond had finished, lying across the rail panting and spitting, Camille was standing alongside Rogan with the tape recorder in her hand.

She'd rummaged it out of the drawer, wondering what Rogan wanted it for. Now she watched as he manhandled James around to face them both. Knowing how it felt to be seasick, she couldn't help a pang of pity at the man's pallor and obvious misery. His lips trembled and there were new stains on his designer shirt, along with some red spots she knew with guilty horror she was responsible for. The pin-

prick wound she'd made had stopped bleeding, but a trail
of dried blood ran down his neck into the collar of the shirt.

Rogan's face was an implacable mask. "Mr. Drummond
is about to tell us something."

"I'm not…" James gasped.

"Oh, I think so," Rogan said, in a voice that sent a
shiver down Camille's spine and made James blink appre-
hensively. "Your discarded breakfast will bring the sharks
around. And if I throw you after it the smell of blood will
send them into a frenzy."

"You wouldn't…"

"I promise, it won't take much." Rogan, his hand
bunching the collar of the shirt, pushed him against the rail.
Feeling sick herself, Camille bit her tongue and started the
tape running.

"Who beat up my father?" Rogan demanded.

"I've no idea—"

Rogan's hand tightened. "Yes, you do. Was it Evan?"

Evan's slurred voice came from the mast. "Not me."

Without looking toward Evan, Rogan gave James a
shake. "Who?" He bent the man farther over the rail.

"Let me go!"

"Who was it?"

Camille saw the movement of James's Adam's apple. "It
wasn't my idea. I knew nothing about it until…after."

"Whose idea, then? Who did it?"

"Gary!" James gasped. "Evan's deckhand. He…heard
Broderick's drunken boasting and thought I'd be interested…I'm in the antique business."

"And he knew you weren't fussy about where your stuff
came from…or where it went," Rogan said grimly. "Go
on."

James licked his lips. "Gary walked him back to his
boat. Broderick was in a confiding mood, said he'd found

the *Maiden's Prayer* and its treasure. Gary pooh-poohed that, and Broderick told him he had proof, the drunken fool even described where he'd put the safe holding the evidence.''

''And?'' Rogan prompted as James stopped. There was splashing in the water below, and James gulped, his eyes rolling sideways. He said quickly, ''Gary was stupid—he asked one question too many and the old goat got suspicious and turned belligerent. Gary downed him and took his keys. He emptied the safe, and on the way back found Broderick was dead. He put the keys back on the body and brought the stuff he'd found to me. He was in a panic about killing the old man.''

''What stuff?''

''A…a few coins.'' James tried to twist away, unsuccessfully.

''And…?'' Rogan queried.

''What…what do you mean?''

''I mean,'' Rogan said menacingly, ''a few coins wouldn't be enough to convince you the treasure was genuine and make it worth your while buying the *Sea-Rogue* just to find out where it was. What else was in the safe?''

James didn't answer and Rogan, his expression murderous, pulled him closer, their eyes only inches apart.

''A couple of gold watches!'' James gasped. ''A—a pearl and diamond necklace. A silver bracelet set with stones…''

Camille made a small sound.

A momentary sneer appeared on James's mouth as his eyes swiveled to her. ''Yes,'' he said. ''You had your chance, but you're so pure, so incorruptible—except for *him!* You lied about him finding the log—lied very badly. That's when I started to suspect he had it after all.''

Rogan roughly jerked his attention away from Camille.

"So you had proof the treasure existed. You just didn't know where it was. Who ransacked the boat while we were at the funeral? Evan?"

Evan said quite loudly, "You can't pin that on me. Or hitting the old lady. I wasn't even in town then."

"Shut up," James snapped. "You bloody fool!"

"So it was you," Rogan said, still glaring at James. "You turned over the boat, looking for the log, when you knew everyone around the anchorage would be at the funeral."

"I didn't—"

Rogan pushed him farther across the rail and Camille made a small sound of protest. "Yes!" James admitted. "It should have been there! I thought you must have taken it, or…"

"Or it was at Mollie's place. I guess everyone in town knew she was close to Barney. You hit her on the head and searched her house. There was no danger from a defense-less woman. You might have killed her!"

Camille said, "Mollie didn't say she'd been burgled."

"He was careful," Rogan commented. "He didn't want to arouse any suspicion that Mollie's 'accident' wasn't one. But he put her keys back in the wrong place."

"You can't prove any of this," James said. "It's under duress—"

"I don't need to. The irony is even if you'd found it, the log wouldn't have been much use to you, unless you're way cleverer than I think. You were looking for the wrong thing. One more question. How did Gary die?"

"I don't know!"

"I'm sure you do." Rogan looked so dangerous, so threatening, that Camille exclaimed, "Rogan!"

There was another splash in the water below, and James flinched. Rogan said, "I could get rid of you. I wouldn't mind at all—and it would save a lot of trouble. No one would know, and it would only be justice for my father. If I shove you overboard and dangle Evan as shark bait I'm sure he'll sing like a bird. Did you kill Gary to keep him quiet?''

''I've never killed anybody! Camille…'' James bleated, appealing to her.

Rogan said, ''What happened to Gary?''

''I had nothing to do with it!''

Camille didn't even see Rogan move, but James's eyes suddenly widened and he said quickly, his voice high, ''I told the stupid bastard to make himself scarce. He didn't have the brains to get himself out of trouble if the police got hold of him. I don't know what happened to him.''

Without turning Rogan said, ''Evan?''

''All I did was what he told me,'' Evan said. ''Everything was his idea. Everything.''

''Including murder,'' Rogan told Brodie, sharing a six-pack with him and Granger in the *Sea-Rogue*'s saloon some weeks later. ''Evan finally confessed to the police that Drummond told him to get rid of Gary before the cops caught the kid and he told them everything. So Evan took him out to sea with the story that he was helping him evade arrest by putting him aboard a trawler bound for Taiwan with some of Drummond's stolen merchandise, a regular trip for them. And in midocean he hit the guy over the head and dumped him overboard. The autopsy showed the blow.''

Funnily enough, now he knew his father's assailant was dead, Rogan was vaguely sorry for the weasely little crook, who'd been small fry compared with Drummond.

Granger said, ''Even if Drummond gets away with his story that he didn't intend Evan to kill Gary, he'll likely be put away for a few years and his business will be down the drain. Plus his reputation.''

"Yeah.'' That would give Rogan some satisfaction. He picked up a can and pulled off the top to swig some beer down.

"Pleading guilty to receiving and smuggling is the best thing he can do,'' Granger said, "after his boat skipper spilled the beans. That stunt of yours with the tape recorder—'' he added reprovingly "—no court would admit it as evidence.'' He'd been shocked when Rogan played him the tape.

"I didn't do it for the court,'' Rogan said. "I needed to know who killed Dad. Drummond's lucky I didn't feed him to the sharks.''

"Were there any?''

Rogan shrugged. "No idea.''

Brodie regarded him thoughtfully. "You don't seem happy. You've found your treasure, got investors falling over themselves to fit out the *Sea-Rogue* as a proper salvage tender, even persuaded me to come in as a partner—and thanks again for the opportunity. I'm looking forward to joining the dive team. So what's your problem?''

Granger suggested, "He's a man of property now. He's not used to it. The burden of responsibility…'' Pouring beer into a glass, he asked his brother, "Have you seen Camille lately?''

Rogan scowled. "No.''

After the navy guys had removed Drummond and Evan to the naval vessel and taken the *Catfish* in tow they'd instructed Rogan to follow them into the nearest port that had a police station. They'd also put a couple of men aboard the *Sea-Rogue*, presumably to make sure their instructions were followed.

Rogan had hardly had a chance to be alone with Camille.

When he did manage to trap her in her cabin one night she was aloof and tense, while claiming she was perfectly fine.

"Are you upset about Drummond?" he asked, and she laughed—a brittle little laugh.

"Obviously I'm not a good judge of men."

He wondered if that went for her judgment of him too. He didn't want to ask.

"He used me," she said. "Pumped me for information, and I never realized...I thought he was interested because he liked me. He even sounded me out about...persuading you to sell the *Sea-Rogue* to him."

With sex, Rogan guessed. He remembered uncomfortably he'd almost accused her of using it after he found the sale agreement. "And you said no."

Camille nodded. "He offered me a bracelet—I think from the *Maiden's Prayer*. I suppose he thought it amusing, piquant—that he could give it to me and neither of us would know where it came from."

"And maybe he was testing you," Rogan guessed.

"Testing me?"

"Plenty of people can be seduced by money and jewels into doing things they wouldn't normally do. He would have used you, if he could, in any way possible."

"I suppose..." she said.

Then she told him she was tired and made it clear she'd like him to leave.

Once all the red tape had been cleared at Rarotonga, Drummond and his skipper were returned to New Zealand under guard, leaving Rogan free until he and Camille were needed to testify at the trial.

Then Camille had announced her intention of flying out.

"Where are you going?" he'd asked in disbelief.

"Home. I do have one, you know. Most people do."

He'd never needed one himself. Not since his mother died. He supposed the *Sea-Rogue* was his home now. The only kind he wanted—not tied to a house and mortgage but able to up-anchor at any time and sail away on a moment's whim.

Except that he was committed now to raising Barney's treasure and returning the money that various investors had put into the venture; he was fully occupied equipping the boat and gathering an expert dive team. He hadn't seen Camille since he'd seen her off at the airport in Rarotonga.

He tried to ignore the hollow feeling he'd experienced when he brought the *Sea-Rogue* into her berth at Mokohina and finally had to relinquish the half-formed hope that Camille would be waiting for him. She had already collected her car from Brodie, who'd hot-wired it on Rogan's instructions and moved it to his place, and then she'd left, long before the *Sea-Rogue* arrived.

He told himself he'd get used to not having her on board, that in time he'd forget her. But daily the aching void she'd left in his life grew larger and more painful.

No woman had ever left him feeling this way. As if half his heart had been summarily removed, leaving a gaping wound.

He kept reminding himself of his resolution never to get involved with a woman who wanted—deserved—any kind of commitment to a normal life, remembering his mother's sacrifice, his father's total unsuitability for marriage or anything resembling it.

And he was like his father—wasn't he? He had no business even thinking about a woman like Camille.

It was just that he couldn't help it.

He put down his beer morosely and caught Granger's eye, an eye that held a disconcerting glint of concerned sympathy. Damn, his brother knew him too well.

* * *

Camille turned into the short driveway of the little house she'd bought, and nearly drove into the fence, jamming on the brakes just in time, her heart thudding. Rogan was leaning against the porch, arms folded, wearing jeans, his sleeveless jacket and his stubborn look. He strode to her and jerked open the car door.

At first wordless with shock, she climbed out and simply stared. Then, the reality of his solid presence, the faint, remembered scent of him assuring her she wasn't dreaming she said, "What are you doing here?"

"I came to see you."

"Is it about the *Sea-Rogue?* The business?" Granger had told her the sale agreement she'd signed with James was null, and she'd had regular bulletins from him detailing the setting up of a company to garner the necessary investment to fit out the boat and recruit the recovery team, and the complex process of complying with the regulations designed to ensure that valuable archaeological material wasn't damaged or destroyed by salvors.

"It's about us," Rogan said.

"Us?" That sent her heart into overdrive. When she'd told him she was leaving—but not that it was sheer self-preservation, tearing herself away while she still could—she'd harbored a foolish, futile hope that he'd ask her not to go, say he loved her and couldn't do without her.

Of course he hadn't. He'd never said he loved her, never suggested she meant more to him than any other woman he'd loved—or slept with—and left. So she'd left him first.

She'd known the first time she laid eyes on him what sort of man he was, that she could expect nothing but heartache from him. And she'd realized that the sooner she made the break the less long-lasting the resulting pain was likely to be. But that hadn't stopped her from crying most of the way back to Rusden. And it hadn't stopped the dreams that tormented her, dreams where she sat with him again on the deck of the *Sea-Rogue,* where yesterday and tomorrow were beyond the limitless horizon, and today was all they had, and all she wanted.

Trying to be normal, not to fling herself into his arms and sob her heart out, she made for the kitchen, asking prosaically, ''Do you want a cup of coffee?''

''No,'' he said. ''I want…''

She turned to face him, her hand clutching at the back of one of her kitchen chairs because she felt unsteady, ''What, then?''

He made a strange, choked sound and reached for her. ''I want…I *need*…this!''

The last word, muffled but with an urgent, despairing undertone, was uttered against her mouth. Then he was kissing her in the same way, almost clumsy, lacking his usual confidence and finesse, but with a hopeless passion that pierced her.

She couldn't help but respond, her body shaping itself to his, her hand stroking his hair, her mouth answering the movements of his with unguarded passion of her own, but even as her heart sang with gladness her mind was telling her that no matter what this was leading to it couldn't last, and when Rogan lifted his head hot tears spilled onto her cheeks.

Consternation in his face, he said, ''I hurt you!'' He loosened his hold on her, touched a trembling thumb to her cheek. ''I'm a stupid, selfish oaf. I didn't mean to be rough.''

He looked so anxious and contrite she laughed shakily. ''You didn't hurt me.'' It was the thought of the hurt waiting in the future that caused the tears. ''It's all right.''

''It's not all right! I made you cry. I'm sorry.''

She didn't tell him how many times she'd already cried, secretly, longing for him, his kisses, his arms about her just like this. Pulling away, she rubbed at her wet cheeks with her hands, and gave him a poignant smile. "It isn't your fault." He couldn't be blamed for making her love him. He'd made no promises, and it had been her own mistake to sleep with him. She'd fought the temptation to repeat the experience, tortured day and night by his nearness, knowing that if she gave in she'd never be able to break free. That she'd spend her life pining for a man who would forget her as soon as the *Sea-Rogue*'s sails disappeared over the horizon.

But unbelievably he had followed her, he was here, and...

Warily she dared to look at him again. "Why did you come?"

"Because I had to," he said somberly. "I had to know if you love me the way I love you."

Camille's mouth soundlessly opened, her throat locking. He *loved* her?

"I'm taking a desk job in the new company," he said. "There's plenty of shore work organizing equipment and crews, and a hell of a lot of paperwork and red tape."

"Isn't Granger—?"

"He looks after the legal stuff and finances but he can't do all the administration himself."

Camille couldn't imagine Rogan behind a desk all day. "Why not hire someone else? Surely the company can afford it."

"Because," he said as though she had missed the obvious, "you need a proper home and security and a man who's always there for you—all the things your mother missed out on."

Camille blinked. "*I* need...?"

He smote his forehead with a fist. "Oh, hell! I've got things back to front. I'm sorry. You love me, Camille— you wouldn't have kissed me the way you did just now if you didn't. And you'll never know how thankful I was for that. I meant to talk…but when I saw you I had to touch you, and you came into my arms so naturally…and then you cried. I hate that. Darling, I don't care what it takes to make you say yes. I swear I'll be the kind of husband you want…need…and spend my life making up for what your father did to you. So please—will you marry me?"

How could any woman not love a man like this, who offered to sacrifice his whole life, go against his nature, simply to give her what he believed she needed?

"You can't do this!" she said, and as he started to protest she put her fingers over his lips. "I won't tie you to a desk! Or a house. You'd hate it!"

He snatched her hand away and held it tightly in his. "You don't understand! All I want is you…I'll do anything if only I can have you in my life forever."

"Give up everything you are?" she said. "You wouldn't be the man I fell in love with. Rogan, you've no need to pay for my father's sins…or my mother's."

"Your mother's?"

"She told my father to stay away. Every time he visited and then left when I was little it would be days before I stopped pining and settled down, and she thought I'd be better not seeing him at all. At first he did send letters and presents, but she returned them unopened until he stopped. She hoped I'd forget him. But he did send a little money occasionally, to her bank account. She never told me." Camille blinked, and sighed. "I'm trying to forgive her."

Rogan pulled her back into his arms, an embrace of comfort. "I never did understand how Taff could have just abandoned you," he said. "If we have children I won't be leaving you to bring them up alone." He loosened his hold to fish in the pocket of his jacket. "I brought this...I meant to make it an excuse for visiting, while I tried to work out how you felt."

A photograph. Her father, laughing at the camera, looking young and strong and eager for life. "Thank you," she said softly.

"I have a few more of him, with my father. And the carving he did of you—I keep it in my cabin on the *Sea-Rogue*." Granger had noticed it there, sent him a quizzical look but refrained from comment.

"You can't take an office job," she said. "I won't let you."

"Camille," he groaned, "please—"

"No! I'll marry you, but there are conditions."

"I told you—*anything!*" But he looked worried.

"You take me with you when you go treasure-hunting. And you never leave me. At least not for long and only by mutual consent."

"Your job..." He stared at her, apparently stunned.

She said, "I'm a historian. I can be useful to you—to the company. Pacific Treasure Salvors needs a researcher, Granger said."

"Granger...?"

"He offered me the job weeks ago. I turned him down but he said he'd keep it open."

"Oh, did he?" Rogan said, chagrined. "The cunning b-brother." He could imagine the I-told-you-so grin on Granger's face when he heard the news of Rogan's engagement.

Camille smiled. "Do you object?"

"Hell, no! It's a *great* idea...if you're sure you want to do it."

"I'm sure. We won't make the mistakes our parents did.

I loved being at sea with you. And diving…quite apart from finding treasure, the reef and the sea life were breathtaking. I miss the *Sea-Rogue*.''

''You were furious with me.''

''Do you blame me? That was a pretty drastic thing to do.''

''I know. But I don't see what else I could have done. Am I forgiven?''

''I suppose so. I always knew you were a pirate. Just don't ever try another trick like that.''

Not that he'd need to, she thought as he kissed her again, at first more gently, but soon exploding into a fierce possession, plundering her mouth, her heart.

Somewhere in his ancestry there was definitely pirate blood. She knew it as surely as she knew he'd keep his promise—that no matter what seas they sailed, what rough waters they encountered and storms they weathered together, she'd be always safe and loved in the harbor of his heart.

* * * * *

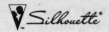

INTIMATE MOMENTS™

is thrilled to bring you the next book
in popular author

CANDACE IRVIN's

exciting new miniseries

Unparalleled courage, unbreakable love...

In January 2004, look for:

Irresistible Forces
(Silhouette Intimate Moments #1270)

It's been eleven years since U.S. Air Force captain
Samantha Hall last saw the man she loved...and lost.
Now, as Major Griff Towers rescues her and her colleagues
after their plane crashes in hostile territory, how can Sam
possibly ignore the feelings she still has for the sexy soldier?

And if you missed the first books in the series look for...

Crossing the Line
(Silhouette Intimate Moments #1179, October 2002)

A Dangerous Engagement
(Silhouette Intimate Moments #1252, October 2003)

Available wherever Silhouette books are sold!

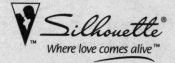

If you enjoyed what you just read,
then we've got an offer you can't resist!

Take 2 bestselling love stories FREE!
Plus get a FREE surprise gift!

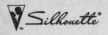